Anointed

Anointed

Patricia Haley

URBAN
CHRISTIAN

Urban Books, LLC
97 N18th Street
Wyandanch, NY 11798

ISBN 13: 978-1-62286-817-9
ISBN 10: 1-62286-817-X

First Mass Market Printing October 2015
First Trade Paperback Printing October 2012
Printed in the United States of America

10 9 8 7 6 5 4 3 2 1

Distributed by Kensington Publishing Corp.
Submit Orders to:
Customer Service
400 Hahn Road
Westminster, MD 21157-4627
Phone: 1-800-733-3000
Fax: 1-800-659-2436

"Phenomenal. . . Haley did an outstanding job on each person's outlook and how, without forgiveness, no problem can truly be solved."
—*Urban Reviews*

"Haley has hit the mark yet again! I couldn't put this book down—the characters are believable and compelling."
—*Maurice M. Gray, Jr., author of All Things Work Together*

"The story grabs the reader from the beginning, drawing you in . . . and keeping you on the edge of your seat as the plot takes unexpected twists and turns."
—*RT Book Reviews* on *Let Sleeping Dogs Lie*

"The perfect blend of faith and romance."
—*Gospel Book Review*

"Haley's writing and visualization skills are to be reckoned with. . . . This story is full-bodied. . . . Great prose, excellent execution!"
—*RAWSISTAZ*™ on *Still Waters*

"A deeply moving novel. The characters and the storyline remind us that forgiveness and unconditional love are crucial to any relationship."
—*Good Girl Book Club*

"*No Regrets* offered me a different way, a healthier way based in faith and hope, to look at trying situations."

—*Montgomery Newspapers*

Anointed is also available as an eBook

Also by Patricia Haley

Acknowledgments

I'm grateful for each reader. My writing is for you. I hope that every book, including *Anointed*, inspires you to appreciate the power of forgiveness and to remember that everyone makes mistakes, but life goes on and there is hope in Jesus. Just as the main character, Dave Mitchell, had an undeniable calling on his life, a purpose that would not be silenced, so do you. Find out what it is and get about the business of fulfilling God's purpose for your life—blessings to you.

How can I honestly and thoroughly thank each person who has supported me during my writing journey? It's impossible. So, I will state upfront how grateful I am to so many for attending my literary events, providing encouragement, showering me with well wishes, and praying for me. Thank goodness the Lord knows you by name and has the ability to bless your acts of kindness far beyond what I could ever do.

Acknowledgments

There are several people who I have to call out by name. With tremendous love, I honor my beloved husband, super-supporter, and best friend, Jeffrey Glass. I'm also blessed to have such a wonderful daughter, "Sweetie Pie," who's my biggest fan and always encourages me in her own sweet way. Thanks to the rest of my phenomenal circle of loved ones—relatives (Haley, Glass, Tennin, and Moorman), sister-friends, fellow believers, sorors, friends, four beautiful goddaughters, god sisters/brothers, book reading nieces Azhalaun, Michelle, Ashley, and my parents—Fannie, Deacon Earl Rome, and Jeraldine Glass who continuously pray for me and show up at my events. Without fail, I honor the memories of my daddy ("Luck"), brother (Erick), and father-in-law (Walter). There are some who have literally gone the extra mile, like the Martin family (Eddie, Regina, Sierra, and Mariah) who drove hundreds of miles from Maine to surprise me at my book signing—you're the best. Thanks to my dear cousins Alesha Russey and Mia James, who are much better at announcing my books on Facebook than I am.

I couldn't possibly forget my freelance editors. You've truly challenged me to sharpen my craft and deliver stronger stories. Thank you Emma Foots, Laurel Robinson, Kirkanne Moseley,

Acknowledgments

Tammy Lenzy, Dorothy Robinson, and Renee Lenzy. Thanks to my hubby and Leslie Walker Harding for hosting me run my story ideas by you and always showing such excitement. Special thanks to Andrew Stuart, Joylynn Jossel-Ross, and the Urban Books team (great book cover). I also have to thank Shirley Brockenborough, Maleta Wilson, and Audrey Williams for the years of support. Thanks to Sirius Web Solutions for keeping my web site. Thank you to my Delta Sigma Theta Sorority sisters, especially my chapter Schaumburg-Hoffman Estates (IL), Rockford (IL), Valley Forge (PA), Milwaukee (WI), Louisville (KY), Madison (WI), Greater Cleveland (OH) Alumnae Chapters, and Omicron Chi (Stanford, CA). Many thanks to my church families at Beulah Grove (GA), New Covenant (PA), Church of Acts (PA), World Overcomers Church (IL), and Trowbridge (CA). I'm grateful to a long list of book clubs, media venues, booksellers, and ministries who have blessed me: First African-Sharon Hill (PA), Circle of Hope-Jones Memorial (PA), Sharon Baptist (PA), CLC Ministries Int'l (PA), Women of Character (FL), PWOC (FL), Towne Book Center (PA), Women of Valor (IL), Sista's Empowered and Making a Difference (DE), Susan Jarrett and The Bookees (MD), Sherry Zabikow at B&N (IL), and Rockford Public Library (Staci and Faye).

I extend a special shout out to: my big brother Fred & Gloria Haley, Bob Thomas, Lorena Skelton, Frances Walker, Little Freddy Deon Haley, and my fellow author, Kimberla Lawson Roby, who's always been more of a sister than a cousin to me. I'm always grateful for your prayers and support. I love each of you dearly.

Anointed is dedicated to a special group of women in my life (my "other moms") who have showered me with an abundance of love and support over the years. I was blessed from birth with my incredible mother, Fannie Haley Rome, and a host of wonderful aunts who have loved me unconditionally every day of my life. To have an extra dose of motherly love and prayers from these honorable women is one of God's abundant blessings.

Mary (Don) Bartel
Emira (Leroy) Lymons Bryant
Emma Collington
Dottie (Ron) Fisher
Norma (Al) Foote
Emma (John) Houston Foots
Soror Thelma (Freddie) Robins Gould
Carolyn (Pastor Gus) Howell
Ann (Michael) Jarvis
Dorothea (Ravi) Kalra
Rosa L. Lawson
Joan Vaughn Walker
Dear Washington (grandmother)

Then the Lord said, "Rise and anoint him; he is the one."

. . . and from that day on the Spirit of the Lord came upon David in power.

1 Samuel 16:12–13

Prologue

Dave wasn't blinded by the moment. The spring breeze danced across the river, brushing across his face as he sat on the park bench. "I can't marry you," he told Madeline.

"Why not? This isn't fair to me. We've been together for over a year. I finally ask you to get serious about our relationship and suddenly you clam up?"

"I have my priorities. I've committed my life to serving the Lord, and I'm not asking you to take my journey with me," he said.

"But you can't decide for me. I know who you are and what you stand for, Mr. Dave Mitchell. Don't you understand that I love you unconditionally?" Dave wasn't sure she fully grasped what was at stake. "You have to understand, there will be sacrifices."

"So what, I get it."

"I'm not sure you do. There will be times when I have to put my calling front and center, both personally and professionally." Dave leaned forward on the bench and peered into her eyes. "It sounds like no big deal as we sit here and talk, but what happens ten years from now when we have kids? You'll want me home with you and the kids, and many times I won't be able to respond the way you want. Trust me, you won't be as calm as you are right now."

"Try me. I know what it will take, and I'm not afraid to go after what I want."

"And I don't want to rush into a decision." Dave's heart wanted to say "yes, let's get married today." But wisdom wasn't jumping up and down. He'd have to reconcile his head and heart. Prayer and fasting would be the key.

"Dave, you're talking to someone who juggled three part-time jobs when I was getting my bachelor's and master's degrees in business. You don't have to explain to me about how to bring a vision to fruition. I've lived it. Besides, you shouldn't worry too much. I'm not the needy type, clinging to your every word or trudging so close behind you that I can see the hairs on the back of your neck. That's not me. I plan to have my space, and you can have yours to do what you must."

Her argument was compelling. Even though she was in her early twenties, it was clear

Madeline knew exactly what she wanted and didn't mind stating her case. Her strength shoved him toward a proposal, but not completely. Dave wasn't an impulsive man. He lived by the leading of the Lord. Peace and wisdom guided him like guardrails on an open road, nudging him in the way he should go when making decisions. "Marriage is a sacred union, a lifetime partnership, not to be taken lightly."

"I know that, and it doesn't change my position."

"You're tough, Madeline," he said, softening as the gentle breeze continued stroking his face and his resolve.

"Have to be."

There was no doubt that she sparked his creative flame. She was smart, funny, and carried a persona that stood up and made him take notice. But was she the one for him down the road? A wrong move in marriage could derail his mission of taking financial management and leadership training to as many churches in the world as he could reach. Pouring wisdom into those on the frontlines and restoring credibility in the religious sector was his number one goal.

He waited to get a warm feeling or voice of confirmation about marrying Madeline. No lightning bolts shot from heaven. The earth didn't shake. The head of God didn't pop through the clouds and speak. Dave had long since passed the thunderbolt revelations. He'd learned to hear God in the stillness of the moment and the quiet whispers of His voice. Madeline felt right. She was challenging but he could manage that. Besides, he was also wired to handle adversity.

They proceeded with a wedding service four months later, followed by the ribbon cutting ceremony at Dave Mitchell International (DMI). The push forward gave Dave an immediate chance to prove just how much his thirty-one years of life experience could handle.

Chapter 1

"Amen," Dave echoed, closing out his prayer as he opened the office door and asked the gentlemen sitting in the hallway to come in. "Mr. Jefferson, please have a seat," he said, gesturing for him to take a seat at his conference table. "I know you've been working with Madeline, but she's not able to join us today."

"Oh, I'm sorry to hear that, but I'm sure I'll be in good hands with you."

"That's for sure. Can I get you anything?" Dave asked, allowing his client to get comfortable before swooping in like a hawk to close the deal. Jefferson had no clue as to how close he was to being caught in the DMI net.

"Nothing for me," Mr. Jefferson said.

"Then let's get down to business," Dave said, straightening the cuff of his sleeve and glancing up at the photos of Presidents Carter and Reagan. He'd met both of them during the last election. "Your church is drowning in bills and money problems. You need help and I'm the one to give it to you."

"Maybe, but at what price?"

"Well, how much is a credible reputation worth to you?" Dave grabbed a pad of paper from his desk and a pen. He jotted down several numbers. "Let's see here. You have forty churches and at least half your staff needs to be trained," Dave said, getting his calculator. "By the time we lay on a few administrative costs, we're looking at three hundred twenty-five thousand."

"Come on, where are we going to get that kind of money?"

"What were you expecting?" Dave asked, laying his pen down and locking his fingers. He'd seen guys like Jefferson countless times. They wanted something for nothing and he wasn't the one to give it to them.

"I was expecting something more like ten thousand dollars to get nine or ten people trained."

"Well thanks for stopping in. Sorry we can't help you," Dave said, extending his hand to Mr. Jefferson.

"What, that's it, no negotiation?" Mr. Jefferson asked, appearing surprised.

"Nope, that's not how this works," Dave said.

"Okayyy," he responded. "You got me, I'm listening."

"I'm not here to sell you a boatload of services. I'm not here to twist your arm, but it seems to me that you're the one with the financial problem and need my help. If that's true, fine, let's work a deal," Dave said, leaning his elbow on the table. "However, I'm not going to waste your time, and I'm certainly not going to let you waste mine. Ten thousand isn't even close to what I'm looking at for the kind of mentoring and training that you need. If you can't come up to six figures, this conversation is over. No harm, no foul," Dave said, dropping back in his chair, sporting a grin.

"That's fair. I can come up to one hundred and fifty thousand," Mr. Jefferson said, as Dave anticipated.

"Great, now we're getting somewhere."

"Are you saying that's a number you're willing to accept?"

"No way," Dave said, laughing loudly, then cutting it off instantly. "But at least it lets me know that you're serious and not here to waste my time, because that, my friend, would end up costing you."

"You're a tough cookie."

"I have to be if I'm going to help clients like you," Dave said, relaxing in his chair, silently thanking God that there would be one more band of churches getting their acts together and averting bankruptcy. Another one down, many to go before he could rest.

Chapter 2

September was bold. The autumn light splashed itself into the foyer, refusing to be hidden by the floor-to-ceiling blinds. Madeline sat at the bottom of the winding staircase dressed like she was going for a jog, but looks were deceiving. Her tired bones could barely walk up and down the stairs let alone contemplate running. Her days and nights were beginning to feel the same—exhausted when she lay down and the same when she got up in the morning. She didn't anticipate today being any different. The days of relaxing and being in control of her time had long since passed. Juggling priorities had become her gift from the moment their first child arrived seven years ago, followed by two more.

"Where can I find the third quarter cost projections?" Dave asked as Madeline pressed the phone tighter into her ear. The children running in and out of the foyer made it difficult to hear him, but she was doing the best she could.

"Look under the file labeled third quarter costs," she said with her eyelids widening, and enunciating each word sharply.

"That was the first place I looked. It's not there, and I could really use the plan before my meeting kicks off in an hour."

"Wait, what's today's date?" she asked, perking up.

"The fifteenth," he said.

"Our anniversary, oh my goodness, I've forgotten about our twelfth anniversary."

"I didn't," he told her. "I've already made an eight o'clock reservation tonight for us at our place."

"Mommy, Mommy, come quick. Don got his blanket stuck in the toaster and I can't get it out," her daughter said, darting toward her and tugging at Madeline's leg.

"Is the toaster turned on?" Madeline blurted out.

"No, it's not, but he's going to keep crying if you don't help him."

"Just one minute, dear, and I'll be there."

"No, no, you have to come now, right now, Mommy, right now," she said, pulling at her mother's pants leg.

"Dave, I'll have to take a rain check on dinner tonight. How about we settle for coffee and donuts down the street when you get in? After twelve years, you don't have to impress me."

"Mommy, come now, please, please."

"Come on, Madeline, we can't keep pushing off personal time together."

"Tell that to your children."

"I'm sure we can take two hours out for dinner without the kids. We owe it to our marriage."

"We'll see, but I have to go. I'll call you later," she said, eager to avoid an argument on their anniversary. One day could hopefully be stress-free.

"Wait, Madeline, I really need that plan. Is there any way you can come into the office within the hour and find it? I could really use your help on this one."

"Mommy, please help," her daughter continued.

Madeline exhaled. "I have to go. The children are into something." She exhaled again. Madeline rose slowly; clearly not fast enough for her daughter, who continued pulling. "Now you see why I can't make any promises about going out tonight."

"We can always get another nanny to help out if it's too much," Dave told her.

"You mean I can get another nanny," she fired back at him. "We know you're not going to have time to find one," she let fly out of her mouth without trimming the edge on her attitude.

"Sounds like you're upset."

Madeline reined in her tone, attempting to balance between the call with Dave and her daughter's tugging, a position she found herself in more frequently these days.

"Tamara, dear, go tell Don that Mommy is on the way."

"But, I want you to come too," Tamara responded.

"All right. Go on now so he doesn't get scared." That seemed to satisfy her daughter because she left without any more demands. One catastrophe was close to being solved. If Madeline could fix Dave's problem as easily, then maybe, just maybe, there would be a shred of solitude in her day. Since it was only eight-twenty, there was hope that the next twelve or thirteen hours would settle down. They hadn't yesterday or the day before, but she wasn't giving up, not yet. "Let me check on the children and then I'll go through my briefcase to see if I still have an older version. Will that help you?" she asked, wanting to get to the kitchen.

"Anything you can give me will help. Madeline, I sincerely appreciate what you're doing for our family. I know you have the children, and I'm so sorry to put this extra pressure on you. But I really need those numbers."

Madeline could have accepted Dave's comment as flattery and walked away feeling valued, appreciated, and needed. The words sounded nice, but something must have gotten lost in the translation because it didn't make her feel great about the situation. She was torn. The strong pull toward the office and the one coming from Mayweather Lane were stretching her beyond recognition. Something had to change. "Dave, I have to go. I'll call you in a few minutes."

"Thank you, and, Madeline, you're the best at getting the job done. I don't know how you do it."

"I don't do it well" was what she wanted to say, but didn't bother. There was no time for idle chitchat in her schedule. Sitting in his office with one job to do, Madeline knew he had no idea of the burden she was juggling.

There was a brief pause on the line and then Dave said, "Madeline, that new account I was telling you about is on the other line. I have to take his call. Get back to me as soon as you can."

At the same time, Madeline heard a crash coming from the kitchen followed by a loud scream. "Mommy!"

Chapter 3

By ten-thirty, Madeline was dragging herself into the office, feeling like she'd already put in eight hours. Her seven or eight o'clock quitting time seemed so far off in the distance. The office was in full swing, charging her energy level with each step. The adrenaline began flowing and her pace quickened in her four-inch heels as she approached her newly decorated office. With the dramatic increase in business over the past couple of years, DMI was forced to expand the operation and started by leasing two more floors in the building.

Madeline greeted employees en route to her safe haven. It was as if she could hear birds chirping. The air was clear. The sun was shining, and she was in one of her favorite places in the world: the company she and Dave had built from nothing. She set her keys on the desk and tossed her purse into the drawer. She'd already escaped from the children long enough to find the cost projections for Dave and had faxed them prior to his meeting. The new account represented solid revenue and a stamp of approval from big churches on the East Coast. She had no choice but to come through earlier. They couldn't blow the deal just because she couldn't get the children settled.

Madeline rushed to Dave's office, eager to find out how the meeting had gone. When they'd initially scheduled the meeting last week, she had planned on attending. Turned out the children had other plans for her, but she was at the office now. It was time to take care of business. A few doors down the hallway and she was in Dave's office, where she found him staring out the window.

"I finally made it in," she said, relaxing in a chair. "The children had a rocky start this morning. I think I'm going to have the nanny start much earlier in the morning. Otherwise, I'll never get in here before noon," she said, tickled. Dave didn't respond, which was odd, as much as they chatted all day about everything and anything. He didn't even turn around to face her. "Dave, do you hear me talking to you?" she asked, mixed with a little irritation and concern. She stood and went toward him. Dave slowly turned away from the window with tears streaming down his face. Madeline rushed to him. "Dave, oh my goodness, what's wrong?" she said as her heart raced. What could be so terrible that it had him weeping? She hadn't seen him this rattled since his father died. Her thoughts instantly shifted to Mayweather Lane. "Is it the children? What happened? Something happened? What is it?" she frantically belted out, gripping his forearms and piercing her gaze into his. "Tell me," she yelled.

"No, it's not the kids."

Relief swooped in but worry didn't completely vanish. Dave was visibly upset, and it couldn't possibly be about DMI. He was committed to the business. She was too, but not to the point of drawing tears.

"It's Jonathan. He suffered a massive heart attack and passed away a little while ago."

Madeline's heart wept. "Oh, Dave, I am so sorry," she said, wrapping her arms around him and resting her head against his chest. Outside of his God, there weren't too many greater loves on earth for Dave than his devotion to Jonathan. Madeline wasn't even certain where she and the children ranked when it came to Jonathan. They were more than friends, more than buddies. They were spiritual brothers, kind of like those identical twins who can feel the other's pain. She continued hugging him, not knowing what else to say or do. Words were too inadequate to give him the comfort he needed. She could only do so much. She figured his God would have to do the rest.

After several minutes, he pulled away and went to get the hanky from his suit coat hanging in the closet. Madeline used this as an opportunity to close the door. There weren't many employees on, what was becoming, the executive floor. But there were enough to make her uneasy about leaving Dave exposed to the public at such a private moment. She eased the door closed and leaned on the handle as Dave buried his face into the hanky. He wept openly, took a seat, and wept some more. She stood close by without crowding him. Finally, she said, "I know this is a trite question, but I have to ask. Is there anything I can do for you?"

Dave lifted his head, folded the hanky, and stared into her eyes. "I have to get Andre. He must be devastated about his father."

"You're right. Maybe he can come and visit with us for a few weeks. I'm sure that will help him through this awful ordeal, and the children will love having their god brother in town, especially Sam."

Dave cleared his throat as he fumbled with the hanky. "I'm not talking about a visit. We should have him come live with us permanently."

"What do you mean, permanently?"

"I mean we should assume guardianship for starters and move immediately toward a full adoption."

Madeline's back stiffened, but she held her words until they could line up in a way that expressed what she wanted to say without offending Dave. This was a sensitive moment that she didn't want haunting her for years to come. "Aren't you jumping the gun? Doesn't he have other family who might want to take him?"

Dave peered at her with a look of steadfastness. "I am his relative."

"I know you're his godfather, but I meant blood family."

"I am his closest relative. He doesn't have anyone else, except us, and we can't leave him out there alone."

Madeline wanted to fire off a round of "whatifs" and "why not's" but realized this wasn't the time. She could see the resolve oozing out of Dave. When he felt confident about a matter, there was no way to change his mind.

"It's what Jonathan would want me to do. It's what God wants me to do."

With those words, Madeline took a seat. There was an itsy bitsy chance that she might have persuaded him to reconsider, that was until he threw God in there. Once he believed the Lord was leading him in the decision, the discussion was over. Nobody, living or dead, was going to influence him differently. It often drove Madeline crazy. But she had to admit Dave's reliance on his God had made them successful. There was no reason to knock what was working, but this guardianship and adoption business was tough to blindly accept as a leading of the Lord. Madeline needed more proof.

She continued struggling for words. Reaching out and placing her hand on top of his clutched fist, she said, "Dave, you know I love Jonathan and Andre. He's my godson too. And you know I'm sensitive when it comes to the needs of children. Heck, we have three at home and I'd quickly give my life for any one of them."

"Then you know how I feel right now."

She had some idea and wanted to be supportive without overcommitting. She could barely get into the office before lunchtime with a nanny at home to help out with the ones they already had. Where would she get the energy to handle four? To openly say yes would be disingenuous, not a label she cared to have. "Let's think about this. If we get Andre, how am I going to manage home and the office? I might be good at a lot of things, but superwoman I am not."

Dave placed his hand on top of hers, sandwiching it. "Let's face it. You are the glue in our family."

After years of marriage, Dave could still melt her resolve, not that he was trying to manipulate her. It wasn't his style, but either way, the words of appreciation saturated her soul, softening her emphatic no to a strong maybe.

"I can't imagine our children being without us. Can you?" Dave asked.

He was right. Andre shouldn't be in the world alone when there were people out there who claimed to love him. That was it, done, he'd won. They had to take Andre in. What was love if it didn't transform into tangible help when needed? "Okay, I'll go along with you."

"Doesn't sound too convincing," he said, caressing her hand.

She pulled her hand away and gently slapped it against her other one. "No, I really do mean it. Let's get him, because you're right. I can't imagine our children being alone when there's someone out there who could help them. It's the right thing to do." Dave stood to give Madeline a hug with his arms extended. She stood too. Before falling into his embrace, she said, "Just because it's the right thing to do, doesn't make it the easiest."

"I understand." he said. "So, let's figure out how to make this work for you, because I don't want you under too much pressure. I know we've talked about this many times, but what about having a nanny live in? As a matter of fact, if Ms. Jenkins can't extend her hours, well then, we'll find two or three other nannies to help out. Whatever you need, I want to get for you," he said, placing his hand on her shoulder.

"Dave, you know how I feel about relying on someone else to take care of my babies," she said, taking a step back so their gazes could connect. "Plus, it's more than the children at home that's making this difficult. It's also DMI. I can't walk away from my fourth child after so many years of us nurturing the company and building it from scratch. I look forward to coming here every day, rolling up my sleeves, and getting into the trenches with you and the team. DMI is as much a part of my life as taking care of our children." She went to the windows and stared out. "But honestly, I'm already struggling with keeping all the balls in the air. Adding one more ball to the mix is bound to be too much for me." Before Dave could respond, Madeline continued. "But look," she said, pressing her index finger across his lips. "Don't worry. I'm not going to rehash the discussion. Andre is coming to live with us and that's final. I want him here, and I will do everything I can to make him feel welcomed."

"If you need to take a sabbatical, do it."

"No way, you need me here," she immediately responded. Dave didn't have to tell her how much he relied on her at DMI. She'd crunched numbers, created fliers, developed plans, and had done everything else short of washing windows. She would have done that too if necessary for DMI to get to where it needed to be. Leaving her professional baby was going to be hard.

"I do need you here, but I can't ask you to sacrifice unless I'm willing to do the same. I'll be able to manage around here until you can come back."

"Are you sure?" she asked, coming closer to him again.

"I'll have to be, won't I? If this is God's plan, he will provide for DMI," he said as she leaned against him and let the strength of their bond wrestle with the anxiety that was beginning to brew. Mothering a four-year-old, five-year-old, and seven-year-old was hard enough. Just thinking about the chaos that would come from adding a ten-year-old added to the brood was exhausting. Madeline leaned in tighter, recognizing that this might be the last breath of solace she'd taste for a long time.

Chapter 4

At seven o'clock, Dave pulled into the circular driveway, stopping at the front door. Madeline was right behind him until she veered off and went toward the bay of garages. He sat in the car for an extra couple of seconds, not accustomed to seeing Mayweather Lane during the daylight. Even in the summer, when the days were their longest, he didn't catch much sunlight leaving at six o'clock in the morning (sometimes five when necessary) and returning at 10:00 P.M. As the summer yielded to autumn, it was worse. He tapped on the steering wheel, pondering. He hadn't given much thought to the amount of time he spent away from home. After a few more moments of rest, Madeline opened the front door, beckoning for him to come in. Tamara and Don stood near the door too.

"Daddy, Daddy," Tamara called out, flailing her hands in the air. Don was holding his blanket and mimicking his sister. Dave's heart warmed.

God had blessed him and silently he thanked Him. Dave hopped out and walked briskly toward the door. The children met him halfway with Tamara leaping into his arms. As soon as he had her sitting securely with her arms wrapped lightly around his neck, he lifted Don with the other arm, juggling both as he entered the house.

"Since you have them, let me go find Sam. He's probably watching TV somewhere." Madeline walked away as Dave struggled trying to balance the two kids in his arm. They fidgeted, giggled, and incessantly talked in his ear, both at the same time. As chaotic as it was making a few steps into the foyer, he felt alive, appreciated. "Oh, and I'll let Ms. Jenkins know that she can leave early tonight, for a change," Madeline said, turning to him.

"Okay, but remember that I have to go back to the office tonight. We have to get our response back to the new client tomorrow," Dave said, not wanting to dampen the mood.

"No, no, stay with us," Tamara said. "I'm not going to get down. You'll have to hold me right here until tomorrow."

"Me too," Don said in his little voice.

"Knew that," Madeline said and left the room.

He sensed something in her tone, not sure if it was frustration, anger, exhaustion, or all the above. That's why he had to convince her to take the time off and stay home with the children, even though it was going to be tough managing without Madeline sitting two doors away.

Dave eventually made it to the staircase and attempted to sit the children down, but Tamara wouldn't let go. Don was more accommodating and went without much resistance.

"Come on, darling, let Daddy sit you here on the steps."

"No," she screamed out. "You'll leave and I don't want you to leave."

"Darling, I won't leave. How about we all have dinner together tonight? Would you like that?"

"Yeah," Tamara yelled, finally releasing the grip she had on his neck. He placed her on the step next to Don.

"Mommy and I have a special surprise," Dave told the kids.

Madeline returned with their oldest son. "I found the little guy watching TV as I suspected instead of doing his homework," she said, twinkling her fingers on top of his head as she and Sam entered the room.

"Come here, big guy, and give your dad a hug," Dave said, taking a seat near the foot of the staircase. Tamara immediately squeezed in, leaving a tiny space for anyone else. Sam didn't readily fly over. So, Dave went to him and bent down to hug his growing boy. "You know," Dave said, pulling back and taking a good look at Sam, "I think you've grown a whole fraction of an inch since I saw you yesterday. Is that possible?"

Sam blushed and leaned in. Dave was touched. Actually, he'd seen Sam yesterday, but his son hadn't seen him. Dave had sat on the side of his son's bed and watched him sleep for many nights. Getting in at ten and 11:00 P.M. was too late to wake his children, but being close to them, poking his head in their rooms and seeing their angelic faces, was fuel to keep going. Before long, Sam and Don were at their mother's side, with Tamara clinging to her dad.

The work had been hard and the sacrifice huge, but Dave knew he was in the will of God. He didn't claim to understand why his calling required him to be away from his children so much, but God had a reason. Dave was certain and didn't question Him, not yet.

He kneeled and beckoned for the children to come closer as they all gathered around him in the foyer. He loosened his tie and draped it across Sam's shoulders. "Remember I told you that we have a big surprise for you?"

Don and Tamara each responded in their own animated way. Madeline stood close but was quiet.

"Well, do you remember Andre?"

"Yes, he's our god brother who lives in Arizona," Sam said.

"No, he's not. He's Uncle Jonathan's son," Tamara said, seeming upset.

Don kept clinging to Madeline.

"You're both correct. He is Uncle Jonathan's son," Dave said, fighting back his emotions. The kids couldn't see him break down. They wouldn't understand and would probably end up scared. He dug deep for great strength and continued. "And he is your god brother, too." Dave drew in a long breath. "Well, he's going to need our help."

"Why?" Tamara asked.

"Well, his mother went to heaven when he was a baby. Now, his father, Uncle Jonathan has gone to heaven too. So that means Andre will have to live with us, because he doesn't have any parents left."

"For real?" Sam said, showing the first sign of excitement.

"Yes, for real. I'm going to get him in a few days."

"Cool," Sam said. "Can I go pick out some of my baseball cards for him?"

"Sure," Dave said, barely able to finish speaking before Sam was bouncing up the stairs, with Don taking much smaller steps, not able to keep up, but trying.

"Make sure you do your spelling and math facts, mister, before you get those baseball cards," Madeline said, although he probably didn't hear her as excited as he was.

"What about you, little lady, how do you feel about Andre coming to stay with us?"

"I'm very happy, Daddy, because if we get a new brother, that means you'll come to live with us too."

"What do you mean?"

"We'll all get to live together again and we can see you every day and not just some days, right?" Dave was stunned, which quickly converted to hurt, an ache deep within his soul. Was that how his children felt, that their father was a casual visitor who popped in every once in a while? The recurring image of sadness coupled with the raw wound of Jonathan's death was too much, and he struggled hard to maintain composure.

Madeline must have sensed him caving because she grabbed Tamara. "Come on, missy. I need you to go wash up and get ready for dinner."

"But I want to talk with Daddy some more."

"You can talk later, after dinner."

"But . . ." Tamara eked out.

"No buts, let's go get washed up."

Tamara traipsed up the stairs in no hurry, until Madeline put a foot on the bottom stair and acted as if she was coming behind her. Tamara picked up her pace.

"Are you okay?" Madeline asked Dave, kneeling down next to him.

Tears streamed down his cheeks as he sighed. "I didn't realize how much the kids miss me."

"You know how children are. They want attention all the time at their age. Even if you were here with them all day, they'd want more."

"Thanks for saying that, but I know there's more to it. They need their father. I just haven't figured out how to do what my Heavenly Father has called me to do while also being a father to my kids."

"I don't have your answer, but I can say that we've made a huge investment into building DMI. We've worked our behinds off to get where we are. We can't let the company slip away." Madeline squeezed next to him. "We're partners and we have to make this work. So, you stay in the office and do what you have to do there, and I'll take the sabbatical like you suggested and take care of everything here."

They embraced quickly and released. Dave stood, extending a hand for Madeline to get up too. "Let's be honest. I'm definitely going to miss having you at the office. I've seen you every day, all day, for twelve years, thousands of hours together. What am I going to do?" he chuckled.

"Guess you'll have to get another phone line since we'll be talking a lot."

They ascended the staircase laughing and joking, a sensation Dave cherished, but would soon question.

Chapter 5

Dave should have returned to the office last night. Opting to stay at home and make a family night with Madeline and the kids had a price. Up at three-thirty, out of the house before four-thirty, and sitting at his desk by five, he'd been paying already.

The phone rang and it was Madeline. "Don has a slight fever. I won't be able to make the meeting with Mr. Stenton this morning."

Dave sighed. "All right," he told her, although it wasn't. His head drooped as he slowly rubbed the palm of his hand across his eyebrows and closed eyelids. The East Coast was Madeline's baby. She'd created the marketing plan, the list of potential clients, and the cost structure. She owned the East Coast expansion. No one in the company, including him, was more in tune with what had to be done for the new account.

Dave extracted the files from the heap and pondered after ending the call with his wife.

Finally, he sat up tall in his chair and put on his reading glasses. The clock was ticking and fretting wasn't adding fresh minutes. The reality was that Madeline wasn't there to lead her meeting and wasn't going to be, indefinitely. He had to go with his gut on this one. "Lord, help me do what I need to do," he prayed. Reassurance seeped in. God had given him favor and wisdom every step of the way in building DMI. Dave didn't see any reason for him to lose faith in God's ability to get them through this transition period, either.

There was a knock on his door around eight-thirty. "Excuse me, Mr. Mitchell, there is a gentleman here to see you," the DMI receptionist said.

"Oh shoot, already," Dave said, buried in a pile of paperwork. "It should be Mr. Stenton from the Eastern Lutheran Group. Bring him up."

Dave would have preferred more opportunity to prepare but time had run out. His faith meter rose as his surging thoughts calmed.

"Mr. Stenton, it's good to see you again," Dave said as the man entered his office, accompanied by the receptionist. "Thanks for bringing him up here," he said. "Please hold my calls." The receptionist left, closing the door behind her. "Please, have a seat," Dave told his guest.

"Will Madeline Mitchell be joining us? I've had quite a few conversations with her over the past month."

"No, she has a conflict and won't be joining," Dave said despairingly. "But don't worry. I'm going to handle your account personally."

"Well, fine then," Mr. Stenton said.

"Have you gone over the proposal that we sent over to your office last week?"

Stenton rustled around in his chair appearing uneasy. "I have and the revised numbers are better, but six hundred thousand is still steep for our budget."

Dave sat down. "Tell me this, do you value the services that we offer? In other words, can we help you?" Dave knew the answer, and Stenton should have been shouting a big fat yes given the highly publicized leadership challenges they had been experiencing for over a year.

"We do."

"Then we need to cut to the chase and work out a deal. You're wasting time haggling over dollars while your organization falls apart. What are you willing to do to get back on track? For goodness' sake, I'm handing you a lifeline, man, take it," Dave said in a raised voice.

"I can't afford to spend funds that we don't have."

"Quite frankly, you can't afford not to," Dave said emphatically. "What number do you need to see in order to make this work for you?"

Stenton rustled more and finally said, "I can't be a penny over four hundred and twenty thousand."

"Done," Dave said, slapping the table and sitting back.

Stenton seemed dumbfounded. "What do you mean?"

"I mean done, we have a deal."

"But how can you afford to give such a deep discount and not impact your bottom line?" Stenton stammered.

"Because I'm not driven by the bottom line. My goal is to help churches who need it."

"Sure, but you're in business too and you're not doing this for free," Stenton said.

"I could do it for free, because I'm not in it for the money."

Stenton grunted. "I'm not sure how you can cut the price on a whim, but I'm willing to take it."

"I make my decisions based on the leading of the Lord. I'm not worried about my bottom line, and you shouldn't either." He reared back in the chair, locking his fingers over his head and pulling them down behind his neck.

By noon he'd sat in two meetings, done the preparation for four, and was ready to take a quick break before heading to the next meeting. He popped into his office, hoping to sneak a call to Madeline. She'd want to know how the East Coast meeting had gone. The phone rang. Dave hustled to the desk, figuring it was probably Madeline thinking the same way he was. He grabbed the phone. "Dave Mitchell."

"Mr. Mitchell, I'm Field Agent Tim Stephens from the Internal Revenue Service."

Dave's spirit dropped. He'd had this call four times in the past eight years. Today, of all days, wasn't the time to get a call from the IRS. "What can I do for you?" he said, as if he didn't already suspect what they wanted.

"We have several questions about your recent corporate filings."

"What kind of questions?" Dave asked, staring out the window.

"I'd rather not get into details over the phone. When can we come out and take a closer look at your financial records?"

No time was convenient. He was booked. Dave should have been totally flustered by the notion of the IRS constantly riding DMI, but he was only mildly agitated. Other than poor timing, he understood their concern. DMI had gone from operating at a loss in the first few years to grossing nearly $200 million in twelve years. The growth was miraculous. He knew it and understood the probing eyes. Dave took comfort in the realization that if God orchestrated the growth, He'd also fight the flurry of battles that seemed to daunt their journey. It was his only answer.

Chapter 6

Dave was writing on a legal pad of paper at his conference table when Frank, the oldest of the Mitchell men, rapped on the door. The clock hanging near the door showed six forty-five.

"Heard you were looking for me?"

"Have a seat," Dave offered.

"What's going on?" Frank asked. "You look as if there's something on your mind."

"It's the IRS. They're going to do another audit."

"What? Come on, you've got to be joking. Why do they keep harassing us?" Frank drummed his thumb on the table, shaking his head. "Aren't there a thousand other companies out there they can pick on for a while and give us a break? We don't have time to keep messing around with them."

Dave had the same sentiment, which was why he had to make some changes. "I hear you, brother, but what can we do?"

"We should be able to do something. I refuse to be helpless, even if it is the government. Shoot, we pay their salaries and I'll be darned if they rake us over the coals and take our money. Maybe we can file a complaint or fire up a set of lawyers who can put the IRS on defense. Let them be the sitting ducks for a change. How about that?" Frank said, relaxing in his seat, seeming satisfied with his response.

"That's precisely why I wanted to talk with you. I have a full plate with Madeline's East Coast and my southern region expansions."

"Yes, and I saw your note about getting the Church of God in Christ national account. COGIC is actually the acronym they use."

"Well, congratulations on the COGIC account, and don't worry about operations. We'll be ready to take on the extra business. My team is fired up and ready to go. Bring it on," Frank said, lightly slapping the table.

"I hear you. This is precisely why I need you to take on the financial role in DMI, too."

"What do you mean?"

"I want you to become chief financial officer. It has to be someone I trust completely." The decision was easy for Dave. Growing up, the two of them were as close as brothers four years apart could be. No matter how busy he was or what was going on, Frank had always made time for him. Dave hadn't forgotten Frank teaching him how to ride his bike, to chuck pebbles into the creek, to catch frogs, and to hit his first baseball. "Put together your own team; completely take on the financial aspects of DMI, including the financial audits. I just don't have time to do it and also keep growing at the rate God has allowed us to realize. This is a critical juncture for DMI and I don't want to fall short because we're drowning in a sea of audits and red tape."

"What about the accounting firm that you have on retainer?" Frank asked.

"Like you said, they're on retainer. We can pull the work in-house at any point. You'll have to put together a simple transition plan but I'll leave that to you, and let me know if there's anything you'll need from me."

"Are you sure this is the route you want to take?"

"Certain."

"Okay, then I'm your new CFO," Frank said, extending his hand to Dave for a shake. "When do you want me to assume the role?"

Dave glanced at his watch. "Oh, about eight hours ago when I got my call from the IRS."

They were both amused.

"I got you, little brother. What about operations? Who's going to do that?"

"That's the bad news. For the moment, I need you to remain chief of operations, too, especially during the expansion. We have to maintain stellar customer service and training programs for the new accounts. It's what we're known for and we don't want to see a dip in quality during the growth period. So, I need you steering the operations ship until we can find the right replacement. As busy as I am, you'll probably have to find your own replacement."

They were amused again.

"Now that you've doubled my workload, I better get moving, otherwise, I'll be spending a lot of late nights here."

"Tell me about it."

Frank tapped the table one last time before standing. "I don't know how you get away with being here late every night. Madeline's the right wife to have if you're going to run a business like this, because you know how mine is. She wants me home by dinnertime. Chief operations officer doesn't mean a hill of beans to her. As far as she's concerned, I'm Frank Mitchell, the husband and father who better get home if he knows what's good for him."

"Madeline is definitely very understanding, mostly because she loves the thrill of our business and the smell of victory. This is her company too, and I know how difficult it is for her to step down."

"Step down?"

"Yes, she's going to take off for a while to spend more time with the kids. And, I didn't tell you yet, but Jonathan passed away."

"Oh, man, you can't be serious. He's the same age as you. What happened?"

"Heart attack," Dave said, fast, before his emotions could catch up.

"Wow," Frank said. "You have my condolences. I know how tight the two of you were."

"We were, which is exactly why I'm going to adopt Jonathan's son."

"Whoa," Frank said, leaning on the back of the chair and letting his head bob a bit. "You're better than I am, because I'm not sure how I'd feel about taking in another man's child and raising him. It's a big step."

"It is, but Jonathan would have done the same for me. It's the least I can do to honor him." Grief wanted to have a public display but Dave refused to let it surface. "So, once we get him here, Madeline's hands are going to be full at home with four kids. Throwing DMI into the mix is going to be too much, even for her, as wonderful as she is. That's why she's stepping down."

"Gotcha," Frank said. "We're definitely going to miss her around here. I know for certain I'm going to miss her. She's feisty, but brother, you already know that. We'll see how long the stay-at-home housewife gig lasts."

Dave grinned. Truth be told, Dave wouldn't mind more evenings at home with the kids, especially after being with them last night and seeing how starved they were for his affection. He was saddened but didn't let it show with Frank. His heart was at their estate on Mayweather Lane but his calling was at DMI. The time with his family would come, but for now he had to do the job he was created to do.

Chapter 7

Madeline planted her cheeks in the first available seat at the smaller of the two kitchen tables, plopping her notebook down, too. She let out a huge yawn around ten-thirty. Catching Dave before he left in the wee hours of the morning had broken her rest. Dosing in and out for three to four hours had worn her down. Getting Sam up and out of the house claimed what drive she had remaining. She scooted closer to the table and tried collecting her thoughts. At best Madeline had an hour before Tamara would be running around wanting attention, with Don following close behind.

After several minutes of basically doing nothing but sitting, she decided to move to Dave's study in the rear of the house. There was a desk and, most importantly, a door she could close off from the children. Since this was her first official day at home, Madeline preferred to slowly make the adjustment. She'd let the children continue

spending the day with their nanny. Madeline
would pop in and out without distraction. There
would be plenty of time to take on the full day-
to-day responsibility. She was more eager to
hear what was going on in the office. So much
was happening with COGIC coming onboard.
There was plenty of movement at the office
with the expansions and several big accounts in
discussions, including a few of hers. She couldn't
wait any longer. She dialed the phone, wanting
all the details.

Dave didn't answer. It was okay for a little while.
She could eat up the time by refining her original
marketing campaign for the Eastern Lutheran
Group. Her pride warmed thinking about the
hard work put into courting the half-million dollar account. Madeline stared at the door, taking in
glances of the room as she looked up periodically.
To see her efforts pay off were both rewarding and
equally melancholy. Honestly, she had wanted
to be at the final presentation. She'd wanted to
take the proposal all the way from the inception
to the "cork-popping" celebration phase. That
didn't happen. Sam, Don, and Tamara flooded
her thoughts, making it easier to shake off the
tinges of disappointment. Her babies were
the ultimate prize. She hadn't lost sight of them.

Even in her stretches of professional euphoria, they were most important. That's the hymn she played over and over in her head until it calmed her ambitions.

The ringing phone caught her off guard. Peering at the wall clock, forty-five minutes had passed as she labored over the marketing campaign. It was her drug of choice. She knew it and was glad that the cost of her indulgence was free. She grabbed the phone after finishing her comment on the page, happy to hear Dave's voice. "Hey, you, I tried calling you about an hour ago."

"I was in a meeting with Frank. How's it going with the kids? Are you enjoying your day off?"

Madeline snickered. "If you consider being sequestered in your study a day off."

"What?"

"Never mind," she told him, opting not to try and explain her weak attempt at being funny. Her interest immediately shifted back to the reason she'd called him earlier. "What's going on there?"

"Remember when we talked about the CFO role a few months ago?"

"Yes, you were thinking asking Frank to take it on."

"Well, I did."

"Good move. What did he say?"

There was a brief silence. "Oh, he said yes," Dave replied in a way that bothered Madeline.

"What are you doing? You seem distracted."

"Excuse me, I'm sorry. It's just that I have papers everywhere. I can't find anything. With my secretary out and now you too, it's a little crazy around here."

"See, I knew this wasn't a good idea for me to take off without planning it out. I need to get back in the office and figure out something else for the children. Maybe we can have a nursery or private school teach them at DMI? That's probably not feasible but what do you expect? I get paid for thinking outside the box," she said, serious about her recommendations, or at least kind of.

"We made the right decision. The kids need you more than I do right now."

"If you don't want my help—" Madeline said, seasoned with emotion.

Dave interrupted. "That's not what I said."

"Sure, sure, okay, but the reality is that your secretary is going to be out for who knows how long on sick leave. Why don't you at least bring in a temp to keep your desks and papers organized?"

"That's not a bad idea. She could help me keep track of this onslaught of meetings and handle quite a bit of administrative tasks. Next you'll want me to find a marketing manager to replace you, too."

"Absolutely not," she said, with her voice elevating. She was ready to jump from the chair. "You can't replace me so easily. I'm definitely not thinking about handing over my spot."

"Now you're talking. We'll stick with the temporary secretary, but I don't have time to interview anyone."

"I'll take care of it."

"No, I don't want to add more work for you," he told her. "This is my problem."

Madeline wanted to do it. Only out of the office one day and she was suffering heavy withdrawals. The charge, the fast pace, the challenges, she missed all of it. Finding a secretary for Dave would be a nice way to stay connected. "I want to," she told him.

"If you're sure it's not going to put a burden on you."

Madeline heard a knock on the door, assuming it was one or both of the children. "Dave, hold on a minute. I think my hiding place has been discovered." She set the phone receiver on the desk and went to the door. Don and Tamara were standing there. She bent down to greet them. "Hello, sleepyheads. Mommy's on the phone with Daddy. Do you want to say hello?"

Tamara ran to the phone yelling out yes with each leap. Don followed her.

"When are you coming home?" Tamara asked.

Being with the children, Madeline could see how depleted they were. It was clear. She'd have to fill the void until he could give them more.

The setting sun beamed into Dave's windshield, almost blinding his path. He was in the house a few seconds when Madeline came in from the kitchen.

"What are you doing home?" she asked, going to Dave and leaning her cheek in for a peck.

"I wanted to spend some time with the kids and give you a break," he said as Tamara and Don ran into the foyer.

"But don't you have Georgia Evangelical coming in tomorrow? I faxed the high-level marketing strategy to you around five. Did you get it?"

"It will be there in the morning," Dave said, picking up Don and then Tamara.

"Humph, that's a surprise coming from you," Madeline said, reaching out for Don and Tamara. "Come on. It's time for your baths."

"I'm staying with Daddy," Tamara shouted out, gripping her father's neck tightly.

"Me too," Don added.

"See what you've done coming home early?" Madeline told him, coming across as mostly frustration.

In that moment, Dave didn't know what to do. He'd disrupted the flow of a household that didn't include him. His goal was to give his wife a break, play with the kids, and be present for at least one night before inserting Andre in a few days. The plan was failing. "What if I give them their baths and put them to bed?"

"Yeah," Tamara and Don shouted.

Madeline laughed. "Come on, you don't have a clue about how to get them ready for bed."

Sadly, she was correct. Time and circumstances had created a complex puzzle. He reflected on the past, unable to pinpoint the precise time when he'd become so far removed from the day-to-day life of his kids. His fatherly heart wanted to ache, but Tamara didn't allow time for wallowing. She had him in the clutches of her grip and didn't appear to be relinquishing her moment for acts of the past.

"Just for tonight, please, let them stay up a little longer. I need to spend the evening with them."

"It might not seem like a big deal, but they need consistency." Madeline eventually acquiesced. "All right, but only thirty extra minutes." She gave Tamara a look that must have been interpreted correctly because his daughter didn't plead for more time.

Dave put both kids down. "Come on, Daddy," Tamara said, pulling his hand and leading the way.

"You better warn me next time you plan to come home this early so I can prepare for this craziness."

Dave's soul was soothed. The surge of harmony erased the peeks of guilt, confident in his decisions. Madeline was the perfect mother for his kids. Soon she would be the same for Andre.

Chapter 8

The four-hour flight from Detroit to Phoenix yesterday hadn't been long enough to mend Dave's shattered spirit. Saying good-bye to Jonathan—his best friend, his brother, and confidant—was an unbearable burden. Only God could help him place one foot in front of the other and ascend the seven or eight steps to the pulpit. Finally, after a teary-eyed jaunt from his front-row seat, he was standing before the congregation. Overcome with emotion, he delivered the eulogy, letting his own words provide comfort.

"If God had taken my life, it would have been easier to bear." Dave paused. The grief was balling up in his throat, making it difficult to speak. He cleared his throat forcefully and continued. "I always believed we'd become old men together, watching our kids and grandkids grow up." Dave paused again. This time he took a sip of water and prayed silently for strength, the only place he knew to go. The congregation seemed patient with him, so he took the extra seconds to gather himself. *Breathe, breathe* he told himself, followed by a deep sigh. Dave felt the blood rushing through his veins, careening to his legs. He was rejuvenated and able to stand firm in the pulpit. "Yet, may God's will be done in my life, in Jonathan's life, and yours. Yesterday was the time to mourn. Today is a day of rejoicing." The congregation was quiet but he continued, feeling the best he had since getting the news. "Jonathan is resting in the Lord. We too will have to take our rest one day, that is promised, but glory to the man who has prepared for his journey; the one who has made the proper reservation in heaven. As Jonathan repented his sins, and confessed Jesus Christ, the Son of God, as his Savior, he made the proper reservation. His soul was saved. So, Jonathan, my beloved friend," Dave echoed, this time without any shakiness in his voice. "Take your well-earned rest, and I won't say good-bye. I'll just say that I'll see you when I get home. To God be the glory for all He has done," Dave said and took his seat as the congregation applauded. His weary bones had found favor.

Andre wasn't as restored as Dave. The young man clung to him, not allowing more than two inches between them before, during, and after the service. Grief-stricken and despondent, Andre concerned Dave. His fatherly instincts kicked in and he instantly wanted to protect the boy, but from what—the will of God? It was evident that the boy would need a great deal of constant support, something Dave had in short supply.

Dave broke away to call Madeline. He wanted to hear the sound of her voice, a simple comfort he'd grown to cherish. He needed her now, but more so, Andre needed her. He would do all that was earthly possible, but a mother's nurturing was the most effective medicine for broken-heartedness. Secure in Jonathan's library, Dave had Madeline on the line.

"I can't talk long," he said, wanting to get back to Andre.

"How is everything going out there?" she asked.

"It was a bit rough this morning, but we're managing. I plan to be home by tomorrow afternoon with Andre. We have a few loose ends to tie up here with the reading of the will and meeting with the real estate agent."

"Won't that take more than a day?"

"Probably, but I figured it was best to get Andre out of here. I can come back over the next couple of weeks to close out Jonathan's estate."

"I know it's tough being there, but you sure sound better."

"I had to. There was no sense in sitting around, pining over what God has already done. I loved Jonathan while he was alive, and he knew it. I have no regrets in our friendship and no doubts about God's will. In those two facts I have regained my strength."

"Okay, then that's good enough for me."

"How are the kids?"

"Their usual active selves, wanting more time and energy than I can give."

"Are you sure you're up for the new addition?" Dave hated laying the extra load on Madeline.

"What choice do we have? We can't leave Andre there alone to be put into some private school or worse, to end up as a ward of the state," she told him.

"I agree. I couldn't live with myself if we didn't take him in."

"We'll do the best we can, that's all we can do."

There was a knock on the library door. It had to be Andre since there wasn't anyone else in the house. "Andre is looking for me. I better go. I love you. Give the kids a hug for me, and tell them Daddy loves them."

Madeline thought she heard a thud come from down the hallway. She waited to see if it was followed by screaming or crying. Nothing came and she was temporarily relieved. Whatever the noise was, she figured it wasn't serious since no one had called to her for help. "I'm sorry, what did you say?"

"I was saying that Andre is looking for me. I'd better go and let you get back to the kids."

That's exactly what she was going to do. The noise hadn't settled with her. Right before hanging up, she said, "Real quickly, I wanted you to know that I've found some candidates for the secretary's position, through the temporary agency. With any luck, I'll select someone today and have them on board when you get back."

"That would be a dream. I'd better go. Andre needs me. We'll talk later."

"Yes, sure, go, go, and tell Andre we're looking forward to seeing him."

Madeline and Dave ended the call. She slowly placed the receiver on the phone base. Andre was going to need a boatload of attention and patience, rightfully so given his situation. The tricky part was that she didn't have either in excess. Tamara and Don were consuming their share and most of Sam's too. *Brush away the flurry of worry.* Madeline couldn't let the mere thought of her obligations weigh her down. There was so much to do before Dave and Andre arrived, and fretting wasn't getting the job done.

   The morning marched on. Madeline drove to
the office, speeding a good portion of the way.
Sam was in school. Ms. Jenkins was keeping
Don. Tamara was getting on the bus at noon
for kindergarten. Madeline was exhilarated and
eager to get to DMI. The rush of being behind
her desk made her giddy. A half hour was all she
had before the candidates would begin filing in
one by one. Her day was going to be filled with
six interviews on the schedule, but Madeline was
thrilled to be where she was.

   The late morning and early afternoon zoomed
by, leaving her with three strong candidates who
seemed to possess the right mix of dedication,
flexibility, organization, and an ability to work
long hours. Pleased with the choices, Madeline had
a slight preference for the last person she interviewed, a young lady named Sherry Henderson.
She was very young, but something about her resonated as a good fit for DMI and Dave's working
style. Madeline reviewed her notes several times
but couldn't come to a decision. It was getting late
into the afternoon and Madeline had to get a few
more things done before going home. She had to
set the secretary search aside and let Dave make
the final decision since he was good at assessing
character. Besides, he would be the best judge in
determining who had the right chemistry for the

role, given the new hire would have to work many long hours with him. Madeline shoved Sherry's resume and the others into the folder, pleased that she'd done her job. Now it was up to Dave to choose one.

Chapter 9

Each family member was present and accounted for: Don, Tamara, Sam, and their frequently uninvited guest, chaos. Hustle, bustle, rapid movement, outbursts, laughter, and heaps of continuous activity brewed a concoction of uncontrollable excitement.

"When are they getting here?" Tamara yelled out, tossing confetti into the air and twirling around as it floated to the floor.

"Soon, my dear, so we have to finish up very quickly." Ms. Jenkins popped into the foyer and asked if they needed help. "I think we're fine. The children are having a ball," she told Ms. Jenkins, who then returned to the kitchen.

"Mom, I'm going to give Andre my super racer," Sam said.

"Really, you're giving away the model car that you got for your birthday?"

"Yep, I sure am."

"Are you sure? Because you don't have to."

"I want to. He doesn't have any parents and I have two. So, it kind of makes sense that if I'm going to share my parents, then I should share my favorite toys, too."

Madeline went to her son and bent down to make direct eye contact. "You are quite a young man. I'm impressed and incredibly proud," she told Sam, enveloping him into her embrace.

"Mom, let go. You know, I'm really sort of too big for hugs now."

"Oh you are," she said, pulling away from him with her hands softly clutching his forearms. "Face it, buddy, you'll never be too old for me to hug, never."

"Okayyyy, but can I get back to my gift? I want to have all my new batteries in before Andre gets here."

"Fine, go, my little man."

Don ran up to her, tugging at the bag of balloons in her hands. "Mommy, I'm going to give him my blanket."

"I don't think you want to give him that."

"Yeah, unh hmm, I do."

"Why is that, mister?" Madeline asked, pausing from the hectic flurry to hear her son more clearly, bending down to his level.

"Sam gave him something special. I want to give him something too."

"That's very sweet and shows that you're a big boy," she said, wrapping her arms around him. "Tell you what; let's think about what else you might want to give him. You have lots of choices, and it will be fun to figure out what will be the perfect gift, okay?"

"Okay," he said, still seeming excited about the entire business of having a guest. Tamara didn't offer a special gift. She was too absorbed into drawing and coloring her welcome sign.

Suddenly the front door opened as the children froze. Dave walked in. "Hello, everyone."

"Daddy," Tamara said, rushing to him. Don was in hot pursuit. Sam casually followed. Madeline waited for them to get their greetings in. She didn't dare try to jump in front of the herd of super-hyped children.

"Where is he?" Sam asked.

Dave went back to the door, briefly stepped outside, and came back in with Andre. The young boy stood in the doorway, visibly frightened.

"Come on in, Andre," Madeline said, slowly walking toward him. "We have all been waiting for you to arrive. We're very glad to have you here."

"Oh boy, do we have some fun stuff for you. Do you like putting together model cars?" Sam asked.

"He's giving you his super racer," Don blurted.

"Shut up. Mom, nobody told him to tell," Sam said, stomping to the base of the stairs and plopping down.

"Don, that wasn't very nice. You should only talk about your gift and not someone else's," Madeline told him, trying to maintain the celebratory atmosphere.

"I'm sorry, Sam," Don said, tearing up.

"It's okay this time, but don't do it again."

"I won't."

"Andre, you remember Sam," Dave said, closing the door and pointing toward his son on the stairs. Andre's gaze wandered around the room, but he didn't respond. "And Tamara."

"Hi, Andre, we made a sign for you," she said, holding up her masterpiece that was 90 percent complete with only a small amount of coloring left to do. Tamara seemed pleased, which was good enough for Madeline.

Don went to Andre and handed him his blanket. Madeline wanted to intervene, knowing Don had an unusually important connection with the blanket. She didn't have any idea how he'd react one night without it. She was about to reach for it when Andre hurled it to the floor. Don jumped back and began wailing.

"Why did you do that?" Tamara asked him with a very mean look on her face. "That's Don's favorite blanket," she said, scooping it up and taking the cherished blanket to her younger brother. They were only one year apart, but sometimes it seemed as though Tamara was his second mother the way she looked after him. Madeline was going to rush in and diffuse the storm, but Dave beat her to it.

"Let's calm down. This is new to Andre, and I imagine he's a bit scared coming into a new house, new family, and being away from his friends and things. So, let's do the best we can to make him feel welcome. Can we do that?" Dave asked.

Each of their children either nodded or said yes. Peace was restored, catastrophe averted, and the party resumed. Tamara went to Andre and attempted to hug him. Without warning, he pushed her away, and she fell on the floor, creating quite a stir. Don clung tighter to Madeline as Andre fell to the floor kicking and screaming. Sam leapt from the stairs and was about to pounce on Andre just as his father snatched him up.

"Let me go, Dad. He can't push my sister. Nobody hurts my sister and gets away with it. Put me down." Dave didn't, thank goodness.

Madeline stood speechless without a plan. She really was rendered helpless, mostly stunned. This was not the reaction her children had expected when they were decorating Andre's room and heaping colorful decorations throughout the foyer and kitchen. She wanted to do something but wasn't sure what, hoping Dave had better insight.

"I need everyone to take a seat. Let's settle down. No one is going to hit, shove, or say mean things to anyone in this house, and that includes you, Andre," Dave said to the boy who was still sprawled out on the floor. Dave put Sam down and asked him to go back to the stairs. He then extended his hand to Andre. "Come on, son, get up."

Andre got up and latched on to Dave. Each step Dave took, Andre made the same, burying his face from the looks of three seemingly frightened, mad, and confused children.

After what felt like forever, order was restored. Andre and Dave sat at the kitchen table while the other children played in their rooms. The climate of change was sweeping through the Mitchell household. Madeline could feel the coolness and it didn't sit well. This wasn't the time to question their decision. They'd done what was best for Andre. Making the situation work was a different story; one she hoped would have a happy ending.

Chapter 10

The throbbing sensation in Madeline's head wasn't subsiding. She couldn't remember if it was her turn to check on Andre or Dave's. Running back and forth to his room most of the night left her drained. The boy's nightmares and incessant crying were more than she expected. Even if it was her turn, Madeline's body was in full rebellion, refusing to move. She stretched her arm toward the center of the king-sized bed, feeling for Dave. He must have heard her patting the covers and rolled over from the other side.

"I'm here," he said, touching her hand.

"Can you check on him for me?" she uttered. "My head is killing me."

"Sure, I'll go." She heard the covers swoosh back and his feet plopping to the floor. "Can I get anything for your head?"

"A cool towel would be nice."

"What about an aspirin?"

"I took two a few hours ago. They didn't seem to help, but I have to wait before I can take any more."

"A cool towel it is then," Dave said. She heard him rise from the bed. Her eyelids wanted to open but the effort heightened her headache. If she could have it her way, Madeline was opting to stay in bed and bury her head under the covers. Dave could take care of Andre, Sam would be in school, and Ms. Jenkins could handle Tamara and Don. She had the plan figured out and decided to see if Dave could accommodate.

"We have to get Andre registered in school today, but I don't think I'll be able to get out of bed, at least not based on the way I'm feeling. Can you carve an hour or so out of your schedule today and take him to school? I can get Ms. Jenkins to help with the other children."

"Oh, that's going to be tough. I'm backed up after being in Phoenix those two days. And with you out, I'm swamped. Today won't work but let me see what can be done tomorrow."

Madeline wanted to be angry but it would only exacerbate the headache. "I need help right now, not tomorrow, Dave."

"I know, and I definitely don't want to put the brunt of Andre's responsibility onto you," he said, coming around to her side of the bed and sitting on the edge. "This is going to take some getting used to. I'm sure that once Andre adjusts, he will get past his nightmares and take on a pretty normal kid's life. He's going to need some patience, and we'll work together to give it to him," he said, as she felt his hand touch hers in the darkness. Five A.M. and the sunlight hadn't quite decided to get moving either.

Madeline was twisted. She didn't want to load Dave with the challenges of the household while he was shorthanded at the office, but he had to acknowledge her needs, too. They were both stretched like a rubber band. She couldn't speak for him, but hers was about to snap. "How about this, why don't you stay here until eight or nine? You can get Sam off to school. Ms. Jenkins will be here by seven-thirty. I can get a few hours of sleep and then get up and take over. You can be on your way by nine."

Dave was silent, which deflated her increasing composure. "I can't, not without creating a mess in today's schedule. My first meeting is at seven-thirty."

"Why so early?"

"Like I said, everything is squeezed into today and tomorrow to make up for the time I was gone."

Madeline knew it was pointless to push further. Dave wasn't going to help. He didn't have time. She had to figure this chaos out on her own. As he stood, she snatched her hand away from his and rolled over, keeping her back close to the edge of the bed. Dave left the bedroom as anger festered in Madeline. She was fixated on how he had the easy job of running their multi-million dollar company, leaving her alone to perform the harder task of managing four rambunctious children. She didn't allow her mind to rehearse the decision to take in Andre. She'd better not if there was any chance of continuing to believe it was a good idea. Understanding that he hadn't asked to be orphaned offered no consolation. Madeline buried her head into one of the extra pillows, hoping her worries and impending day of stress would vanish.

Chapter 11

Dave squeezed in a cup of coffee and a bite of food wherever he could. He was engrossed with the business at hand but Madeline stayed on his mind. After the night that Andre had, he couldn't stop thinking about him, either. There were a few more meetings and then he'd steal away to give them a call.

"Brother," Frank said, entering the office. "I've been trying to catch up with you since early this morning. You're a tough guy to find," he said, taking a seat without waiting for an invitation. Frank sailed a small set of stapled papers onto the table. "Consider the IRS a closed subject."

"As we expected," Dave said, giving Frank part of his attention.

"You were that confident?"

Dave shrugged his shoulders and continued reading an article.

"Why?" Frank asked.

"It was out of my hands from the beginning. Let's face it. I'm a small business owner. The IRS is a long-reaching arm of the government. There was no way I could beat them outright. I did what has always worked for me."

"Don't tell me, you prayed to God for guidance, help, and who knows what else?" Frank said, half mocking. Dave could tell. He wasn't bothered by the comments. He knew what he knew. God had been the definitive source of his strength and guidance from the day DMI was conceived. God alone had supplied the inspiration, the resources, and Dave wasn't ashamed to shout his testimony from the rooftop. Fortunately for him, Frank wasn't on the roof. He was sitting right there.

"Why bother worrying? It doesn't help solve the problem. I might as well stay positive and hope for the best."

"Can't argue with that," Frank said, resting his elbow on the table. "The proof is in the pudding, and you, my brother, have plenty of pudding," he said, sealing the comment with a chuckle. "I have to give it to you. Your God routine is working for you. Great wife, kids, and look at this place," Frank said, looking around the room.

"I wouldn't call it a routine," Dave said, peering up from the article.

"Ay ay ay, don't take it like that. I didn't mean anything by the comment, except that your thing with God has produced results—plain and simple. A sane man has to take notice. That's why I'm sticking with you, little brother, to see if your Midas touch can rub off on me. Never know. I could stand a good wife too."

"You already have a wife."

"I specifically said a good wife, one like Madeline who can work side by side with me in the office, take care of home, and the kids, and stay sassy. That's not an easy combination to find, let me tell you." Frank picked up his papers, preparing to leave. "You know you hit the jackpot with Madeline." Dave did and nodded in agreement, knowing Frank didn't mean any disrespect. "She's one of a kind. Be sure and treat her right." Frank said, reaching the threshold of Dave's office.

"You know I will." Dave picked up the phone to call his wife. Much of the day had passed, but he wasn't going any longer without speaking with her.

The phone seemed to ring and ring, so long until Dave briefly forgot who he was calling. Madeline picked up, triggering his memory. "I was just about to hang up and dial again thinking I'd called the wrong number."

"No, I'm here, pooped of course. I managed to get Tamara and Sam off to school. Don is taking his afternoon nap and Ms. Jenkins is watching Andre while I'm barricaded in your office again."

"Maybe I can work the schedule around over the next couple of days and give you a legitimate break. You deserve it," he said, picking up the family photo sitting on his desk.

He was concerned about Andre. The way he acted last night required more than Madeline had to give. "Are you getting Andre registered in school today?"

"I decided to let him relax. We can take him tomorrow. I figured another day won't make much difference in the grand scheme of things. School started a month ago. He hasn't missed much. They usually fool around a few weeks rehashing what the students forget over the summer."

"You're probably right." He set the family photo back in its place. "Just let me know when you're getting him registered, and I'm there."

"Well, we'll see. By the way, have you interviewed those secretaries I set up for you?"

Dave let his head press against the high-back chair and closed his eyelids. "No, not yet."

"Dave, come on, you have to get it done so you can get some help. Get off the phone this minute and call the temp agency. They can get the ladies in today."

"It's already after one o'clock, might be too late today," he said.

"Not for someone who really needs the job."

"Good point, I'll call." Dave could achieve two goals for the price of one. He'd put an end to Madeline's worrying while also getting the help he desperately needed in the office.

He made the call. It took a bit of doing, but two of the three candidates were willing to come in on short notice. The other would come tomorrow.

By three-ten, the second interview was well underway. "Miss Henderson, tell me what kind of secretarial experience you have?"

The young lady shifted her weight from one arm of the chair to the other and then said, "I don't have very much experience." Her gaze fell to the floor.

Dave was short on patience and couldn't understand why Madeline would recommend someone with no experience. She knew how critical it was for him to have a top-notch person in the office. He pressed on with the interview, annoyed. "You understand that I'm looking for a secretary with several years of experience, a person who can start today and handle quite a bit of responsibility. Does that sound like a job you can handle?"

"Yes, Mr. Mitchell, I can," she said, sliding to the edge of her seat quite convincingly. "I can do any job you need me to do. You see, I must get this job. I really must."

Her spark of enthusiasm claimed his attention. Passion fueled Dave. It was how he ran his life, in the pursuit of goals and dreams. He wholeheartedly believed in being totally and passionately committed to whatever task was being undertaken. Miss Henderson didn't have the experience but she'd earned a chance to present her case. Dave was actually intrigued. "If you don't mind me asking, why are you so eager to get this position?"

Miss Henderson remained at the edge of her seat. "I had to put my college studies on hold last year due to financial reasons. I must get a job now."

"But if I hire you, how soon will you quit and go back to school?"

"I have no idea when I'll be able to go back. I can't think about the future. I have to get a job today."

He sensed sincerity in her answer. Since he placed high marks on loyalty and trustworthiness, Sherry was quickly moving to the top of his candidate's list.

Dave was deemed to be a decent judge of character. Something about Sherry Henderson resonated with him, although he was unable to pinpoint exactly what it was. They spoke for twenty more minutes before concluding the interview at four.

"Miss Henderson, thank you for coming in."

"When will you make a decision about the job?"

"You will hear one way or the other by tomorrow." Sherry's demeanor appeared to turn somber. Dave stood and came from behind the desk. "But you are our top candidate." The color returned to her cheeks. "If you are selected, how soon can you start?"

"Tomorrow or even today."

Dave glanced up at the wall clock and laughed. "Since it's already four o'clock, perhaps today wouldn't be realistic but I get your point. You're available to start right away, which is great for me."

They said good-byes and she left.

He'd have the temporary service cancel the third candidate tomorrow. Between the two ladies he'd met today, the job could be considered filled. He got Madeline on the phone. He valued her input and wanted to get her recommendation before closing out the selection process.

"You'll be pleased to know that I've interviewed two of the three candidates."

"Wow, that's good. Who did you pick?"

"I'm leaning toward Sherry Henderson. She's enthusiastic and has the kind of positive attitude that I'd like to see on my team."

"I knew you'd like her. She was my pick too. The only reservation I have is her age. She seems very young, like in her early twenties," Madeline said.

"And somewhat inexperienced as a secretary, too, but she didn't come across as immature."

"No, she didn't, as a matter of fact just the opposite. She presented herself very well," Madeline added.

"I get the feeling she'll catch on quickly, and the selling point for me was how keen she was to start. We need that kind of enthusiasm in the office. That's important to me."

"I agree, and we can always put her on a trial period for six months. If she doesn't work out, we let her go. On the other hand, we don't know what's going to happen with your secretary, and her medical leave. You might end up keeping Sherry permanently."

"Exactly, there's no risk," Dave said.

"So when does she start?"

"You know me. Once I make a decision, it's full steam ahead. Let's get her in here as soon as the agency can make it happen," Dave said.

"Good idea."

"You sound relieved," Dave told his wife.

"I am. Sherry will be good for us. I'm glad you're getting the help."

Chapter 12

Sherry heard the phone ringing as she fumbled with the key to her apartment. She dashed in by the fourth ring, hoping to catch the call.

"Miss Henderson, I'm calling from the temporary employment agency." Sherry's stress skyrocketed. She wasn't expecting to hear back until tomorrow. She prepared for the disappointment. "I have good news. Mr. Mitchell would like to hire you for the secretary's position."

"Oh my goodness," Sherry blurted, unable to contain her emotions.

"Apparently he was quite impressed with your interview." Sherry was bursting with joy. She couldn't wait to get off the phone and tell her fiancé. This job was the miracle they'd hoped for. "Can you start on Monday?"

"Yes, absolutely," Sherry said, although Mr. Mitchell had given the impression that she could start tomorrow. "I can start sooner if you'd like."

"We'll need you to come into our office and complete paperwork. I figured since tomorrow is Friday, it will be more practical for you to start fresh with DMI on Monday. I believe the client will appreciate the gesture."

"That's fine with me." Actually, it wasn't fine. If Mr. Mitchell was okay with her starting Friday, the agency should have been okay with it too. She needed the money and one day was definitely going to make a difference, but the decision wasn't hers. She'd make no trouble. "Thank you for the opportunity. I'll be there Monday."

"Great, Mr. Mitchell will meet you in the DMI lobby at eight A.M."

"Thank you, thank you," Sherry bellowed, resuming her joy. There was no containing her glee. She had to get to Edward.

Twenty minutes later and she was parking her car in his parking lot. Each step taken toward his apartment building was taken with ease. It felt like she was floating. Their worries had fallen away and she was free again to enjoy the thought of their future plans. She couldn't get to his door fast enough. After several rapid knocks, he came to the door. Sherry wrapped her arms around his neck. "I got the job. We're going to be okay. Isn't that wonderful?"

Edward pulled away. "Yeah, that's nice." He walked into the living room, leaving Sherry standing at the door.

She closed it and went to him. "What's wrong? I thought you'd be happy."

Edward placed his hands on her shoulder and stared into her eyes. "I am happy for you, but it doesn't change the fact that I'm still out of work."

He was pulling away again until she took his hand and said, "You'll get something very soon. I know you will."

"Ah, you say that but I'm not so sure. It's tough out there right now."

"General Motors is a big company. Just because Buick didn't work out, can't you go to Cadillac or Pontiac?"

"Don't you think I've tried that by now?" he said with a sharp edge that caused her to lean back. "I don't have enough seniority to approach any of the other plants."

"Okay, so General Motors is one company in Detroit. There are plenty others."

"Don't you get it? None of the big companies are hiring junior pipefitters. On top of that, you know how it works. Once they find out that I didn't complete my apprenticeship from General Motors, places like Chrysler and Ford won't hire me either."

Edward took a seat on the couch, covering his eyes with his hand. Sherry eased next to him. She wanted to console him but didn't know how, short of getting him a job. At least she had one, which was going to be a huge help. Edward was happy for her. Deep down she knew he was and understood his frustration. With their wedding ideally happening next summer, she imagined his depression was fueled by the pressure. Sherry was committed to getting a job and she had. Next, she'd work super hard and make as much money as possible to help Edward through this rough patch. It wasn't going to last long. Before they knew it, the wedding and unemployment would be behind them and a bright future lay ahead. She relished the thought and snuggled in next to Edward, hopeful but guarded.

Chapter 13

Madeline pulled the covers over her head when Dave got up at five. He was getting used to her sitting up in the bed and talking with him for twenty or thirty minutes before his feet hit the floor. She had changed her routine the last couple of days. He looked over at the mound sequestered under the covers and grinned slightly. She was tired and he wouldn't bother her. They'd catch up during the day, although it had been difficult for both to find time to talk on the phone. He stopped reflecting and got up. Duty was calling.

An hour later he stepped into the hallway and found Andre lying next to the door—two mornings in a row. He scooped up the lad and returned him to his room. Andre didn't wake up, which eased Dave's ability to exit and get to the office without incident.

Nine-thirty rolled in and Dave had several notes strewn across his desk stating that Madeline had called already.

Patricia Haley

He was about to dial her at home when Frank walked in and asked, "You busy?"

He was, but when Frank came to his office, it was usually very bad or extremely good news, with room for nothing in the middle. He'd want to hear what Frank had to say. "Come on in, have a seat. I can make my call after we finish."

"I don't know what it is about DMI, but the vultures love this place. Every time we turn around somebody is out to get a piece of this company. If it's not the bloodsucking vultures at the IRS, it's a crippled group of vagabond shysters trying to hustle a buck. When will it end?"

Dave listened as Frank vented a while longer. When he stopped talking, Dave asked, "What's got you so riled up this morning? I thought you'd resolved the IRS situation. Did they change their minds and decide to proceed with the audit?"

"No, we're good with the IRS, at least for now," Frank said, grimacing. "This is a fresh attack. I just got a call from Attorney Davis." Dave was on alert. It was never a favorable sign when the senior principal of the law firm was involved. "We're being sued by Train Them Up, Inc."

"For what?"

"Trademark infringement."

"You have to be kidding," Dave said.

"I wish I were. Nope, it's for real."

"What do they want?"

"Money and publicity, of course, the same as what each of our other adversaries want."

"I just don't understand the basis of their suit. They must mean a concept was infringed upon, and how can you own a concept? That's simply crazy. That's the same as saying we stole their idea," Dave said.

"I know it's crazy, and you know it's crazy. My job is to make sure Attorney Davis and the courts think this suit is just as crazy too."

Dave shook his head. "I know you'll handle it."

"I'm on it."

Dave couldn't help but to snicker under his breath thinking about his DMI journey. "What is this, like lawsuit number thirty-four?"

Frank didn't find the matter funny. He kept a staunch disposition, appearing irritated by the lawsuit. "It's been at least that many in the past ten years."

"Remember the last suit, the one where our former employee claimed we fired him without just cause," Dave said.

"Man, that was ridiculous. The guy was late something like seventeen times in a month. There's only twenty working days in the month, so I don't know what he was talking about with

no just cause. He should have been glad we
didn't dock his pay. Come to think about it, he
owes us money." Frank loosened up and laughed
along with Dave. Then Frank shook his head.
"This has got to end at some point. Why don't
these cats get the message? They aren't going to
win."

"They never do."

"Eventually they'll stop wasting their energy
and mine, because we're not handing out money
from the company like it's Halloween," Frank
said in a stern tone, meaning every word and
ready to enforce.

"Chalk it up as the cost of doing business."

"This isn't about business. It's purely greed.
These animals need to find another watering
hole, period. Can you imagine how much money
we'd be out of if we'd lost any of those cases?
DMI would be crippled financially. That's why I
take each one of these frivolous claims seriously,
because if we lose to one, the rest of the vultures
will be on us in a flash, ready to draw more blood
and pick the bones clean."

"That's not going to happen. We're still standing strong," Dave said, empowered in his role.

"You bet it's not going to happen, not on my
watch, not so long as I'm chief financial officer,
or chief of operations, or so long as you're my

brother. The attacks will stop with me. They'll never make it to your desk. That, you have my solemn promise about," Frank said with such fervor that Dave claimed an extra dose of reassurance. Between God and Frank, DMI was well protected. To seal his assurance, Dave would say a prayer as soon as Frank left and then go on with the business of the day, worry-free.

As Frank was closing out his conversation, the phone rang.

"Go ahead and get that. I'm leaving anyway. I'll keep you posted on the case," Frank said, leaving Dave's office.

Dave answered the call to find Madeline on the other end. "Perfect timing. I was just wrapping up a meeting with Frank, and I was going to call you shortly. How's your morning going with the kids?"

"Not good, did you forget about taking Andre to school?"

"Oh, shoot, I did." Dave couldn't believe he'd forgotten about getting Andre registered in school. He'd promised Madeline that they'd go together.

"It's already Friday. If he doesn't go today, we'll miss the entire week," Madeline said.

"You're right. Let me carve out a few hours this afternoon. I can pick up you and Andre around one o'clock."

"Are you sure? I'm okay with going Monday so long as you promise to lock it in and show up. But Dave, Monday is the absolute latest that we can wait."

"No, let's go today. This is too important to push off. I'll see you and Andre at the house." Dave and Madeline exchanged "I love you's" and got off the phone. Dave stared at his calendar. He had to review contracts for the expansions and meet with the marketing team to finalize their upcoming campaign. He barely had a free moment to go to the bathroom let alone leave the building, but he wasn't going to tell Madeline. Without complaining, he began shuffling his appointments and would keep at it until the three-hour block of time was free. Madeline and Andre deserved his commitment, and they would have it, no matter what. Everything else was going to have to wait. He finally took a break to pray for his guidance and Madeline's strength, faithfully believing God would deliver both.

Chapter 14

Sherry tossed and turned much of the night. She popped up before the alarm rang Monday morning, eager to get to work. DMI was her miracle job and she'd do her utmost to be a success there. Her tiny closet held her four dresses and two skirt suits, the ones most appropriate for the office. That would cover a week. She'd planned to take her first check and buy another outfit and continue the pattern until her closet held two weeks' worth of clothing. Sherry hurried, dressing and grabbing a quick breakfast, and got on her way.

She entered the building and waited in the lobby. When Mr. Mitchell didn't show up by ten after eight, the security guard sent her upstairs. She got on the elevator, feeling energetic and ready to get started. She got off on the fourth floor and approached the receptionist. "I'm Sherry Henderson. I'm here to see Mr. Dave Mitchell."

The receptionist looked at a list and said, "I don't see your name here. Please take a seat while I contact Mr. Mitchell."

Sherry's enthusiasm cooled. She'd rehearsed many tasks that could go wrong, but having Mr. Mitchell forget about her starting today hadn't been one. She took a seat but didn't find it comfortable. By eight-thirty, anxiety ratcheted up and she popped out of the seat, no longer able to contain her concern. She approached the desk again. "Did you speak with Mr. Mitchell yet? Is he expecting me today?"

"I've tried to reach him several times. He's quite busy, but I'll try him again."

The receptionist picked up the phone. Sherry interrupted, "Would it be possible for you to go see if he's in his office? I'm sure he wanted me to come in today." Sherry could tell the receptionist was about to say no, so she cut her off. "Please, this is my very first day here. I was hired as Mr. Mitchell's secretary. I could see how busy he was during my interview last week. It seemed to me that he could use help right away. I'm here and eager to help him. Could you please go see if he's there? Please?"

The plea must have resonated with the receptionist because she agreed to go. "Wait here and I'll see if I can find him for you."

"If you want, I can fill in for you at the desk," Sherry offered.

The receptionist hesitated and then said, "Thank you, but we better not do that. Let me go find Mr. Mitchell," she said. "I'll be right back."

Sherry paced until the receptionist returned fifteen minutes later. "I found him. He's on the phone now, but he told me to bring you up to his office."

"I know where he sits. If you want, I can go up to the sixth floor myself and save you from having to keep running around."

The receptionist's eyelids widened, followed by, "Are you sure? Because that would be wonderful."

"Sure, no problem." Sherry thanked the receptionist and went to the elevators. She was so thrilled. The stairs would have worked too, whichever was faster.

Mr. Mitchell's door was partially closed, so she sat at the empty desk in front of his office. Thirty minutes later, which actually felt like two hours, he emerged from the office.

"Miss Henderson," he said, extending his hand to shake. She popped to her feet. "I'm sorry for the delay. It slipped my mind that you were coming today."

"It's okay."

"No, it's not. I have quite a lot of juggling going on these days. My secretary normally takes care of things like this for me. Since she's on sick .leave, you can see that I'm not doing as well with her job as she does, which is why I'm glad you're here. Perhaps you can save me from myself," he said, lightening the mood. The lingering anxiety she'd felt while waiting was completely erased. He'd seamlessly put her at ease.

"Where do you want me to sit?"

He patted the back of the chair where Sherry was sitting. "Exactly where you are. This is where my secretary sits, right outside my office. So, this is now your desk."

Sherry's anxiety was gone but it seemed to be replaced by intimidation. Throughout the interview process, she was so focused on getting hired that there hadn't been an opportunity to stop and think about who she was working for: Mr. Dave Mitchell, the head of the company, the top guy. Her nerves began sizzling, moisture accumulated in the palm of her hands, her knees trembled. She wasn't afraid of who he was but was deeply concerned about the quality of work he'd expect. She probably couldn't make mistakes like the other secretaries in the building. She desperately needed the paycheck, but had she been set up for failure already? What had she gotten herself into? "Can I please sit down? I feel a little woozy all of a sudden."

"Sure, absolutely," Dave said, pulling the chair out for her like a perfect gentleman. He reminded Sherry of her father, not solely in age but also in his mannerisms. She appreciated the gesture, trying to remember when the last time Edward had done that. He used to pull out her chair and help her out of the car routinely. When he got laid off, there was a change. That's why this assignment was a blessing. They could get married as planned. Her heart beat smoothly thinking of Edward. She sat down.

"Where would you like for me to start?"

The dumbfounded look on Dave's face made her nervous again.

"Honestly, I don't know. When my secretary is out, my wife normally helps me keep organized. As you can imagine most of my day is filled with meetings, which means I won't have very much time to help you get going. I know that sounds crazy. I need your help but don't have time to get you started."

"I understand, really I do. Is there someone else who can help me?"

"Let me think," he said. Shortly afterward he said, "I got it. I'll have our receptionist help you. She can show you around the building, where to find the washrooms, the copy machine, fax machine, and other areas you'll need. Oh, just a minute," he said and went into his office. He returned with a tall stack of papers. "If you don't mind, I could use three sets of these for an upcoming presentation."

She was elated. "I will get it done right away."

"No hurry, I won't need the copies until Wednesday."

Mr. Mitchell's phone rang. He excused himself, went into his office, and closed the door. Sherry had officially started and dove right into the work. She found the receptionist and had her explain how the copy machine operated. The morning was clicking by. Sherry went back to her desk periodically to see if Mr. Mitchell needed anything. He happened to catch her on this round.

"Sherry, good, you're here. Can you please go and tell Mr. Jefferson that I'm running behind by a half hour? I'll catch up with him and Frank later this afternoon to finalize the deal. He's in our legal department on the third floor."

"Okay," she said, jumping up.

"Also, when you get a minute, I'd like you to schedule these six meetings. I've put down the names and numbers of who should attend. You'll have to find a slot that fits everyone's schedule.

These meetings should happen within the next two weeks. Let me know if there's a problem with getting any of them scheduled, and I'll see what we can do," he said. "I'm sorry to be dropping so much on you without much guidance. Let me know if you need help."

"Oh no, sir, I'll be just fine." Whether she believed it or not was irrelevant. She was going to make this assignment work.

Chapter 15

Noon had come and gone. In the beginning of the day, she'd only had a stack of copying to be done by Wednesday. As the morning zipped along, Dave had emerged several times with additional requests, including more copies, setting up meetings, cancelling meetings, typing, and running errands inside of DMI. Sherry had a list of questions for him but every time she considered knocking on his door, his phone-in-use light indicator was on. That was the case most of the day. If there wasn't someone physically in his office, he was on the phone. His time was jam-packed to the point where he'd stepped out and asked her to take his calls earlier.

By the tenth call in two hours, Sherry had her speech down pat. When the phone rang, she answered, ready to spew out her greeting. "Good afternoon, you've reached Mr. Mitchell's office. Can I please take a message and have him return

Patricia Haley

your call as soon as possible?" she said, taking pride in her efforts.

"Sherry Henderson, is that you?"

"Yes," she uttered, surprised anyone would be calling her there.

"It's me, Madeline Mitchell. Welcome aboard."

Sherry was in a chipper mood. She'd liked Madeline the moment they met in the interview, being intrigued by her knowledge and personality. "Mrs. Mitchell, I want you to know how grateful I am for you and Mr. Mitchell hiring me."

"You have a great attitude and that made the decision easy for us. How's it going so far?"

"It's very busy here, but I'm doing okay I think."

"I'm sure you are. Like I said, we're certainly glad to have you on board, especially me. My husband tends to take on a lot without asking for help."

"I plan to do my very best with as much as I possibly can. You won't be sorry."

"I'm sure I won't." They spoke for a few more minutes and Sherry could hear yelling in the background. "I better go," Mrs. Mitchell said abruptly.

The noise was so loud and unsettling that Sherry couldn't ignore it. Without filtering her reaction, Sherry asked, "Is everything okay?"

"Have Dave call me back as soon as he can," Mrs. Mitchell said and got off the phone.

Sherry was left pondering what could possibly be going on. The mound of work that Dave had heaped on her throughout the day quickly ushered her back into the DMI world. The short conversation with Mrs. Mitchell floated away.

Chapter 16

"Andre, you're going to school. We don't get a choice. It's the law," Madeline said, pleading with him. She stood in the doorway, speaking, but her words weren't getting over the threshold. She'd tried getting close to him and providing some type of comfort, but he didn't let her enter the room without a ruckus. She was ready to give up.

"Ahhhhhhh, ahhhhhh," Andre wailed as Madeline went to the top of the staircase and sat down with her hands completely covering her earlobes. *Count to ten, to twenty, to a hundred.* If that was the answer to getting Andre calmed, she'd count to a trillion with no complaints. Reality had set in early in the day. She didn't have the answer. Handling irate clients was a cinch. Controlling an emotional ten-year-old was out of her league. She felt beaten. Madeline had called Dave many times, unable to catch up with him. She needed him. He had to come home if for no other reason than to give her a sanity check. The family was suffering. Don was sequestered downstairs with the nanny. Tamara and Sam were in school, but they'd be home in a few hours and Madeline couldn't have Andre still acting out without impacting the other children.

Andre continued wailing. He wouldn't stop.

She slowly rubbed the palms of her hands across her eyebrows with her eyelids shut tightly.

"Andre, I'd like for you to come downstairs with me," she said, returning to his doorway after claiming a twenty-minute hiatus. She wouldn't dare pretend to be fully rejuvenated, no way. But she had restored enough gumption to try reaching out to him again. The thought of Dave dashed in. Jealously brushed against her. She knocked it away and shifted her waning conviction to Andre again. His actions demanded all that she could offer and more. Since she couldn't get a hold of Dave, Madeline didn't know where the "more" was going to come from. She'd gotten herself into a mess.

"I figured you might be hungry." He hadn't eaten breakfast or lunch, which was disturbing. She couldn't let him wither away in her care. Something had to be done and fast if this arrangement was going to work. "Would you like a snack before the children get home from school?"

He was despondent. The boy sat in the corner playing with a miniature basketball that Dave had bought him on their way from Arizona. He'd clung to the ball for several days, refusing to put it down. Madeline didn't want to push him. They'd gotten through the past ten minutes without him acting out. She wasn't about to disrupt the unfamiliar sound of quiet. She went downstairs to prepare for her other children, leaving Andre for Dave. After all, bringing the boy into their home was his decision too, which meant he had to share the load.

Chapter 17

Sherry was pleased with her day. She was quickly learning that keeping busy wasn't difficult to do at DMI. Dave emerged from his office ten minutes shy of three o'clock.

"Miss Henderson, can you do this filing for me?"

"Of course I can."

"You'll have to get the key from the secretary in legal. She'll show you where we keep critical documents and acquaint you with our filing system." He set the stack of files on top of her desk. "Let me know if you have any questions."

He said that every time, but there hadn't been a single free minute for her questions. She didn't bother asking.

Dave glanced at his watch and rested his fist on the stack of files. "I'm going to grab lunch. Please hold my calls for me." He was about to walk away, then turned and asked, "How has your first day gone?"

"Very busy, but I like that."

"Well, if work makes you happy, you'll be extremely satisfied here every day," he said with humor. "As you can see, there is plenty of work to go around."

Sherry wasn't fully at ease talking to Dave with him being an executive. She appreciated his humor, conscious of not crossing the unspoken set of boss-and-employee rules.

"Are you finding your way around pretty easily?"

Not sure if he wanted the real answer, she grappled with what to say. Sherry had plenty of questions, but if she asked them, would he see her as a dependent secretary who couldn't figure out what had to be done without his constant input? She couldn't take the chance. She told him, "Yes."

"If there's anything you need, don't hesitate to ask," he said, tapping on the stack. "I'll be back in a few minutes. By the way, what did they have in the cafeteria today?"

"I don't know. I haven't gone to lunch yet."

"What, are you kidding me?"

"I have too much to do."

"Nonsense, you have to eat. Let's go," he told her in a "don't bother refusing" kind of tone. So she didn't resist. "This works out well," he said.

"It gives me a chance to welcome you aboard properly." She followed along, grateful. "I hope the cafeteria is okay for you. They'll only have snacks left this late in the day, but I can't take the time to go out for a decent lunch today. With the Church of God in Christ coming in later this week and the Georgia Evangelical deal closing, I'm up to my ears in meetings and contracts, as you can see. I'll owe you a rain check for a nicer venue."

"The cafeteria is fine with me," she said, not planning to eat much regardless of where they went. He could eat. She'd spend the opportunity getting questions answered. That was more important.

Sherry was beaming, walking several steps behind Dave.

"Am I walking too fast for you?" he asked, causing her cheeks to blush.

She couldn't figure out what to say or do around him. Being his secretary, Sherry realized she had to boost her comfort level quickly. She didn't want him to question his decision on hiring her. She would muster the courage and act as if going to lunch with him was commonplace.

Dave grabbed an apple and a couple of leftover tuna sandwiches. She opted for a cup of coffee and a pack of cheese and crackers.

"This is awful," he said. "This isn't a meal. This is a survival kit," he said, slicing at chunks of her shyness. "Be sure and put a lunch date on my calendar. I can certainly do better than this."

"I don't mind, really I don't."

Dave must have accepted her answer, because he didn't mention the food again. The conversation carried on for nearly forty minutes, which translated into hours for him based on the tightness of his schedule. He stayed and answered most of her questions, which she thought was pretty incredible. She concentrated on looking at every object in the room that took her focus off Mr. Mitchell. It was difficult not to be swept up in his presence, given his way with words, engaging disposition, and knowledge. She especially liked how down-to-earth he acted, not superior or condescending. Sherry couldn't wait to see Edward and tell him about her first day. Finally there was something wonderful worth celebrating. Edward would be pleased.

Chapter 18

Madeline was irritated. It was well after three o'clock in the afternoon and Dave hadn't returned her call yet. Andre had calmed, allowing her to breathe. After a period of drama-free thinking, she was able to put the chaos into perspective. How should they expect a little boy to act after losing his last parent, moving across the country, and then being dropped into the middle of a strange family? Being overwhelmed was natural. It was difficult for her to deal with his outbursts and withdrawn attitude. That was true, but she couldn't be mad at him. Instead, she'd concentrate on increasing her patience.

"Mommy, can I get a snack?" Don asked, tugging at her.

"Sure, tell Sam and Tamara they can have one too."

"Andre too?"

"No, honey, don't bother him, okay? Go to the kitchen and have Ms. Jenkins help you. Mommy has to make another call," she said, hiding her aggravation with their father.

Madeline went into Dave's office and closed the door. She was practically boiling with anger by the third ring. When Sherry answered the phone, Madeline harnessed her attitude, intent on not publicizing their personal business. "Hi, Sherry, does Dave happen to be free?"

"He should be. Let me check, Mrs. Mitchell. I know he just got back from lunch."

What in the heck was he doing at lunch when she was ducking and dodging chaos being hurled from every direction at home? Enjoying lunch would have been a dream for her today, yesterday, or the day before. After a brief wait, Sherry returned to the line. "He told me to tell you that he'll call you back in a few minutes."

Madeline wanted to tell him to get on the phone, but again she refrained from letting Sherry get a glimpse of their discord. Personal matters had to stay private. "Okay, well tell him I'll be waiting," she said in the cheeriest voice she could muster. It was so convincing, she impressed herself. *Dave had better call,* was what her thoughts were really saying.

Several minutes later the phone rang and she snatched it up. *Better be Dave.* She answered and it was. "Where have you been? Didn't you get the message earlier that I called? I needed your help with Andre."

"Hold on, let me close my door," Dave said.

She didn't want to offer any courtesies. Madeline was mad mainly because she felt alone in the battle. But she kept a tight grip on her anger. "I guess the only way to get a call in to you is to get on your calendar. I can't seem to catch you any other way."

"I'm sorry. There's a lot going on here, but you know that better than anyone."

Madeline cut him off. She didn't want to squander precious time talking about DMI. It would just make her day worse. "I've been trying to get in touch with you all day about Andre."

"What's wrong, is he okay?"

"No, he's not okay. That's what I've been trying to tell you. He's a mess and as a result I'm a mess too."

"What's going on with him?"

The fact that Dave didn't know made her want to stretch her arm through the phone, pull his face into their house, and let him see what she'd been wrestling with for days, but she didn't want to pursue that line of discussion either. She settled with saying, "Andre isn't ready to start school, not yet." Each morning she'd approached Andre about going to school, and it had lit a firestorm. The house was in constant uproar. He just wasn't ready, simple as that.

"You're with him all day. You know what's best. I support your decision."

She was primed to argue with him, but he didn't give her a chance. He was too agreeable, which irritated her. "Fine," she snapped. "I'll call the school." Another week at home. Now that Andre was registered, the principal wouldn't like it, but tough. She had to do what was best for Andre even if it was unconventional.

One topic could be checked off her list. There were several more items she planned on discussing with Dave. She was content in her seat, gearing up for a long conversation.

"Excuse me, Madeline. Someone's knocking on my door. Give me a minute and I'll be right back. Don't go anywhere, hold on." He didn't have to worry. She wasn't going anywhere. Dave returned and said, "I'm sorry, but negotiations with Georgia Evangelical have broken down. Frank needs to run the new numbers by me and then get the package sent out this evening. It may be another late night for me."

"We've been on the phone five minutes and you have to go already? You had time for a lunch break but you didn't have time to call me? What's gotten into you? We used to talk constantly."

"And I miss that, but I honestly need to get down to finance and get this issue resolved or the account will be in jeopardy."

"Go, bye," she said with a sting. Madeline remained sitting as the phone buzzed, indicating that she should place the receiver on the base. She didn't. The call was over. Dave was gone. She was upset and empty. He hadn't provided the sounding board she craved. Forget the promise she'd made to him before they got married about accepting the demands of his job no matter how intense it got. That promise was made during her naïve years. That was then and this was now. Resentment festered.

Chapter 19

Sherry stared at the inch-thick packet of notes that had to be typed. She peered at the clock flashing four-fifty and then back at the copies that had to be done in preparation for Mr. Mitchell's big presentation tomorrow. She toyed with the time and amount of work left to do. There was no way she could finish by five. Her zeal was squashed. This was her first day on the job. Sherry couldn't conceive of telling Mr. Mitchell that she needed to leave early. Well it wasn't really early. Five o'clock would be leaving on time, but tell that to the typing, filing, and scheduling left to do. She felt like the wife who'd been busy all morning and looked up at three o'clock to realize she still needed to cook, clean, and wash before her family walked in the door. Sherry was dazed in the moment and didn't know what to do.

She slumped in her seat. Getting off late was going to be a problem this evening. Her countenance lit up thinking about Edward and their date tonight, although she didn't view their moments together as dates any longer. They were a true couple, planning to be married soon. Sherry sat up in her seat again, rejuvenated. The mounting stack of papers didn't scare her. She'd work as fast as she could to get done and get to Edward. The thought of telling him about her day sparked her batteries and boosted her speed. She couldn't wait to tell him about the conversation she had with Mr. Mitchell. Her delight was bursting and must have shown when Mr. Mitchell walked past her desk.

"Oh, Mr. Mitchell, I have a few papers that need your signature."

"Are these the ones for the Georgia Evangelical deal?"

"Yes, and a few for the Eastern Lutheran Group," she said, scrambling through the stack, trying to find the paper and appear organized. It didn't pop up right away. "I know it's here," she said, starting to panic.

He put his hand on top of the stack. "Don't worry. I'm headed to a meeting with the CFO, so I'll be here late. When you find the paper, please set it on my desk and I'll sign it."

"But it has to go out in the packet that's getting shipped this evening," she blurted out, not sure if she should have said it. She was hoping to get off at least by six or six-thirty. If she had to wait for Mr. Mitchell's meeting to end, then her evening was over. The perfect time for her and Edward to discuss wedding plans would be crushed. She couldn't let that happen. Not now, not when she had money coming in and they could reconfirm the date. The wedding had been on hold for several months, since Edward was laid off. That's why her employment was so important.

Sherry kept digging feverishly as Mr. Mitchell stood, but she could tell he was preparing to leave. There it was, finally, that pesky paper. "Found it," she said. Sherry plucked it from the pile, practically out of breath, and glided it to the edge of the desk with one hand while whipping out a pen in the other. Poof, she'd saved the day, or more like the evening. Her galloping heart slowed to a controlled trot with her anticipation rising. The wedding plans were on again, thanks to Mr. Mitchell. Sherry had to acknowledge Mrs. Mitchell too, maybe more, because she was the one who brought her to DMI. Sherry had to find a special way to repay the kindness one day, but tonight, she was too busy. The work wasn't going to get done by itself.

Chapter 20

Madeline didn't wait for Dave's alarm to sound off at four-thirty. She was wide awake by four, having drifted off to sleep shortly after putting the children to bed last night around nine. The plan had been to wait up for Dave, but her depleted body rebelled. With seven hours of sleep, Madeline was rested and ready to tackle the day. Her first order of business was Dave. He had to be told about the tenuous situation at home. She'd tried her best to manage the household, but with Andre's fragile condition, there was no hope of doing it alone. Madeline called out to Dave softly so as not to startle him from his sleep. He didn't respond. That's when she rubbed across his shoulder and continued calling his name until he woke up.

"What time is it?" he asked.

"Time to get up, we have to talk."

"All right, give me a minute."

She rubbed across his shoulder again. "No, come on, I need you to get up now, otherwise, the time will run out and we won't get to talk until tomorrow morning."

"All right," he said, rolling over so his back was flat on the bed and hands clasped under his head. "I'm up. Let's talk."

"Dave, I'm at my wit's end." She paused, careful not to say something that could be hurtful or misinterpreted.

"I was afraid this was going to happen. Let's get you some help today."

Madeline cackled but not in a ha-ha way. "How are we going to get help just like that?" she said, snapping her fingers in the air. "If the solution was that simple, don't you think I would have fixed it? We certainly wouldn't be having a four A.M. discussion. Come on, Dave, you know me better than that." Her dissatisfaction with his curt response simmered.

"Madeline, I'm sorry, dear. I didn't mean to offend you. That was not my intent," he said, drawing closer and resting his hand on hers.

"What can I do to make this better for you?"

There were a thousand tasks he could take on around the house but that wasn't going to get at the problem. "I need you present in my life."

"What do you mean? I'm right here," he said, caressing her hand.

"You're not here most of the time." Before he could say a word, she raised her voice and continued. She was finally getting his undivided attention and was intent on commanding the stage. He was going to get an earful. "When we agreed that I would stay home with the children, it didn't mean that I would become their only parent." Dave tried to interject but she kept talking faster and louder. "I love my children and I'm okay with staying at home to give them what they need, as long as you are giving me what I need. And right now, you're not."

"Okay, what do you need, another nanny, another housekeeper, cook, what? Just tell me and it's done."

"Stop, Dave," she shouted. "How many times have I told you that I don't want my children raised by nannies? They have two parents. They have us. That's our job, and I'm the only one who's doing my job," she said. Dave sat up. She appreciated him being smart enough not to interrupt. A wise listener was what she needed him to be. "I miss our interaction in the office." She didn't consider herself the crying type. If she were, this would have been the moment for tears to flow. Her eyelids were dry and she continued purging. "I didn't realize how much I'd miss my work at DMI. It's hard for me to have a meaningful adult conversation. I really miss that."

"Are you saying that you want to come back to DMI and get someone else to take care of the kids?"

"I'm saying that I totally underestimated the effort required to take care of four children and a household without my husband."

"But you know I'm doing my part at the office."

"Are you kidding me? DMI is a thousand times easier to manage than this bunch. Andre alone is a handful. Remember him, the boy who has already lost one father? He can't lose you too, and I'm sure that's what it feels like to him since he never sees you. Heck, I never see you. If nothing else, you're going to have to make plans for him. I can't help him. He needs you. Sam needs you. Don needs you. Tamara needs you, and I need you. If you can't make the time for me, at least do it for them."

"You know I love my family, and I want to be present for them. You know that," he said with his voice deepening. "My hands are tied. Somebody has to keep the company running. Don't think I'm sitting at the office twiddling my thumbs. Between the expansion efforts and constant attacks from lawsuits, the IRS, and competitors, I'm constantly on the defense dodging bullets. With you out of the office, it's even more intense. Thank goodness Frank is handling the finances and operations; otherwise, we'd be in a pinch."

Madeline had yielded her position to Dave's calling years ago, which was why being his partner at the office meant so much. In a sense, his calling and vision had become hers. Honestly, DMI deserved proper attention, but she wasn't going to let Dave forget that they had a partnership. She was willing to spend 80 percent of her effort taking care of their home. The other 20 percent of her passion was reserved for DMI. If she could split her priorities, he could too. "I don't want you to take me for granted. What I'm doing here is just as important as what you're doing. As a matter of fact, it might be more important, because what I do frees you up to do what you do. This is a one hundred percent partnership."

"Agreed."

She appreciated Dave swallowing his words during their talk. The slightest offensive comment might have heated her mounting discord and sparked an argument that neither wanted.

The clock sitting on the nightstand displayed four forty-five. Dave got up from the bed and she didn't stop him. She'd stated her case. The bottom line was that Dave couldn't continue being a hands-off father, not if he valued his children's stability. She didn't know how he was going to do it, but he had to find a way. The strength of their relationship depended on him.

"And don't forget that Andre is probably waiting outside the door for you. He refused to go to sleep last night until you got home. Seeing that you didn't get home until who knows when, I suspect he fell asleep," she said, shaving some of the thorns from her words, not wanting to argue.

She heard Dave's voice as he moved toward the bathroom. "He was lying by the door last night and I took him back to his room and put him to bed. You're right, I'm sure he'll be at the door this morning, and I'll carry him back to bed like I've done every day," he said, closing the bathroom door.

"At least one child is getting some of you," she muttered and pulled the pillow tighter to her head.

Chapter 21

Dave was supposed to be finalizing a new proposal, but he hadn't gotten very far. Home had him bound.

Frank walked in. "I knew you'd be here. Is there ever a time when you're not?" Dave gave him a rapid glance that didn't stick. "Don't the long hours ever weigh on you?" Frank asked.

Dave shrugged his shoulders and wrenched his hands. "I don't like it, but what can I do?"

"You're the chief. You call the shots in here. Go home whenever you want."

"I wish it were that easy."

"Make it that easy."

Dave understood his brother's perspective, which was seen through the eyes of self-reliance. Dave had chosen a different path, one guided by faith and trust in the almighty God. Dave's choices weren't always right and by no means perfect, but he could accept the outcome, knowing that he was trusting in God to make up the difference.

"I didn't choose this path on my own. It was selected for me. Because of that, I have to succeed."

"Better you than me," Frank said, shaking his head.

"I don't know why you're talking. Many nights you're here late too, so don't act like I'm the only worker bee sitting in this room."

"Yeah, but I don't have a wife who wants to be around me," he said. "Anyway, how is that adoption situation going, any problems?"

Other than Andre taking time to get adjusted, there were no problems. "We had to take the guardianship step first and then the adoption comes next. Surprisingly, the paperwork has gone pretty smoothly. The legal aspect was a piece of cake since Jonathan designated me as Andre's guardian in his will. Since there aren't any other relatives to contest the will, we're sailing through the process. In a couple of months he'll officially be my son."

"Wow, I have to give it to you, that's all right. I honestly don't know if I could do it. Those two I have are plenty. Another three years and the last one will be in college. I can't wait to get them out of the house."

"You don't mean that," Dave said, laughing.

"You bet I do, most definitely. 'Bye' is what I'm waiting to say. I already have the good-bye speech rehearsed. I practice it every now and then to make sure I'm ready when the time comes," Frank said, laughing too. "When that last one is gone, I'm not adding any new ones. That's some of the reason my wife is so mad at me. She always wanted more kids. Two is good enough. Maybe one of them will bring me a cool drink of water in my old age but there's no guarantee. With two, my odds are doubled."

"Why not have three and triple your odds?"

"Oh no, three is when the cost starts to outweigh the benefit. Taking care of three kids, I can afford to get my own cool drink of water with that price tag."

"You're something else," Dave said as the brothers roared in amusement.

After a good chuckle, Frank asked, "You're cool with this, but what about Madeline? How's she doing?"

Humor was sucked out of the room as Dave thought about the sacrifice Madeline was making for him and their family. "She's amazing. What else can I say?" Dave wouldn't elaborate by telling Frank that his wife was stretched with running the house and managing Andre's emotional challenges. Based on what Dave saw, though, Madeline was gaining control. Frank didn't need to know details. "Without her at home, I wouldn't be able to do what I do here, that's the bottom line. She's my anchor at home."

"She was your anchor here too. When's she coming back?"

"I don't know." He hadn't spoken to his wife about DMI lately. Actually, if Dave discounted the constant arguing, they hadn't spoken much at all. "She's thrown herself totally into the kids and their schedules. There doesn't seem to be any time or interest left for DMI."

"That's surprising. She loves this place. Even I know that much."

Dave hated admitting that Frank was right, but he was. "I know," he said, taking on a somber feeling. "She's making a sacrifice for the kids." Dave pulled his seat up to the table and grabbed a pad of paper. "I owe them some of my time." Perhaps he could speak it into existence, although realistically it was wishful thinking at best. Neglecting his family wasn't his heart's desire, but what else could he do during this phase of DMI's growth? Every time he got a break between expansion opportunities, there was a frivolous matter scarfing down the free time he was expecting.

Frank slid a folder to him. "Good luck with that," he said with a strange look on his face.

"What is this?"

"More of the same, but don't worry about this lawsuit. I got it. I'm just letting you know so you won't be blindsided if someone asks you a question, Frank said."

The lawsuit didn't generate a reaction. It would be taken care of like the others had, but Madeline and the kids resonated. His thoughts were troubled.

In the end, his family was paying the price of keeping his ministry on track. His hope was that DMI would settle down and soon he'd be free to go home at a decent time each night. The notion of being at home with Madeline and the kids, eating dinner together, playing games, and talking until they fell asleep on the sofa was soothing. Normally, this would be the time to pray for confirmation and direction, but he'd wait until later, since Frank was there. In the meantime, he believed that God had a plan for his family, had to; otherwise, Dave wouldn't be able to continue. He pushed family aside as he got to the pressing business sitting before him.

"Thanks for stopping in, man. It was good being able to talk," Dave told Frank.

"That's what I'm here for."

Dave checked the wall clock. "I have to get going. I have an arbitration hearing at eleven."

"Really, who's representing you?"

The latest general counsel had resigned—number three in two years. The constant barrage of legal issues seemed to run them off. "I'm going solo."

"Are you sure? Because it doesn't sound wise to me. You know they're gunning for you every time you set foot in the courtroom. Ask for a continuance and get an attorney. If we can't hire one, we'll rent one."

Dave didn't find the comment funny. He didn't mess around when it was time for battle. He was focused, able to completely block out distractions. "I have no fear. My lead counselor is always with me." He went to the closet and grabbed his suit coat.

Frank stood. "Well, your record does speak for itself. You've won the other cases decisively. When you think about it, those don't count as legitimate fights. Each one was over before it got started."

Dave agreed as he adjusted his collar and cuff links on his sleeves. He pointed up toward heaven with both index fingers. "It's not me. It's Him, all the way."

"Like I often tell you, I might not be as religious as you are, but I definitely respect your game. Do me a favor and keep those prayers going and remember to mention your big brother once in a while. Maybe God will let some of what you have rub off on me," Frank said. "What is this case about anyway?"

"A church in the southern region is claiming that DMI mismanaged their funds, although we didn't have direct access to their money. It's a clear case of extortion, and they're not getting away with it."

"A bunch of crooks hiding behind the name of the church," Frank said.

"Well, that's why God has called us to this ministry. Their kind of stinking thinking and fiscal mismanagement have to be rooted out of churches."

The brothers walked out of Dave's office together. "Hang on while I run to my office and grab a few things. I'm coming with you." Dave was preparing to respond when Frank cut him off. "Don't bother telling me to stay here. I'm coming with you. I know you have God, but you'll have me there too."

Dave didn't argue. Once Frank made up his mind, that was pretty much it. His brother and wife were alike in that way.

Chapter 22

Dave and Frank sat on one side of the table in a cramped office. They were in an older wing of the courthouse, the part that sat below the jail. It felt like a dungeon to Frank. He couldn't wait to escape. An hour was as long as he wanted to be that close to a jail. His thoughts were scattered but he could tell Dave's were not. On the other side of the table were the church's pastor and at least two attorneys he figured. He wasn't sure who the fourth person was. It didn't make a difference; they'd all be dealt the same loss equally. Frank relaxed and waited for the fireworks to begin.

About ten minutes later, the judge came in. Both sides of the table prepared to rise as he said, "No need to stand. We're going to be informal as long as everyone plays nicely." Chuckles circled the room.

Once the hearing got underway, it moved with lightning speed. Both sides pleaded their cases.

"Your Honor," Dave said, "we had no access to the church's money. This case is a scam."

"Wait a minute, mister," the pastor rose up to say.

"Hang on, everyone," the judge said, extending his hands like an umpire calling the runner safe. "Mr. Mitchell, are you telling me there's no merit to this case?"

"That's exactly what I'm telling you." Dave plucked a file from his briefcase. "I have the contracts and the checks we've received from them. I also have the DMI financial records showing transactions in and out of our corporate account as far back as six months before and up to five months after the alleged funds were taken." Dave opened the folder and placed it in the center of the table, as if to say that DMI had nothing to hide. "Ask them to produce records for the same timeframe. We'll soon see who's lying."

Sparks didn't flare until the judge asked for the church's bank statements. It turned out that the fourth person on the other side of the table was an attorney too. They fumbled among a mound of papers before huddling in a muttered conversation. The pastor appeared concerned. Frank was licking his lips. He could smell the fireworks getting lit.

"Excuse me, Your Honor, but we seem to have misplaced some records."

Frank couldn't react openly. He'd wait.

"How can you come to an arbitration hearing and not bring critical documents?"

Frank knew why. They hadn't expected to be put under the spotlight. Their plan was most likely to roll in with a team of high-paid attorneys, talk a good game, and run away with a payday. Frank smirked. Clearly they hadn't heard about his little brother and his personal counselor. There were a few details that had to be finalized, but Frank wasn't paying much attention. His stomach was growling. He'd moved on to lunch plans. That was more interesting than watching the pastor and his entourage grovel.

"We'd like a continuance."

"For what?" the judge barked.

The look of concern flushed across the faces of Dave's accusers. "We need to get the proper documents."

"This was your day in court. If you didn't come prepared, that's your fault. I won't let you waste the court's time with your incompetence, counselors." The judge set the pen down on his pad of paper. The judge was mad, regaining Frank's interest. He could tell something good was about to happen. The other side must have sensed it too because they squirmed and fidgeted relentlessly. The pastor sitting closest to the judge was fuming. Dave was calm. "After careful consideration, I find there to be some truth in Mr. Mitchell's claim that this is a frivolous lawsuit brought before this court, with little shred of solid evidence." He hurled his words directly at the plaintiffs. "I find this to be an egregious abuse of the court's time. Therefore, I not only find in favor of the defendant, I'm also awarding damages for defamation of character in the amount of one million dollars."

"What, Your Honor? There's no precedent for your decision," the lead attorney said in a raised but controlled voice. His outrage was quite visible.

"Then consider it an unprecedented act."

"Your Honor, that's absurd and extreme," another attorney yelled. The others conversed among themselves. "The original claim was only for six hundred thousand. How can you award them more than we were asking in the first place?"

"If the number doesn't sit well with you, I can always raise it to two million."

The attorneys shut up. They didn't seem happy but at least knew when it was no longer feasible to keep fighting a battle that was over.

Frank didn't expect DMI to see a dime of that money, at least no time soon. He fully expected the brood of attorneys to file an appeal. Frank didn't care if the preacher wanted to keep spending money on attorneys instead of his congregation. That was between him and them.

Dave gathered his belongings. Frank too. Dave shook the judge's hand and then the pastor's. "My mission at DMI hasn't changed, Pastor. I'm in business to help you, because by helping you, I'm glorifying my Father," he said, pointing up. "Isn't that the business you and I should be about?" he said and left.

Frank couldn't wait to get outside. He never tired of seeing Dave in action. They headed to the office, invigorated.

Back at DMI, Dave said, "Frank, let's recap the arbitration over lunch. We might as well capitalize on the momentum for our next case."

"Which case?" Frank asked.

"Don't worry. It's on the way," Dave said as they roared.

"Cool, lunch it is," Frank said.

He was walking toward the elevators when Dave turned to say, "Sherry, why don't you come to lunch with us? I'd like for you to take notes as we hash out a strategy."

Frank hadn't noticed how young she was until now. He peered at his kid brother, amazed at how lucky and successful Dave was, even when surrounded by inexperienced, and at times, incompetent people. Whatever luck Dave had, Frank looked forward to the day when he would have the same.

"Are you coming, big brother?" Dave asked.

"Right behind you," he said, content with being in the midst of a great man.

Chapter 23

Madeline couldn't remember the last time she'd awakened refreshed. No nagging headache, or lingering exhaustion, or inescapable issues were waiting to latch on this morning. She was free. She lay quiet for what must have been a good fifty minutes, wondering if it was for real. Dave was still in the bed too. She glanced at the clock on her nightstand. Four fifty-three. She considered going back to sleep but decided against it. She and Dave hadn't enjoyed very many pleasant conversations in recent weeks, especially when it came to what the children needed.

"Dave," she whispered, turning on her lamp. It took several calls before he responded. "Are you awake?"

He groaned. "I'm up, everything all right?" he said, letting his back lie flat on the bed.

"Yes, everything is fine. I just thought that since I'm wide awake, we could get a chance to talk before you go into the office."

"Okay, that sounds good."

Madeline was pretty sure she'd gotten up early one day last week to speak with Dave about Andre's upcoming parent-teacher conference, or maybe it was the week before. She couldn't recall. Getting up between four and five wasn't as appealing as it had been several months ago when she'd left DMI. Back then Madeline was willing to get on Dave's calendar anywhere she could. DMI was like a drug she craved. She'd wanted to know what was happening with sales in her region. She wanted to hear about the new deals brewing, about what activity was happening. As the days passed, her zeal was replaced with Tamara's piano lessons, Don's registration in preschool, and managing Andre's bouts with nightmares.

"Did I tell you that Andre and Tamara's parent-teacher conferences are tonight?"

Dave rustled around on the bed. "No, you didn't tell me," he said, seeming upset. What did he have to be upset about? At best he only had to show up.

"Hmm, I thought I had. Oops, I guess I must have forgotten, sorry."

"That doesn't seem like something you'd forget, Madeline. It's pretty important, don't you think?"

Okay, she'd forgotten to tell him, whoopee-do. *Move on.* "Dave, you don't even want to go there with me. Many things are important, like getting home for dinner every once in a while, tucking our children in bed every blue moon, calling them after school to say hello. That's what I consider important."

"Madeline, I'm not trying to fight."

"Good, I'm not either but don't come down on me because I forgot to give you a date. With as much as I do in the house and for this family, it's a miracle I can remember anything. You have a secretary to handle your schedule, I don't. Now that's what you need to remember," she said, folding her arms, sitting up, and pressing back against the headboard.

"What time are the conferences?"

"One is at six and the other seven."

"Which is which?"

Her temper heated. "What does it matter? You need to come to both."

"I didn't mean it that way."

"Oh well, that's how it sounded. If you can't take the time out for one child, don't do it either," she said, slumping down on the bed.

"I'll be there," he said, getting up.

"We'll see, but I'm not going to hold my breath."

"Madeline, you know I'm doing the best I can. You act like I'm staying away from home because I don't want to be here.

"Humph."

"And you know that's not the case." He sat back on the bed. "What do you suggest I do, Madeline? You have all the answers. What would make you happy?"

"Don't you dare try to make this about me. I understand that you're the CEO and have to run the company, but you're also the one in control there. There is no one who ranks higher than you, which means you can do what you want to do. If the CEO wants a few hours or a few days off, who's going to tell you that you can't? That's what I want to know, huh, tell me that, Mr. Dave Mitchell."

"Sounds easy, doesn't it, seeing this from where you're sitting? Wasn't that long ago when you were at DMI, helping to fight off the attacks and lawsuits, while watching the place grow like crazy. You don't seem to realize what a vital role you played at DMI. When you left, we had a massive hole to fill, but I don't bother you with that business. I handle your absence the best way I can, because this arrangement is what we agreed was best for our family and for DMI. I'm doing my best to uphold my end of the bargain."

"Don't try to put this on me. No way, mister, I still say you can get the time off if you want." She did remember the workload and it wasn't easy to fill her spot. She'd been there from the beginning and had a wealth of knowledge that a replacement would take years to obtain. But her disdain for his absence didn't diminish. Maybe it was selfishness, maybe need, or maybe resentment because he got to taste the corporate action daily. Being away from DMI was like fasting. Initially giving it up seemed impossible to survive, but as each day passed, her tolerance increased. But make no mistake, the taste wasn't completely gone—she'd just learned to manage the cravings. The thought of it all caused her to get agitated. She didn't know what the source of her irritation was, except that it was there and didn't appear to be going away.

Dave reached for her hand. She pulled it away. "I'm sorry you're unhappy, but I want you to know how much I appreciate what you're doing. You've whipped this place into shape, just like you did with the marketing department at DMI."

Madeline found the compliment empty. She wasn't in a receptive mood. She was sure that would change, but Madeline didn't want to let Dave off so easily. Letting him stew was gratifying.

"Oh, I meant to tell you that Andre hasn't been sleeping outside our bedroom for the past couple of days. Is he doing better?" Dave asked.

"Ask him yourself" was what she really wanted to say, but there was no fruit coming from that kind of response. "For three months he has fallen asleep waiting up for you. Since you never showed up, he had his nightmares practically every night up until a few weeks ago. After going back to sleep, he'd get up in the wee hours of the morning and camp out by the door hoping to catch you. I guess he's finally given up, like the rest of us. Looks like his nightmares are gone, along with his chasing you."

Dave stood and walked toward the bathroom. "I was just asking the question."

"And now you have your answer."

"Madeline, don't give up on me. God is going to see us through this rough patch."

"Humph, apparently God is the only one getting your attention. Maybe that's who you should have married, became a priest or monk or something like that," she said, turning off the lamp and scooting down under the covers. She'd thrown away a good hour of sleep on worrying and arguing. Hopefully she could get a little more rest in before her day kicked off with the children. Irritations had to be marginalized.

Chapter 24

Dave stood at the large windows framing his office, peering outside, as he uttered a few words of prayer. Madeline hadn't been the most tactful in her lashing this morning, but what she said rang with truth. That was one of the many characteristics he appreciated and had come to depend on: her knack for honesty. He could work with the truth; didn't mean it would always sound good or put him in a comfy position, but knowing the truth was required if he was going to fix the problem. He went to his desk and picked up the phone, ready to call Madeline again. He'd called to apologize to her earlier but she was in the middle of getting the kids off to school and didn't want to talk. He was disappointed, but understood. He rested the phone back on the desk. He'd give her space to cool down. He was confident that she'd call when the time was right.

He had another idea. He was in charge and decided to call his CFO.

"Hey, Frank, how about lunch on me today?"

"What, you're going to lunch? I better check the weather because there must be a tornado or hail storm headed this way."

"Ah, come on, I'm not quite that bad."

"Yeah, you are."

According to Madeline he was. Now he had confirmation from his other truth marshal. Between his wife and brother, he was never at risk of living in denial. They made sure he had a healthy dose of reality dumped in his lap frequently. Admittedly, their style of delivery was rough, but his love for them smoothed the edges.

"Let's get out of here, man, and grab a nice lunch. The break will do you good. You work just as hard as I do."

"Oh no, I don't," Frank said, amused. "No way, but as much as I hate to pass on a free meal, I'm going to have to. These IRS people are breathing down my neck."

"I thought we were finished with them." Dave wasn't alarmed, only curious. He knew Frank had the matter under control.

"Exactly, which is why I don't understand how they can keep bugging me. I guess since you put your special touch on them, they don't know what to do with us. I get the feeling they cancelled the audit so fast that they're having second thoughts."

Faith had a way of bringing resolution to a tumultuous situation overnight. Dave had experienced it time and time again. Every time he heard a testimony like the one Frank was sharing, Dave was increasingly convinced. No matter how much turmoil was trying to surface at home, he'd remain focused and let God handle the storms. "Well, looks like you have it under control. You don't need me involved."

"Nope, I got it. So, I'll definitely take a rain check with lunch, and don't think I'm going to let you forget," Frank said.

"No worries there."

Dave ended the call and returned to the windows. The sun was sitting high in the noonday sky, almost tugging at him to come outside, to take a well-earned break. He plucked his suit jacket from the closet and headed to the hallway. Even if he had to walk around the building for fifteen minutes, he was getting out of the office to enjoy the beautiful day his Father had created.

He stepped past Sherry's desk, who seemed preoccupied with typing. Then it dawned on him what to do. "Miss Henderson, don't I owe you a welcome lunch?"

She stopped typing and looked up at him. "We already went. Remember when I joined you and Mr. Frank Mitchell after the hearing?"

"Oh come on, that doesn't count. That was work for heaven's sake. You were there to take notes."

"Don't worry about it, really." I totally understand how busy you are and it's okay. He could tell she was eager to get back to her typing. "I'm settled into my job, and I'm not new to DMI anymore anyway," she said with her fingers returning to the typewriter. Three months ago she wasn't certain about her responsibilities at DMI and asked questions every chance she got. That seemed like a long time ago. Sherry was organized and filling the role as if she'd been there for years. Dave was glad to have her on board, especially since his former secretary was extending her medical leave for another six months. Dave grinned, thinking about Madeline. His wife had saved him by hiring Sherry at a time when she was most needed.

"I'm taking you to lunch. Grab your coat and let's go."

"Where?" she said with a dumbfounded expression.

"To lunch."

"Right now? But I have to—"

"Stop right there. We're going to lunch and that's a direct order," he said, allowing his grin to widen so she'd relax.

"Are you sure? Because I have a ton of work to get done before I go home tonight."

"I'm positive. Let's go; the work will keep until later." Dave felt satisfied. He'd heard Madeline's appeal and would do his best to make meaningful changes.

He and Sherry stepped onto the elevator. Dave pushed the ground floor button.

"Mr. Mitchell, the cafeteria is on the third floor," she said, reaching for the button. He placed the weight of his hand on hers before she touched the buttons.

"We're not going to the cafeteria." She looked puzzled again. "We're going out to one of my local favorites. It's only a few blocks away. Do you mind walking?"

"No, I don't," she said with her puzzled look dissipating, as a content expression formed. That's what he wanted to see.

They walked through the turnstile. "And I have one request," he said. "Please call me Dave."

She hesitated but didn't seem bothered. Then she said, "Dave, do you mind calling me Sherry? I'd like that."

"Sherry it is," he said. She put on her coat as they exited the building. The sun was even brighter outside than it had been filtering into his office. This was a new day, a new start, and Dave was pleased with his efforts.

Chapter 25

Sherry was grateful to Mr. Mitchell—or Dave, as he preferred—for taking time out of his busy schedule to take her to lunch. She didn't feel like a high school student around him any longer. They'd spent so much time working together that her initial awkwardness around him had faded.

Dave poked his head out of the office. "Sherry, please hold my calls."

"Sure, Mr. . . . . I mean, Dave. How long would you like me to hold them?"

"Oh, I'd say about a half hour. I need to call my wife."

"Okay," she said, making sure he'd finished talking before returning to her work. He closed his door and she tapped a few buttons on the phone to send the calls to her desk. She couldn't help but to think about Edward, her sweet and kind fiancé. That's something he would have done in the past, stop all activities just to give her a call in the middle of the day for no reason. Her soul tingled thinking about how fortunate she was to have Edward. He was going through a difficult time, but it would pass. With her love, support, and a decent paying job, he'd be fine real soon. A series of unpleasant conversations with him recently attempted to sway her opinion about how soon he'd regain his positive outlook, but she refused to give up hope.

When she started, the job was a lifesaver and still was. Edward didn't quite see it the same way, but she understood. Once he found employment, then he'd be able to appreciate her help. She'd tried several times, but he'd yet to accept money from her. It bothered her more than she acknowledged. They were supposed to be getting married in the summer. Her money was his and his was hers; at least, that's how Sherry believed it went with married couples.

She couldn't take the fretting a second longer. *Better to give him a call and push doubt aside.* She could tell that Dave was still talking to his wife. The red light was lit, indicating that a call was in progress. *Great.* That would afford her a good five or ten minutes to call Edward without appearing to be on a personal call in the presence of her boss. It would take some getting used to, calling him Dave, but eventually she'd hammer it into her head. He was kind and easy to talk to, but she hadn't forgotten that he was the CEO. She was only a secretary. Her income meant too much to jeopardize over a careless mistake. She'd been mindful of every word, but at this moment, Sherry wasn't worrying about DMI. Edward was at the top of her agenda.

She called him at his apartment. Unless he was out job hunting, she knew he'd be home, sitting on the couch, waiting for their date this evening. There wasn't much else for him to do since he didn't like watching soap operas or game shows. She couldn't imagine sitting for hours with nothing to do, but he did.

Edward answered after several rings. "Hello, darling," she said, practically whispering. "I have a few free minutes and wanted to say hi." Sherry covered the receiver with her hand and constantly caught glimpses of Dave's closed door to make sure she was safe. "How's your day going? Find anything that looks promising?"

"Nothing today, but I'll be back out there at seven A.M. tomorrow." She admired his effort. Every morning Edward was up and out as if he were going to work. By nine A.M., he had filled out four or five applications.

"Don't worry. I know you're going to find a good one soon."

"I hope so, but let's face it. There aren't any pipefitting jobs out there. I'm not in the union, which means I can't get back into an auto plant. In Detroit, it's the only game in town."

There wasn't much she could say. He knew his industry better than she did. "Just don't give up."

"Who's talking about giving up? I'm just feeling sorry for myself right now. I'm going to keep looking; that's all I can do," he said solemnly.

Dave's door opened and Sherry instantly tensed. "I have to go," she muttered into the phone. "I'll see you around six." She didn't give him a chance to respond, feeling compelled to end the call abruptly. Dave didn't come outside his office. He hadn't noticed her on the phone, but it was too late to get Edward back on the call. She'd see him in a little while anyway. Sherry got to work, hurrying to ensure she got off on time today, for a change.

The afternoon zipped by. Sherry had watched each second of the last ten minutes click down. Finally it was 5:00 P.M., close enough to quitting time. She opened her bottom left drawer to pull out her purse, eager to go. Dave approached her desk, coming from a meeting he had with legal. He set a stack of what looked like contracts on the corner of her desk. She eased her purse under the desk and turned toward him with full attention.

"Can you believe it? I was in that meeting for two and a half hours," he said, sighing, "But we got it done."

She smiled, hoping he'd finish and go on to his office, allowing her ample room to bolt for the elevator. Her mind was racing. She had to pick up a few items at the supermarket, cook, and be ready for Edward's visit at seven. Sherry was giddy at the notion and couldn't wait.

"I hate to ask," Dave said, "but is there any way you can get these copied and shipped this evening? I realize this is short notice."

Her energy slumped but she was careful not to let it show. "Of course, Dave, I will gladly make the copies and get this shipped out. I'll just need the addresses?"

"Are you sure, because I can get someone in legal to do this if you have to go? I totally understand and it's no problem if you have to go."

"No," she said, reaching for the stack. "Consider it done. I'm fine with time." She let the words crawl out, deciding that dependability and a steady paycheck were better than a consistent five P.M. quitting time.

Dave left and Sherry called Edward.

"Edward, darling, I have to work a little late but not much."

"What, again?"

She pressed into the phone like usual. "It won't be long. I'm going to rush through and get out before six. I'll have dinner on the table by seven-fifteen, I promise." She wouldn't be serving her famous stuffed chicken breast as planned but that was an acceptable sacrifice.

"Why do you have to stay late practically every night? It cuts into our evenings together. Don't they have more than one secretary in that place? I don't want them taking advantage of you. Are they paying you for the extra time?"

"Yes," she whispered. She got that Edward was upset, but his ranting wasn't getting the copying done. She had to go and told him so. He didn't like it but she'd make up for it later.

Sherry felt drained after the call. Balancing Dave's needs at the office with Edward's at home were awkward, but manageable. At least, that was what she chose to believe.

Chapter 26

Edward was already mad, so Sherry was determined to keep her promise about having dinner done by seven-fifteen. It was six-forty when she walked into her apartment. She didn't bother turning on the oven. The safest bet was to fire up a skillet. She tossed in the ground beef, some onions, tomatoes, and peppers for a quick dish that she could pour over mashed potatoes. It wasn't the meal she'd envisioned for them, but it would do. She turned the skillet on high along with a pot of water for the potatoes. Thank goodness the tiny spuds didn't have to be peeled. There wasn't time. Her tossed salad didn't blend well with the meal, but they'd eat it anyway. A meal was a meal at this point. She hurried, pausing only to grab an extra breath here and there. Sherry was pleased that the potatoes boiled so quickly. At five after, she was smashing feverishly. The meat mixture was done and the salad tossed. Sherry leaned against her refrigerator, exhausted yet pleased.

Five minutes later Edward rapped on the door, exactly as scheduled. Sherry had decided at the supermarket that she would keep the date peaceful with Edward. She'd walk delicately around any topic that got him agitated.

"Hello, darling," she said, opening the door and hugging him. He held her tightly. *So far so good,* she thought, kicking her anxiety outside the door and closing it.

"Dinner smells good," he said as she grabbed his hand and led him to the two-seat table in the kitchen.

"Oh, it's just something I whipped up." He had always loved her cooking and paid generous compliments, causing her to love him even more. "The food is ready. We can eat whenever you'd like."

Edward went to wash his hands and returned quickly. "I'm ready."

She sat, ate, and talked. Sherry didn't stir the conversation until he seemed relaxed. "Christmas will be here in a few weeks." She could see Edward tensing and knew why. "Let's keep it simple this year. We shouldn't spend a lot of money on gifts, not with our wedding being the most important. It will be July before we know it. Every dollar we save now will count."

Edward took the napkin from his lap and slapped it across his plate. "Can't we spend an evening together without talking about the wedding? I want to relax for a change."

Didn't he relax all day she thought, but wouldn't dare let those words taste air. He went to the open space that doubled as her bedroom and living room. She followed, taking a seat at the other end of her sofa sleeper. "Okay, but we're going to have to talk about it sometime; might as well be this evening."

"Fine," he bellowed, "what can we talk about?"

"For starters we have to find a way to cut down on our costs so we can save money. I don't need a gigantic, expensive wedding. All I truly want is to be your wife," she said, moving closer to him. "We can go to the courthouse as far as I'm concerned."

"No, we're not going to do that. Before I got laid off, you were planning a special wedding with both of our families, pretty dress, reception hall, the whole business." He closed his eyelids, leaned forward, and cupped his forehead into the palm of his hand. "I don't want you to be forced to settle for a cheap wedding because I can't afford to give you what you want."

"You're what I want, do you get that?"

"No, and that's final," he said, jumping up.

"Then if you're not willing to cut down on the wedding costs, we have to cut somewhere else, because my pay and your unemployment are only covering the basics. What about moving in together to save money? We can either give up your apartment or my studio. Either place will save us at least two hundred and fifty dollars a month. What do you think?"

Edward sat down again. "I have something to tell you," he said in such a sad voice that it nearly brought tears to her eyes.

"What?" she asked, bracing for the worse. She wanted to know, while, at the same time, not wanting to.

"My unemployment benefits are running out. I have one check left, and they're not sure I'll be eligible for an extension."

She shifted to the edge of the couch. "See, that's why we have to give up one of our apartments. It makes sense to move in together right away."

"I can't move into your place and let you take care of me, no way," he said.

"Okay, let's move into your place then."

"Definitely can't let you pay bills in my place, just can't do it. Plus, I might have to move out of there soon, unless my situation changes. I won't have my fiancée or wife getting evicted or carrying the financial responsibilities of our family. I'd rather you stay put for the time being."

This wasn't the time to be full of pride. His decision directly affected her life and future. If they were going to be a team, he had to learn how to accept her input. She'd push for a different answer, not sure where it would lead, but Sherry had to try. "I really think we should move in together, I really do." The look on Edward's face confirmed that his decision was final. They weren't moving in together. "There has to be something we can do."

"There is: I have to get a job."

"But how are you going to do that? You're already filling out tons of applications every day."

"Then I'll have to fill out more. It's time for me to stop looking for a skilled tradesman position. I'm not going to get one of those. Starting tomorrow, I'm going to the supermarkets, fast food joints, and anyplace else I think might be looking to hire."

"You won't make nearly as much at those places as you did before."

"Doesn't matter. If I have to get two or three jobs to make ends meet, then that's what I have to do."

Sherry was crushed hearing their reality spoken so vividly. The wedding and their future were in a holding pattern. She wanted to express her disappointment but didn't. Edward appeared more emotionally deflated than she did. Sherry let him have the spotlight. Her chance would come.

Chapter 27

Dave languished over the sales reports, blown away by the numbers screaming out at him. Twenty percent growth and it was only May. Only the Almighty could make such a mark on a company in record time. Dave's initial instinct was to tell Frank. Then he thought about Madeline. She'd want to know, he guessed but wasn't certain. There was a point when there wouldn't have been a question. Absence had chipped at her interest in DMI. He had to admit that she seemed to have lost interest in him too. Dave balanced the report in one hand and the family photo in the other. He had the answer and called Sherry into his office.

"I need you to do me a favor."

Sherry asked to be excused, went to get her notepad, and returned immediately. "I'm ready. What do you need me to do?"

Dave clasped his hands together, discretely containing his glee. "Next week is very important for my family. You see, it's my wife's birthday, and I want to make it very special for her. She deserves the best that I can come up with for her."

"Do you want me to order flowers or candy like we did for Mother's Day?"

"No, I have something much bigger in mind this time, something very special. I'll need your help with making the arrangements." He leaned his elbows onto the desk. "Have a seat," he said to Sherry and she complied. "I'm planning to give my wife the day off, spa treatment, shopping, and the works."

Sherry gasped. "What an incredible idea."

Dave was thrilled. Sherry's reaction confirmed that he had the right idea. Madeline would be equally pleased with his plans. He wouldn't leave any details up to chance. "This is very important to me that she gets treated like the queen she is."

"Of course, Dave, I can handle this."

He scribbled some notes on the desk pad, ripped the sheet of paper off, and reached across the desk with it, toward Sherry. She took the note and read over it. "See where I've laid out a general schedule for the day?" Sherry nodded. "I figure it will be nice for her to begin with a half day of pampering at the spa. I'd like to have lunch sent over from Tribute Bistro. It's her favorite restaurant." Sherry's smile consumed her countenance. He prayed Madeline would be just as pleased if not more, since she was the actual recipient of the gift he was customizing. "After the spa, I'd like to have a car pick her up and drive over to Canada to spend the afternoon shopping."

"Dave, this is going to be an incredible day for your wife," Sherry said, unable to contain her enthusiasm.

"That's my hope," he said. "So, mostly I'll need your help with getting each piece of the day confirmed." He got up and went to his suit coat. Fumbling around the inside pocket, he recovered his wallet. Dave plucked out his credit card and handed it to Sherry. "Let me know if you have a problem booking any part of this package."

"Don't worry, Dave. I will take care of this right away. You can count on me to handle this very well," she said, practically leaping from her seat. "If it's okay with you, I'd like to get started," she said, practically at the door anyway.

"Sure, go for it," he said, grateful for Sherry's willingness to coordinate his wife's special day. With his schedule, he'd never be able to execute his plan. "Oh, and I'll speak to human resources about making you a permanent employee, effective immediately. I've waited long enough.

Doesn't look like my secretary is returning. If
she does, we'll find another spot for her because
you're staying with me," Dave told Sherry. She
seemed pleased.

Chapter 28

Edward pushed the revolving door, raising his jacket collar outside to knock off the slight chill in the spring air. He crumbled a few papers and tucked them into his pants pocket. Finally, he had good news for Sherry. His second unemployment extension was approved. But, the $200 a week wasn't enough to fully cover her rent, his car payment, and his other living expenses. The glee he felt when leaving the unemployment office had dwindled by the time he reached his car. He turned the key in the lock, slowly. Depression tried gripping him before leaving the parking lot, but determination prevailed for now.

The wedding consumed him. He didn't consider the possibility of robbing Sherry of her dream ceremony. He wasn't going to let her down. There was time left to do something. No sacrifice was too large. He'd already broken the lease on his apartment several months ago. He had to forfeit the $200 security deposit, but it was worth the freedom. He'd found a cheap room in a local boarding house, enabling him to take the savings each month and put it toward Sherry's rent. It was his only recourse with bills mounting. She refused to take the money until he convinced her that it was insulting to him, as a man, not to be able to take care of her. From the moment they got engaged, he felt that she was his responsibility and Edward intended on making good on his commitment. She finally agreed to take $125 each month for half her rent. He was content with the arrangement. Plus it left him enough to keep his car. Thank goodness he'd bought Sherry's car with cash last year. It was ten years old but ran well. That would tide her over until he could get her a better one. Once they got married, then there would be no his or hers. Until then, chivalry wouldn't let him commingle her money with his, in a disguised effort to pay his bills. What kind of a man would he be? Nope, no way. It was the only shred of dignity he had remaining.

Edward backed out of the lot and put the car in drive. He drifted onto the road, thinking. He wasn't delusional. He had to find a way to earn more money and fast. He couldn't keep waiting for tomorrow. Today was the day. Edward pushed on the gas pedal while trying to pull papers from his pocket, the ones he'd crammed in there after leaving the unemployment office. He flattened the balled-up paper on the passenger's seat, looking for the address. After a few drifts into the other lane of traffic, he had the address. He pressed the pedal harder.

He glanced at his watch. Eight-thirty. He was in for a long day. The employment center had given him the addresses of two reliable temporary services. They seemed pretty sure he'd be able to land temporary placement with one of the services. There had been so many disappointments since he was laid off that Edward wasn't going to get ahead of himself. He wasn't going to jump for joy until there was actually a job offer on the table. But he was inspired. Before the end of the day, he was determined to be working. He was serious. With renewed conviction, Edward considered finding a pay phone to call Sherry. Spotting a phone up ahead, he tapped on the brakes, and then pushed on the accelerator. He'd rather surprise her in person with the good news of actually having a job. Hopefully she was getting off work at a decent time tonight and they could celebrate. He winced. His finding a job would be as much of a surprise as her getting off at five.

Normally, the notion of her having to work so hard would send him into a dark place. Not today, he was getting a job or two. Soon enough, he'd have plenty for them both and she could quit hers and go back to school. He was charged and floored the gas pedal. His paycheck and their marriage were waiting down the road. Edward was getting to it as fast as he could.

Chapter 29

The hours sailed past. Sherry became consumed with coordinating Madeline's day of pampering.

"How's it going?" Dave said, walking from his office.

"Oh, very well, Dave. I've made most of the arrangements," she said, giddy as could be. "Sure you don't want me to make arrangements for the flowers or candy too?"

"No, I have to actually handle a few aspects of the birthday; otherwise, it won't seem personal for me."

Sherry understood, but she gladly would have made the extra plans. She was having an insane amount of fun. With the elaborate setup that Dave orchestrated for his wife, it was no wonder Sherry was fantasizing about having a birthday celebration as thoughtful and grand. Her elation was deflated thinking about Edward. He was struggling with money. He couldn't afford to put her in a limousine and send her across the river to Canada for a day of shopping or anything else. He was barely able to cover rent on his room, let alone booking her at a five-star spa for the entire morning. The closest she'd get to a spa treatment with Edward was to take a relaxing bath before the other neighbors in her building used up the hot water. It had happened once about four months ago and not since. Sherry discounted Edward's predicament, which equated to hers as well, and shifted back to happier thoughts: Mrs. Mitchell's gift. One day, Sherry dreamed, she'd be experiencing such luxury. She was certain it could happen.

Quitting time approached. Sherry had been so consumed most of the afternoon with her side project that she hadn't done much for DMI. There was a boatload of work to do. Sherry's phone rang and she answered to find Edward on the call.

His exhilaration leapt through the phone. She was inspired hearing him. "I have really good news that I can't wait to share with you."

"What, tell me. Did your unemployment benefits get extended again?"

"Better, but I'm not going to tell you until I see you in person. Please don't work late tonight."

She looked at her mound of work. "But I do have a lot of work left to do."

"Please, I'm begging you to come home on time tonight, at least this one time, please."

The sincerity rang loudly. She wouldn't refuse his passionate appeal. "Sure, I'll leave in a few minutes."

"You promise? Don't tell me you're coming home early and then get caught up after you get off the phone."

"I won't, I promise. As a matter of fact, I'm putting my sweater on as we speak. I'm grabbing my purse. I'm walking out now. I'll run by my place and be at yours before six."

"Great, but don't bother stopping at your apartment. Come right over. I can't wait to see you."

She might have stopped working at five, but her fantasizing continued in high gear. The thirty-minute drive to Edward's seemed like five minutes. When she parked out front, there were few details Sherry could recall during her drive. Spas, limousines, all of it swirled around, nearly making her dizzy. She climbed the three flights of stairs to that attic apartment and knocked. Edward must have been standing at the door because he opened it instantly. Before she could greet him, Edward had whisked her from the hallway, squeezing tightly.

"My, aren't we in a good mood." She wanted to say "for a change" but decided against it. Whatever had him happy she didn't want to ruin. It was such a rare state for him these days. He set her feet on the floor but held on longer. "My goodness," she said, wanting a little space. It wasn't his welcome that made her gasp for air. His apartment, room, or whatever he called it was the culprit. The place was tiny. She felt claustrophobic and was anxious to get out of there. "What's the good news?" Hopefully he would tell her quickly. They could hug in celebration, and she could then get outside in less than five minutes total.

"Not so fast, ma'am. I want to savor this special moment. We don't get a chance to talk much anymore."

"About what? We talk all the time." *More like disagree, but talking was talking,* she figured.

"Let's talk about how our days went." Sherry grimaced. "I'm serious, I want to hear about your day," he told her.

"I don't know if this is such a good idea, Edward." They'd been down this path and it never ended well. She wanted to avoid the predictable and disastrous outcome. "You don't usually like to hear about my day. You've told me a hundred times how much you don't like my working late or how much focus I give DMI. I really don't want to fight tonight. I had an amazing day and don't want to ruin it with an argument."

"I had a pretty incredible day too, so we'll both have something wonderful to share. You go first," he insisted.

"Are you sure you want to do this?" she appealed.

"I'm sure."

"Okay, well today was amazing like I said. My boss asked me to help him schedule this birthday package for his wife. It was out of this world. You wouldn't believe how much money rich people spend. For one day, he's going to spend over two thousand dollars. Who does that?" she said, bubbling. "I wish I could have a day like that," she said without thinking. Sherry watched the pride drain from Edward's countenance along with his smile. What had she done? Maybe there was a way to salvage the mood. She'd try. "Enough about my silly day, how about yours? I can't wait to hear your great news. Come on, tell me. I can't wait any longer." She laid the charm on extra thick to overshadow her callous comment. He was struggling to pay the bills and she was cooing over her boss's birthday gift. She felt awful.

"I'm sorry to have you living like this," he said, peering around the room. "I can't promise you the kind of birthday present that your boss got his wife, not yet, but one day, I promise to give you much more."

"Don't you think twice about the gift. I want to hear your news."

He reluctantly said, "I got a job."

She screamed and wrapped her arms around his neck.

"That is great news. Why didn't you tell me sooner?"

"I wanted to surprise you but it's no big deal."

"Are you kidding me? It's huge, congratulations. Is it with Ford or Chrysler, where?" She fired off a few more questions before he got a chance to answer.

He looked away and then back toward her. The joy he had when she came in was gone. Sherry knew it but continued clinging to the positive tidbits that she hadn't yet driven out of the room.

"This placement is with the temporary service. I'll be working the assembly line at a small factory on the other side of town. It's second shift, three to eleven. I didn't want to work nights but what choice do I have? It pays two hundred a month more than unemployment. I had to take it. The extra will cover the other half of your rent," he said. That seemed to boost his enthusiasm.

"I don't want you doing this because of my rent. My DMI check can keep covering my rent and more if we need it to."

"We're not having this conversation again. I'm the man in this relationship. If I can't take care of you, what good am I in this relationship? It's done. I'm taking the job and your rent is paid in full from now on and that's final."

She didn't argue. She'd already wounded his spirit once this evening. She wasn't going to twice. Edward was a good man. He didn't have much, but what he did have, he was more than willing to generously share with her. She settled into the tight room and breathed. It was temporary and she could hold out until Edward got stable. She fell into his arms and relaxed.

Chapter 30

Dave was restless throughout the night. It was no wonder his feet were on the floor long before the alarm rang at 5:00 A.M. He ran down to his office and pulled out a single long-stemmed deep red rose that was safely tucked inside his closet. He'd gotten in fairly late last night and figured the flower wouldn't be discovered. He'd decided against giving her a full bouquet since Madeline would be gone for the entire day. Next to the rose was a card. He set the flower down and signed the card, finishing his note with:

Thank you for being a dynamic partner, wife, and confidant. With all my love, I hope you enjoy your birthday. If anyone deserves it, you do.

He tucked the flap into the envelope, grabbed the flower, and rushed to Madeline. He couldn't wait to make her day.

Upstairs, he sat on the bed next to her. She was sound asleep. He softly whispered her name.

After several attempts to wake her, she began rousing.

"Good morning, darling; happy birthday."

"Ah," she moaned, stretching the cover over her head. "What time is it?"

"A little after five," he whispered, poised to give her the rose.

"That's too early. The boys don't get up for another two hours. Go on to the office and let me get back to sleep. I'll call you later or see you tonight or whenever."

Her reaction wasn't what he'd expected but Dave was determined not to be dissuaded. She was tired and he could certainly understand, but that's exactly why today belonged to her.

"I'm not going to work today."

She was quiet at first and then popped up in the bed. "Why, what's wrong? Are you sick?" she said, clearly concerned.

"Nooo, I'm not sick. As a matter of fact, I feel great," he shouted.

"Then what's wrong with you?"

"Happy birthday," he said, handing her the card and rose.

"Thank you, but you're avoiding my question. Why aren't you going to work?"

He drew closer to her. "Because I'm staying at home with the children."

"Oh, quit playing," she said and lay back down.

"I'm serious. I'm staying at home and taking care of the children today."

Madeline had a perplexed look and then out of nowhere, erupted in laughter, to the point that she had to grab her stomach. Each time she tried speaking, her laughter latched on, making it impossible. Finally, after what felt like five minutes, Madeline was able to eke out a response. "You stay home with the children?" She started laughing again, pointing at him.

Dave wasn't feeling the humor, but it was her birthday. If that's the way she wanted to spend her day, fine with him. "This is your day." He drew in even closer, leaving minimal separation between them. He gently stroked along her forehead and down the side of her face. "I've planned total relaxation for you."

"What are you talking about?"

"At seven, a car is picking you up and whisking you off to the spa." The shock resonating on her face was priceless and worth the preparation efforts he'd made.

"I can't go anywhere in the morning. I have to get the boys off to school, and then Tamara has to get on the school bus at noon. I . . ." she stammered. "I can't go at seven."

"Yes, you can. You have to. I'll be here. I'll take care of the kids," Dave said, not doing well at assuring her.

"You don't know the first thing to do when it comes to the children."

"Okay, give me a quick set of directions." He'd have the nanny and housekeeper as backup. How hard could it be? She was taking her gift. He wasn't letting her off without a fight.

"I'm not sure," Madeline said, bending her knees and resting her elbows on top. "I don't think you'll be able to handle it."

"Try me and let's see, fair?"

She sighed. "You're not going to let up, are you, until I say yes?"

"That's the plan."

"Fine, I'll go to the spa. How long is it, a few hours?"

"Actually, it's the entire morning."

"Oh my goodness, what are they going to do, peel my entire body and make me over?"

"Pretty much."

"Okay," she said in a muffled yell. "Just get me home in time to see Tamara off to school and before Don takes his nap."

"No can do. After the spa, the car is taking you over to Canada for an afternoon of shopping."

"There's nowhere to shop across the river."

"Don't worry, I've got that covered. There will be plenty of shopping for you."

Madeline pressed her palms into both sides of her head and wailed. "Whatever, if nothing else, you've piqued my curiosity. I'll go."

"Thank you, Lord."

She flipped the comforter back. "Let me get moving. I can get lunches packed for the boys."

"No, you're not. You're going to rest for another hour and let me fix the lunches." He wasn't sure why the housekeeper or nanny weren't fixing the lunches every day. Maybe they weren't starting early enough to be of full benefit to Madeline. He'd have to check into that later.

Madeline reached out to him and they embraced. "Thank you for being so thoughtful."

"You're more than welcome."

"I honestly think you're getting in over your head with the children, but who am I to stop a self-made millionaire from making a decision? They're all yours," she said, kissing his cheek. "Have fun and don't bother calling me at the spa to report any disasters. I'll be too relaxed to respond."

"Just what I want to hear." Dave was happy, because Madeline was happy. Their marriage had endured a few stretched moments, ever since she'd left DMI last September, but they'd survived and would emerge stronger by God's grace.

Chapter 31

Madeline hadn't completely followed Dave's orders, but she came as close as he could expect. She got up at six and took a bath. He'd planned for her to get out of bed and go straight to the spa where she could take a mineral bath and enjoy the full amenities of the spa. Dave sighed. His Madeline was going to do it her way. There was no sense spending energy debating with her. It was her time to use as she pleased.

"I'll get the lunches packed for Sam and Andre," she said, descending the stairs with her purse and a hanging bag containing the clothes she was changing into after the spa treatment.

"Let me get that for you," he said, reaching for the bag.

"It's light. Don't worry about it," she said and continued descending the staircase.

He was mildly disappointed. Dave wanted to make the entire day whimsical for Madeline, but she was so independent that he realized his vision would be much more difficult to execute than expected. "Don't worry about the lunches. I can make them or the housekeeper can. Between us, we can handle two school lunches."

"I'm not so sure about that. Did you know that Andre doesn't like his sandwich to touch his fruit? You have to put his fruit in a bag and then stick it inside his lunch pail."

"I got it, done," he said, having no knowledge of Andre's idiosyncrasy. Coming behind her, he placed one hand on her right shoulder and the other on her left forearm. "I'm steering you in the direction of relaxation," he said, heading her toward the door.

"It's too early for me to leave. I have twenty minutes left, and I have to sign Sam's field trip note." She draped the bag across the banister and took two steps up the stairs. "I also forgot to get the makeup kit for Tamara's career fair. She couldn't decide whether to be a fashion designer or makeup artist, so Miss Tamara decided to be both."

"Where did she get the idea of being either of those?" he asked.

"Who knows, but I can't stand around talking," she said, taking the stairs faster, but Dave ran up and jumped in front.

"You are getting out of here, Mrs. Mitchell." He took her hand and initially she resisted going back downstairs. Madeline wasn't the only persuasive person in the family. Dave had built a company on the art of persuasion. A few select words and she was standing in the doorway holding her garment bag and purse. "Go and don't worry about us. We'll be just fine."

"I need to say good-bye to the children again."

"No, you don't. You already woke up each of the kids and gave them hugs and kisses. They'll be good for a few hours without you. The real question is, will you?"

"Bye, Mr. Mitchell," Madeline said curtly, but with enough sweetness to let Dave know she was appreciative.

He stood outside as the limo exited the estate grounds.

He went inside and stood in the foyer not sure what to do next. Were the kids getting up on their own or would he have to wake them? In that moment Dave decided that no matter what happened, he was not going to disturb Madeline, not even if there was an emergency. Dave wanted her to relax. But the primary motivation for his decision was to prove that he could look after four kids. He wasn't a fool. Of course he'd need the nanny and housekeeper to help, but Madeline did too.

By seven-fifty, Dave was running around the kitchen in disarray with Sam and Andre looking on. "Here, take these lunches," he said, handing the pails to the boys in no particular order.

"Detroit Pistons is his. Speed Racer is mine," Andre said and switched with his brother. As soon as he looked inside he began crying and shoved the bag off the counter.

"What's wrong with you?" Dave asked, frazzled from the ruckus the two boys made getting dressed this morning. He was certain they didn't horseplay every morning with their mother.

"You probably put his apple in the bag without covering it," Sam said.

Oh shoot. Dave had forgotten that fast. The housekeeper whisked in to pick up the bag and to console Andre.

Dave scrambled, realizing time wasn't on his side. "I think we can pack another lunch before your bus comes."

"We don't have any more deli meat, Mr. Mitchell," the housekeeper told him. "We normally do the shopping on Tuesday."

"That's today?" Dave said in a panic.

"Yes, sir."

There had to be a plan B. The boy couldn't go to school without a lunch. "Do they have a restaurant close to the school?" Dave figured he could buy a meal and drop it at the school before lunchtime.

"We don't know. We ride the bus to school or Mom takes us," Sam said.

Andre shrugged his shoulders. "You can buy lunch at our school," he said, lighting up.

"Great," Dave said, relieved and wondering why he hadn't thought of that from the beginning. He darted upstairs, taking three steps at a time in pursuit of his wallet. He was up and back down in less than two minutes. He searched for a smaller bill but had to settle on a twenty and handed it to Andre.

"Can I have one too?" Sam asked.

"For what?"

"To buy my lunch." Dave didn't see any reason to buy him one when he was holding a perfectly good pail of food.

"Go on, boy, and get out of here, and take your lunch with you." Sam trudged out. Andre was happier than Dave had seen him in a long time. "And bring me my change. That lunch can't cost more than a buck or two," he yelled as the boys ran to the edge of the long driveway. Dave saw the bus already sitting and waiting. He shook his head and went inside.

"We did it," he told the housekeeper. "I was glad to see Andre so happy about the lunch. I'll have to tell his mother that we should let them buy at the school more often."

"I don't think she'll go for it."

"Why not?" If it made the kids happy, he was all for it.

"Because Andre is allergic to nuts and he doesn't like the edges on his bread. Mrs. Mitchell tried the school's lunch program for several weeks until she had to stop." Dave's sense of accomplishment was vanishing with each revelation. "Andre wasn't eating much at school. He came home starved each day until she put a stop to it and starting packing what he likes and can eat."

"I had no idea," Dave said, dejected. "But he was so thrilled about buying lunch. Why didn't he tell me?"

"Oh it's probably like a game to him. He got to pull the wool over his father's eyes."

"Right, I'm the substitute teacher today and they'll try and get away with as much as they can."

The housekeeper laughed. "They're good boys though. Don't you worry a bit, Mr. Mitchell. One day of bad food won't kill Andre."

It better not if Dave planned on living past Madeline's backlash. "At least I did okay with Sam."

"Well," the housekeeper said, gritting her teeth, "the boys will probably get into a fight."

"Why?"

"Because you gave money to one and not the other."

"What?"

"Sounds silly, but to a seven-year-old and a ten-year-old, they're constantly making comparisons and competing with each other."

Dave drew in the longest sigh of his life. *It can't consistently be this hectic,* he supposed. The office was much simpler to manage compared with each passing second in the Mitchell household. Dave leaned against the counter. *One hour down and two kids out the door.* Lucky for him, there were only two more kids and twelve more hours to go.

Chapter 32

The day dragged on. To Dave, it felt as if there were weights on the hands of the clock, forcing the hours to slow to a crawl. His glimpses of sanity came during his routine calls into the office.

"How's it going, Dave?" Sherry asked.

"You don't want to know," he answered, actually not having the energy to recant his morning or afternoon. There had been hope in getting Tamara off to school. He could certainly handle one child and a kindergartener. Not so, he found out.

"At least you're getting a break."

"Are you kidding me? This is not a break. A break is having only three meetings at the office in the afternoon and none of those with the IRS auditors. That's a pretty good afternoon. I can handle that, but here, oh no. Let me tell you how my afternoon got started. Tamara opened the makeup kit without permission. She had it smeared all over her face and the walls."

"Oh my goodness." Sherry giggled.

"It was a disaster. I had to rush and get the makeup off. She missed the bus, forcing me to drive her to school. I bet her mother never has to drive her."

"Well, look at the bright side."

"Is there one?"

"There is," she pointed out. "At least you got to spend time with Tamara. I imagine that was very special to her."

Sherry wasn't aware of how much her comment had blessed Dave. He was centered again, charged and ready to go, at least that's what he believed, until he heard the light tapping on his office door. "How's it going at the office? Any forest fires?"

"Not really. Actually, it's pretty quiet for a change, surprisingly," she told him.

"Well, feel free to call me if you need me." The tapping grew louder. Ignoring the knock was no longer an option. "Sherry, I have to go. It would appear that I have a visitor waiting outside my office."

She laughed. "Have fun with your children, and I'll call you only if there's an emergency."

By then, Don had opened the door and come into the office. "Thanks, Sherry, and I'll check in later anyway." His attention shifted to Don, who didn't appear to be settling for less. "Hello, son, what would you like to do this afternoon?" Dave said as he made way for Don to jump onto his lap. Don's blanket came along with him.

"I don't know."

Dave didn't either. From what he remembered, food was a great pacifier. "How about a snack?"

"Yummy," he replied, beaming too much.

Dave figured this might be one of those situations like he'd encountered this morning with Andre. Dad was letting Don have something his mother didn't. He considered the consequences for a few seconds and decided one snack couldn't hurt. Besides, if the tiny treat kept Don occupied, it was worth Madeline's backlash. He stood and lifted Don to his shoulders just as the phone rang. He set Don down on his seat and grabbed the phone. It was probably Sherry calling with critical DMI news. He wasn't going to miss the call and snatched it up. He was mistaken, hearing Madeline's voice. "What are you doing calling us? You're supposed to be lavished in relaxation and pampering."

"I am, but you know I had to check on the children and see if they've driven you crazy yet."

"I have it under control, piece of cake," he said, barely able to spew out the lie and maintain a sense of honesty going forward.

"Sure. You'll tell me anything."

"Hi, Mommy," Don blurted out.

"Is that my Don? Let me talk to him."

Dave handed their son the phone. "Hi, Mommy, when are you coming home?" She must have said, "later," because their son said, "That's too long. Can you come sooner?" Dave felt invisible. He looked at the little man sitting in his chair. *Traitor,* he thought. Before his mother called, Dave was his best friend. They were getting ready to share a snack together. He guessed that was tossed to the wayside when his mother came on the scene. Dave's feelings were wounded, but he understood.

"Bye, Mommy, I love you too," Don said, handing the phone to his father.

"I'm cutting my shopping short and coming home early."

"Oh, you don't need to do that, come on. The kids are taken care of, you don't have to worry."

"I can't help it. Don's little pitiful voice got to me. He misses me, and I miss him terribly. I can shop anytime. I'm coming home and that's all there is to it."

Dave didn't press the issue any further. Honestly, her coming home was good. He might as well go into DMI and get caught up. The kids had made it painfully clear that he wasn't needed at home, not as long as their mother was there. He'd spend the rest of the afternoon and part of the evening with his fifth child, the one that valued him the most, DMI. "Come on," he told Don. "Let's get that snack before I change my mind," he said, taking his son's hand and meaning nothing but lightheartedness with his comment.

Chapter 33

"Thank goodness it was Friday" didn't ring true. Even the extra boost that should have come from the June sunshine didn't help. Edward shoved the envelope in his pocket, with the check and pink slip poking out. He sat in the car with his forehead pressed against the steering wheel. He wanted to move, but to go where? His thoughts were scattered, not making much sense. Sherry deserved better. He sat for a while longer and then pulled his head up. He had a plan: the car lot, the bus stop, the bank, and then Sherry. Definitely her last. Their wedding date was almost there. Edward wanted as much time and money as he could get his hands on before going to her with his news.

Three buses and four hours later, Edward was at home and exhausted. Instead of taking the fourth and fifth buses, he chose to walk the last two miles under the summer sun and save a few coins. He rested, while going back and forth about what he was going to tell his fiancée. The phone rang. It had to be her. He wasn't ready to talk, but had no choice. Edward answered the call and greeted his future bride.

"I thought we were meeting tonight," Sherry said.

Oops. He was so distracted earlier that he'd forgotten about their date. They were planning to eat and then discuss the final wedding details.

"I stopped by a half hour ago and you weren't home."

"I'm so sorry. I'm here now. Where are you? Can you come back?" he asked.

"I'm at a pay phone down the street. I figured it didn't make sense to go home if we're still getting together, unless you prefer to meet at my apartment?" she said.

Sherry didn't have to spell out her message. Edward knew she didn't like his tight quarters, but it was a roof over his head. He couldn't and wouldn't complain. "I'd prefer to meet here," he said. She probably thought it was some macho move to want them meeting at his place. Not true; his car situation was the sole reason for wanting to meet within walking distance of his room. Sherry didn't know that yet, but it wouldn't be long before she did.

In less than ten minutes, she was tapping on his door. He wanted to hide from his reality, but the room was too small to hide his entire body anywhere. *Might as well open the door, break the news, and deal with Sherry's broken heart. Here goes,* he thought, and opened the door. They did a quick hug and release combo.

"Come in, have a seat. Can I get you anything to drink?"

"No," she said, taking a seat, wearing a puzzled expression. "Why are you being so formal? It's just me." She giggled. If only he could keep her laughing after sharing his news.

"Look, Sherry, I'm not going to beat around the bush. I got laid off of my temporary job today."

"Ah," she moaned.

"The factory had to shut down for maintenance and cut over to a new line. They said I might get called back in a few weeks or a month, but I'm not holding my breath."

"Me either," she said, surprising him.

"Don't you worry none. I'm back out there tomorrow looking for another job. The same way I got this one, I'll get another one. You'll see. Nothing is going to stand in the way of our getting married next month."

"You can't possibly be thinking about a wedding in four weeks. Where would we get the money?"

"I told you that I'll get another job right away. We'll have plenty of money."

"Stop, Edward, who are you fooling? I don't have the money," she said, pointing into her chest. "You don't have the money," she said, turning her index finger toward him. "Which means we don't have the money. If we don't have the money, there's not going to be a wedding."

"Come on, Sherry, it's not that bad. How many times do I have to tell you that I'll get another job?

"Okay, when you get a job and have stayed on it for six months, then we can talk about a ceremony. Until then, I can't deal with the stress of paying my bills and forking out a couple thousand dollars for a wedding."

"Wait a minute. I'm paying your rent," he said.

"You mean you were paying my rent. Remember that your unemployment won't cover your rent, car note, and my rent too. We figured that much out those other ten months you were unemployed."

"You're wrong there. I'll continue paying your rent."

"How?"

"I dropped my car off at the dealer. They didn't give me any money for it since I still owed them twelve hundred dollars, but they agreed to take the car off my hands. At least it's one less bill for me, actually two if you count the insurance that I won't have to pay. So you see, there's plenty left for your rent."

"You can't be serious. We have no choice but to put the wedding on hold," she said as her eyelids filled with tears.

"Nonsense, now let's not get bent out of shape. We've been through tougher times, much together than this. We'll get by."

"Not this time, Edward. The wedding is off."

"For how long?"

"You tell me," she said, taking a tissue from her purse. "Our finances aren't stable. We can't get married on the hope of you getting a job. We have to wait."

Edward dropped to his knees and let his head rest on her lap. "I don't want to wait any longer. I want to marry you today. What if we scale down the wedding? You've always talked about going to the courthouse. I'm the one who pushed for the big wedding, thinking it's what you wanted. None of that matters. I just want to be your husband more than anything else in the world.

Let's get married, tomorrow, right now," he said, clinging to her.

"It's too late. We've told our families and they're expecting a ceremony. If we'd gotten married before getting them involved, then yes, maybe we could do something smaller. But you set their expectations very high," she told him.

"They don't matter. Tell you what, instead of having the wedding and reception at Louie's Inn, we can get married in the park. A permit is, what, twenty-five dollars? We could spend a hundred bucks on flowers. We could have light refreshments with cake, cookies, and punch at home."

"Are you kidding?" she said, shifting the weight on her legs, making it awkward for him to keep his head on her lap. "You couldn't possibly consider having a reception in this tiny room."

He pulled back to meet her gaze. "You're right. We can use your apartment. It's much bigger."

"No ,we can't," she shouted, standing. "Don't you get it? The wedding is off until our situation changes."

"Don't you really mean until my situation changes?"

She didn't respond. She didn't have to. He took a seat.

"Edward, we have to be realistic. We've been waiting on a miracle. At least I have and guess what, it's not coming. We should have cancelled months ago instead of putting down a three hundred dollar deposit at the hotel. That money is as good as gone, money we don't have. Humph, how stupid."

"I understand, Sherry, I do, but I'm not giving up on us. I'm willing to set my pride aside and accept your offer to move in together. I haven't been in favor of it in the past, but like you said, I have to be realistic."

Sherry looked away and said, "I don't think that's such a good idea anymore."

Her reaction came as a total surprise to him. She'd constantly made the offer as recent as two months ago. "Why the change?"

"I don't know, but it doesn't feel right."

Edward might have been unemployed but he was no dummy. He got what she was saying loud and clear. Adjusting the ceremony was easy. That wasn't the problem. She'd lost faith in him. He understood and would work tirelessly until it was restored. Sherry was his life, and he couldn't lose her.

Chapter 34

Wednesday felt like Monday and Tuesday, each miserably draining. Sherry was grateful that she'd survived another day at the office without falling apart. She went to Dave's office and knocked. He was reading at his conference table.

"Excuse me. Is there anything else you'd like for me to do today?" She hoped the answer was yes. Every night this week she'd intentionally stayed late to avoid having to be around Edward. His recurring disappointments and bouts with depression were tiring. She needed air.

Dave beckoned for her to come in. "What are you still doing here? We work late so much that when we can get out at a decent time we should," he said, setting the packet of stapled papers on the table with his pen and pointing to the chair for her to take a seat. She did. "Madeline and my kids would love to see me by eight or nine every night." He glanced at his watch. "Let alone seven; that would be a dream."

"How did Sam do in the chess tournament?" she asked, wanting to talk about something positive.

"Came in second place. He was disappointed, but I told Sam he'll get them in the next tournament."

Sherry and Dave had spent a considerable amount of time together since she started last fall. They'd spoken about his family and her wedding. She no longer harbored the element of intimidation around him. They spoke freely, with her always remaining respectful of his position in the company.

She knew about Andre joining the soccer team, since he missed the cutoff for football, and how bumpy it was for him when he moved in with them. According to Dave's updates in recent months, Andre was adjusting well, and Dave was glad. She knew about Don and his bunny blanket, the one that went wherever he did. She'd heard countless stories about Tamara's Easy-Bake Oven adventures. Sherry didn't have children, but would have loved to have a family like Dave and Madeline's one day. She didn't dwell on the notion, in order to avoid being reminded of her personal crisis with Edward.

"Enough about me and my kids, what about you? I'm sorry, what's your fiancé's name?"

"Edward Hanson."

"You and Edward are approaching your big day. Are you ready?" he asked.

Sherry fought to contain her emotions. "The wedding is postponed," she told him, holding back tears.

"Really," Dave responded, shocked as she expected him to be, especially after seeing her glee for months. "I don't know what to say. I know it's a personal matter, but if there's anything I can do to help, let me know."

Determined to maintain professionalism and not break out weeping, Sherry shared the details of Edward's unemployment history.

"I can appreciate your situation. Maybe I can help."

"How?"

"You've done a fantastic job for me here. I'd like to help with a financial contribution."

"Oh no, Edward would never accept money from someone else. He's very proud that way."

"I understand. So, what if I gave you a five hundred dollar bonus?"

"No way."

"All right, then I can make it a thousand," he said, squinting his eyelids.

"I'm sorry. I didn't mean that five hundred wasn't enough. I'm grateful that you've offered to help. It's far more than I could have expected. Dave, I can't take the money. I didn't earn it."

"Not only did you earn it, you deserve more. When you joined my team, my secretary was on leave and my wife had started her sabbatical. It was an administrative nightmare around here for me. You saved me, Miss Henderson. So, I say that you deserve the bonus, and I'm having payroll cut the check tomorrow. Will that help?"

"Thank you, Dave, but I can't take the money. I just can't." Ashamed and struggling with maintaining composure, she didn't elaborate much more. At this point, it wasn't so much that Edward would be upset about her taking the bonus. Sherry was the one who felt awkward. She would be taking advantage of her boss's kindness to pay for a wedding that wasn't making sense anymore. She wouldn't take his assistance.

"Then what else can we do? You already work late most nights, but I guess we could squeeze in a few more hours, if that's the only answer we have to help resolve your financial concerns."

"That won't work either." She went on to tell Dave that Edward didn't like her working late, and it had been an ongoing problem in the relationship.

"I had no idea DMI was creating such an issue for you personally."

"Dave, it's not this job. My problem with Edward is much bigger than this—much, much bigger—too big to still be talking about getting married." She stopped, wanting to rewind her last statement. "I've said too much already." Sherry was embarrassed and prepared to leave. "Oh, I almost forgot," she said, approaching the doorway. "The *Free Press* is coming tomorrow to do a feature story on you and your family."

"That's right. I'd forgotten. See, that's why you deserve that bonus. You keep this place running." He stood and walked to her. "I don't know what I'd do without your assistance." She was touched. Her world outside the DMI doors was falling apart, but not in here. She was alive, appreciated, and actually happy. She had a future and that's what she'd cling to.

Chapter 35

Dave couldn't let go of the conversation he'd had with Sherry about her fiancé's misfortune yesterday. He wanted to help out as an act of kindness, but admittedly there were selfish reasons, too. He'd come to rely heavily on her contributions in DMI, and she'd blended into the company's fiber nicely. She understood his schedule, his demands, and the sheer volume of work to be done in any given day. He never had to ask her to stay late. She just did, realizing that it was germane to her role as his secretary. If her fiancé had his way, it sounded like Sherry wouldn't be working long hours. Dave could see the tension coming down to Sherry having to decide on keeping her job or keeping her soon-to-be husband happy. DMI couldn't compete with that, but Dave wasn't one familiar with defeat. He had to make sure Sherry stayed on board. He didn't have the patience to train a replacement. It had taken Sherry months to gain the experience necessary to master her role. He didn't have any months to spare, not while DMI was still doubling in size. He sat at his desk pondering on what could be done to minimize the risk of her walking out.

Nothing came to mind. He went to the windows and peered into the afternoon sky, hoping God would give him an answer. It dawned on him that his best angle was to focus on making Edward happy. He seemed like a proud man, based on what Sherry had said. Dave resigned that he needed more information before hatching a plan. This was going to be tricky. If he could help Edward, would it help Sherry? She didn't seem enthusiastic about getting married anymore. As a matter of fact, Dave detected that Sherry and Edward's differences had built a wall that she didn't know how to overcome. What Dave interpreted in the conversation last night was that she wanted out of the engagement, but wasn't sure how to make it happen. Retaining one of his star employees was his duty. He'd have to give it more consideration, but maybe there was a way to make the decision easier for her.

The intercom interrupted his train of thought. "Excuse me, Dave, but your wife is on line one."

He braced for the call. He and Madeline weren't completely at odds these days, but they weren't in harmony either. "I got it, thanks, Sherry," he said, pushing the button to get Madeline on the line. "Is everything okay?" he asked, half afraid to say anything else and kick off an argument. Fortunately for him those had been confined to the early morning and late nights. She hadn't bothered him much at the office, but perhaps that was primarily attributed to her lack of calls.

"I'm reminding you that the children are planning a little party for you tonight. Since you spent the day with them a few weeks ago, they're eager to have another one."

Dave glanced at his calendar and saw several late meetings and phone calls. If he had to guess, his day was ending around eight-thirty, putting him home by nine. He already knew that wasn't going to be acceptable.

"Let me figure out how to move my schedule around and get home by eight."

"I knew it. You had no intention of keeping your word with the children. Dave, you're something else. These children have worked their behinds off planning the party on their own, making decorations last night, and you name it. They will be crushed if you don't get home by six, absolutely no later than seven."

That was going to be close to impossible, but Madeline wasn't going to hear his explanation, so he didn't offer one.

"I'll figure this out."

"You'd better," she said and hung up, leaving him holding the receiver. The disconnection was piercing. He wouldn't guarantee six o'clock, but with a mighty move of God's hand, Dave would be home by seven. This was one time he had to.

Chapter 36

The office was buzzing with a reporter and photographers from the *Free Press*. Sherry had noticed how sharply Dave was dressed. His cuff links were always noticeable but today they seemed to pop even more. His suit coat hung well. It was the kind that looked expensive and specially made for a tall guy like Dave. She wondered how much a suit like that might cost; probably more than her and Edward made in a week combined, possibly in a month.

Dave's door opened and the reporter came out. "Mr. Mitchell, I think we're finished here," she said, folding a small notepad and tucking it in her pocket. "My photographer is going to get a few more photos of you. If I have any questions, I'll get back to you. Thanks for your time," she said, shaking his hand.

"The pleasure has been mine," Dave said with a flair that saturated the room. Sherry hadn't paid much attention before, but it was quite evident. The reporter seemed to think so too by the overly friendly way she spoke to him with extra giggles and all.

The photographer went into Dave's office. He followed and closed the door.

"Well, Mr. Mitchell is quite extraordinary, isn't he?" the reporter asked, standing next to Sherry's desk.

"He's a really good boss."

"So, you work for him, as a secretary?"

"Yes," Sherry said, letting her word drag out. Sherry had never spoken to a reporter and was nervous about saying the wrong thing.

The reporter pulled the notepad from her pocket. "How long have you worked for Mr. Mitchell?"

"About nine months. I started off as a temp last September and then moved to permanent last month."

"And what's your name again?"

"Sherry Henderson," she said, growing increasingly nervous with each question.

"Sherry, would it be okay if I asked you a few questions? I had an excellent interview with Mr. Mitchell, and a few comments from his personal secretary will be just the added touch I need to make the story stand out." Sherry was reluctant. "I promise this will only take a few minutes and then I'll get out of your way. What do you say?"

"Sure, I'll do it," Sherry said, wondering if Dave would approve. It was too late now. The reporter had pulled up a seat.

"Do you mind if I turn on this recorder? It works much better than my memory," she said, smiling.

"It's okay."

By the third question, Sherry had reeled back in her seat with the words flowing like a river. Sharing positive facts about Dave was a simple task. She could share the rest of the day and still not come close to running out of wonderful things to say about him. She felt fortunate to have Dave Mitchell as her boss. She'd learned a great deal about business from working with him. She didn't plan to be his secretary for more than a few years, but it wasn't because of him. She just wanted to finish college one day and become a social worker. That was her dream, but in the meantime, working at DMI was huge. The interview continued for another fifteen or twenty minutes.

The photographer emerged from Dave's office. "Let's get a picture of you and Mr. Mitchell."

"I don't think you need me in the picture. This is Mr. Mitchell's interview, not mine."

"Nonsense," Dave said. "We can take one at the receptionist's desk with the DMI logo in the

background. How does that work for you?" he
asked the reporter.

"Perfect."

"Let's go," Dave told the reporter. Sherry trailed
them although every fiber in her body said to pass
on the photo shoot. The publicity was too much.
She was content sitting in the background. That's
where Sherry felt most comfortable.

Chapter 37

By mid-afternoon, the interview was over but the jubilance remained thick in the office. Sherry bounced around from one task to the other, soaking up the positive energy. She needed as much of it as her soul could cart off at the end of the day. Edward's challenges were draining. He couldn't help being laid off, but his attitude and constant negativity had worn her down and was beginning to nibble at their love.

Dave emerged from down the hallway and approached her desk just before five. "How's it going, Sherry? You getting out of here on time?" he asked.

"No, I have too much to do."

Dave looked as if he wanted to say something else. "What did you think about the interview?"

"It was very interesting for me, even though the interview was about you," she said, giddy. His presence radiated. She instantly felt better around him, encouraged and alive. When she spoke with Dave, it was a taste of freedom. There were no money troubles, other problems, or a sad-looking man sucking the air from the room. Dave was strong and she appreciated his strength.

"Well, I'm glad you were able to participate. Although, I hope it didn't put you behind on your work." He paused and then said, "Is that why you have to stay late?"

"No, not at all," she quickly responded. Initially she wasn't comfortable with the interview but afterward it had been a ball of fun. She'd gladly do another one so long as Dave was involved. His way seemed to make difficult tasks much easier.

"Because I wouldn't dare want you to be penalized for helping me, especially when I know how important it is for you to leave on time."

If he only knew how she really felt about staying late. The extra hours had been a lifesaver, not only financially, but where it really counted, and that was with her peace of mind. "No, Dave, even if I hadn't participated in the interview, I would have been here late."

"I feel awful about you dedicating so much time to DMI when you have a life outside of here. Tell you what, why don't we hire another secretary, kind of like an assistant for you? We might not have enough work to make it a full-time position in the beginning, but I'm sure she can float between us, legal, and Frank to fill her day. What do you say?"

Sherry didn't know what to say. She felt protective of her extended hours with Dave. Most of the nights when she stayed at the office, he was there too. The extra time had allowed her to learn the job and to become really good. She didn't see the hours as a burden and didn't want Dave to feel that they were either. On the other hand, she didn't want to stand in the way of his executive decision. He was super smart and understood business matters. If he thought they needed another secretary, he was probably right.

"I really don't know," she said. "I love my job and don't mind working the hours, but if you think it's too much for me to handle, then maybe you should get a second person."

"Hmm, let me think about it, because whatever I do, the goal is to make sure you're happy. You're invaluable to me and to DMI. I don't want you running off because I overworked you," he said.

Staying late and talking with him was one of the few pleasantries she currently had. Little did he know, there was zero possibility of her leaving the job for any reason or for anybody anytime soon.

"How's Edward getting along?"

"He's still trying to find a job." She wasn't going to tell the full truth. Dave was nice and caring but he didn't want to hear the woes of her and Edward's long list of problems. It was like someone saying hello and asking how you're doing. It was an empty courtesy and she understood.

"What is his specialty?"

"He was in a pipefitting apprenticeship at General Motors before getting laid off. I guess you could say he's good with his hands. Any kind of work like that he seems to enjoy."

"Did he go to college or trade school?"

"No, he didn't, but Edward is a hard worker."

"Oh, I'm sure. Does he have any interest in going to college?"

"I don't know. He's never mentioned going. He was very supportive when I was in college."

"What salary is he looking for?"

"I don't know that either. If I remember, he was making close to fifteen dollars an hour, but with overtime it was twenty-two dollars. When he worked on Sundays and holidays it was thirty dollars an hour. I'm sure he'd love to make that much again, but at this point, he just wants a steady job."

"Where did he grow up, if you don't mind me asking?"

Odd question, she thought, but it was Dave. She didn't mind answering. "On the east side of Detroit." She wouldn't elaborate on how rough the part of town was where he'd grown up. Dave didn't need to know.

"Interesting," Dave said and excused himself.

Sherry wasn't sure why he was asking about Edward's background. When Dave went into his office and closed the door, she returned to her task list. Finally, around eight-thirty, she was ready to go and knocked on Dave's door. She figured he was focused on his big meeting coming up for the Tri-State southern expansion. It had been the bulk of her work for the past month and wasn't going to ease up until the meeting was finished next week.

"I'm leaving," she said when he told her to come in.

"Okay," he said, standing. "The security guard usually takes a break at eight-thirty. So, let me walk you out.

"That's not necessary." Since summer was only a few weeks away, it stayed light outside until almost nine o'clock. "I'll be fine," she said, not wanting to inconvenience Dave. He was there late for a reason and taking time to walk her outside wasn't it.

"Nonsense, I won't take no for an answer. If you can stay late, the least I can do is to make sure you get to your car safely," he said, ushering her toward the elevators.

They chatted along the way. Sherry was grateful while also feeling guilty about pulling him away from his work. Every minute he spent on her was one less that his family was going to get tonight.

In the parking lot, Sherry turned the key and unlocked the door. Dave opened it for her and she slid in. She thanked him and turned the key in the ignition. Several attempts couldn't get her car started. She was so embarrassed.

"Here, let me try it," he said as she got out. Dave tried cranking the car with his head partially hanging out. She wasn't sure what he was listening for. Cars weren't her thing. Edward always took care of hers. "I thought it might be flooded, but there's no gas smell. Let me pop the hood," he said.

Sherry was humiliated. "That's okay, Dave. Thank you for your help, but you don't have to do this." He had on an expensive pair of pants and shirt. She couldn't afford the dry cleaning bill for his clothes, let alone replacing a single garment if gas or oil got on him.

"Sherry, it's no problem, really. Long before I became CEO, I was quite handy with cars, gadgets, you name it. Won't hurt for me to take a peek," he said, raising the hood and securing it. He poked under the hood for several minutes, emerging to say, "I don't see the problem, and obviously I don't have a car lift in the parking lot. So, that means we need to get you a tow truck. I can have it towed wherever you'd like."

"I don't know where to take it."

"You want to go inside and call Edward so he can pick you up, while I make arrangements for the car?"

There was no sense in calling Edward; he'd given up his car and was temporarily relying on public transportation. By the time he took the three buses necessary to reach DMI, it would be midnight. "He doesn't have a car anymore. He can't pick me up. I'll have to call a cab."

"Then I'll give you a ride."

Sherry felt even worse than before. She didn't want him going out of his way for her, especially when he had a very important meeting coming up that required most of his attention. It was mortifying. "I'm going to take the cab, but I really appreciate your offer."

"At least let me cover the cost of the cab, please," he said. She wanted to say no but ulti-

mately gave in. Dave was quite persuasive. "Do you or Edward use a certain mechanic?"

"Not really, he takes care of our cars."

"Then I'll have it sent to my mechanic."

Dave drove a Cadillac most of the time and a Mercedes, too. Her ten-year-old Vega wasn't in the same league. There was no way she could afford an expensive shop. She couldn't afford car repairs, period. Being out of school for almost a year, repayment on her school loans had kicked in. With her other expenses, there wasn't much left. "I'm sorry, Dave, but I have to find a shop that's more in my price range."

"Don't worry. DMI will cover the cost."

"No, I've already accepted money for the cab, but the repairs are too much." Her pride couldn't say yes.

"Consider this a well-earned bonus."

"But I got a bonus and raise last month when you made my position permanent."

"So, consider it an extra bonus. Call it whatever you want, just take the gift. You deserve it, Sherry. When I say that you've been a true blessing, I literally mean it. I would consider this an honor if you'd accept my assistance. Let me help you the way you've helped me."

She wanted to decline, but wouldn't rob him of his opportunity to thank her, not if it meant so much to him. "Okay, yes." She was overwhelmed with his generosity and ability to handle problems so smoothly. Admittedly it felt good not having to fix something on her own for a change.

Chapter 38

Dave was up earlier than usual this Monday morning, but Madeline was set to catch him before he got moving. She was desperate for a vacation. "You know the children are out of school today. I reminded you last week about the family vacation. We can use the break. This has been a challenging year, but we've made it," she said, propping several pillows behind her head. "The children took a vote on where they wanted to go, and it's no surprise that the Disney fun park in Florida won."

Dave snickered. "Best choice."

"So, we're off to the Magic Kingdom Wednesday morning for two weeks. I wasn't sure what your schedule was like. Do you prefer to leave in the morning or afternoon?"

He stammered. "I can't go yet. Remember, the Tri-State southern expansion is happening next week with the possibility of bringing on three key clients. We're in the final preparation phase, and I can't leave the office for another week or two."

"You know I don't keep up with your schedule anymore. I have too much to do here to be spending valuable time worrying about what you're doing at DMI. What I do know is that the children are counting on you to show up, me too."

"It's not that I want to bail on you and the kids. Madeline, I know you know that."

"I'm beginning to wonder exactly what I do know about you. I knew you to be a family man who knew how to set priorities."

"That hasn't changed."

"Apparently it has, if you can't take two weeks out of a whole year and dedicate it to children who are starving for your attention. Why do they have to get in line behind the southern division, the eastern expansion, the west this and the northern that?" she said, sitting up and letting her neck sway with each piercing word.

"That's not fair, Madeline. We agreed on the sacrifices DMI would require before we got married. I was upfront with you from the beginning about my calling. I never tried to change you and up until now, you'd done the same."

"Children change you, Dave. I agreed to make the sacrifice. Your children didn't. They came into this world and into this house innocent. You brought them here. Now, you have to be involved in their lives; otherwise, I fear that you'll regret it down the road. I promise you that, because they'll end up resenting you for putting DMI first."

"I pray that's not true."

"Here we go," she said, falling back on the pillow. "Here, wait; let me tell you what you're getting ready to say. You're going to say that God has a plan and that you're going to pray for direction, right?" Madeline didn't let Dave answer before she was talking again. "Of course I'm right. Tell me this, Mr. Holy Dave Mitchell; do you really need to pray about whether or not to take a vacation with your wife and children?"

"Madeline, there's nothing I'm going to say that will satisfy you at this moment."

"Sure, there is."

"And what would that be?"

"Simple, say that you'll have your bags packed Wednesday and get on the plane with us. I'm not asking for much, just two weeks of you playing husband and daddy. DMI can have the other fifty weeks a year. Sounds like a bargain to me."

"I want to go."

"Then go," she yelled.

"You didn't let me finish. Even if I could take a few days from the southern division preparation, I have another pending lawsuit that's also coming up the following week. I have spent zero effort on due diligence."

"Can't Frank handle it?"

"Yes, to a degree, but when we go to court, I'm the one who gets questioned."

"You are full of excuses, Dave. That's what I'm hearing, a bunch of lame excuses."

Dave got up from the bed. "Let's table this and talk about it at a better time."

"There is no better time. We're leaving in two days."

"Fine, Madeline, you're right, I owe the children some time. You're absolutely right. I'll come down for the weekend, and fly back for the meeting next week. It will be good for us."

"A weekend is not going to cut it, Dave. We want you there for the full two weeks, but if you can't swing that, then no less than a week."

"I just can't do a week right now, but I can schedule the time next month."

"No way, have you been to Orlando in July? It's a sauna, way too hot. I want to go when the children can enjoy the vacation. This is about them and not what's most convenient for you. Put them first for once. Let them see what that feels like."

"No matter how guilty you try to make me feel, Madeline, I can't go next week."

"Well, let me tell you this, if you can't come for at least a week, don't bother coming at all. We don't need your part-time involvement. How about that?" she said, turning her back to him and refusing to utter another word.

Chapter 39

Dave peered into the bathroom mirror. He was convinced that quality was more significant with his kids than quantity. His rationale seemed valid, but Madeline wasn't hearing it. She wanted more, the very position he'd been afraid would rise up from the moment they'd gotten engaged. He'd warned her long ago that one day she'd want him to be available and his calling would take priority. He recalled the conversation as if it happened today, instead of thirteen years ago sitting on a park bench at the riverfront. *Lord, what must I do?* He pondered. Dave wanted to go with his family, but no matter how he tried to rationalize the trip, it wasn't the best time.

The kids deserved a break. He got that part of Madeline's argument, and she was right, no disagreement there. But they had the entire summer. There had to be at least one other week over the next two months when they could squeeze him into their plans. He was willing, just not this week or next. He planned on Madeline cooling down and letting him join them on the weekend. If not, he'd have to wait for another opportunity in the near future. He turned on the water and let the four showerheads pour down on his body as he prayed God would do the same with an outpouring of peace and wisdom into his soul. The water rained down on his head.

Bam, the decision was made. It was final, he couldn't go. He allowed himself to wallow in the disappointment for a matter of seconds and then cast aside his simmering anguish. It was done.

Dave dressed eagerly and was rushing out of the bedroom, but not before kissing Madeline good-bye. He could tell she hadn't returned to sleep quite yet. He bent down and whispered, "I love you and the kids," and sealed it with a kiss on her cheek, trusting that as he took care of God's business, God would take care of his.

"Talk is cheap," she muffled, moving away from him.

He walked out of the room, accepting their reality, and hoping she would come to terms with it too.

Dave's drive into the office wasn't worry-free. The issue with Madeline had been marginalized, not necessarily resolved but discussed. Sherry's fiancé was the other issue bugging him. During the conversation with her last night, Dave had gathered additional information about Edward's background and skills. The man needed a job. Dave owned a multi-million dollar company and recognized his realm of authority. Yet, none of the scenarios he conjured seemed to include DMI as a viable place for Edward. For one, there weren't many pipefitting needs in the building. DMI leased a portion of the facility with expansion plans that would eventually require them to own the entire place, but for now, the needs of a maintenance man or skilled tradesman was minimal. Secondly, and the most significant to Dave, was that Edward could possibly serve as a distraction for Sherry, at a time when her concentration and dedication were critical. Dave required her full dedication. He racked his brain considering various potential employers. Who owed him a favor?

Dave parked in the DMI lot, having fully utilized the thirty-minute drive in. He stayed in the car and pulled out the bulky phone that was mounted inside the center console. He had an idea and didn't see a reason to wait until he was upstairs to put the plan in motion. He dialed directory assistance to get the area code for Texas and then the number for Longhorn Industrial and Manufacturing. After a few diversions, he had the company's president on the phone, a colleague he'd met years ago at an executive conference. They'd maintained periodic contact.

"Joe, it's Dave Mitchell here. How the heck are you?" Greetings and chitchat commenced and concluded in the span of a minute. Both men were busy and time was valuable, Dave knew neither had any to spare. He got directly to the point. "Joe, I need your help."

"What can I do for you?"

"I know a young man here who desperately needs a job. He was recently laid off due to restructuring at General Motors and hasn't been able to land a comparable job since."

"What kind of skills does he have?"

"Based on my understanding, I believe he was in the skilled trades apprenticeship program for pipefitting. I don't actually know him personally, but he comes highly recommended by one of my valued employees. If I can help the poor guy who happens to be down on his luck, then I'm willing to give him a hand. We both remember what it was like in the beginning."

"Certainly do," Joe said. "Tell you what, Dave, I'd love to help you, but we don't have much use for a pipefitter in any of our operations."

"Understood, but I have a feeling that any decent job is going to be of interest to this young man."

"What kind of a salary is he expecting?"

"Well, he's getting in the neighborhood of twenty-five to thirty thousand base."

"We can definitely match the base rate, especially with benefits and bonus incentives. I can't guarantee that we can give him the overtime rates that he might be accustomed to at GM, but we can make a job with us worthwhile for him."

"Hey, if this guy is as smart as I'm hoping, he won't be concerned about the overtime rate. Let's face it, GM might pay more but he's not on their payroll or anyone else's at the moment. If he wants to be employed, he'll see the merit in your offer. I'm not worried. You present the offer and the rest is a done deal."

"Sure about that, huh?"

"Positive." Dave had never met Edward, didn't have to. Dave was relying on the notion that any responsible, unemployed man wasn't going to turn down a permanent position, not with a family depending on him. Dave was counting on Edward's manly integrity.

"Then, I'd say yes, we can find a spot for the young man. What's his name?"

"Edward Hanson."

"I think our supervisor training program would be the perfect start for him. Every year we take two candidates and rotate them through our various sites. We give them extensive operational and leadership training. It's quite a premium position around here, and if he's as serious as you say he is, this will be a prime opportunity for him."

"Sounds great."

"You do realize that the job is here in Texas?" Dave hoped that's where the job was. Based on their talk, he could tell that Edward's struggle was draining on Sherry, but he figured she didn't know how to fix the problem. If his instincts were right, and they usually were, this job for Edward was the break Sherry needed. The distance would create a natural separation. Her problem would be solved, and she wouldn't have to do anything. "We have a few locations in Arkansas and Oklahoma, but headquarters is here. After he completes the three-year program, he'll get his permanent location assigned. Do you think he'll be okay with starting in Texas?"

If Edward was smart he would be. "I'm trusting that this young man will seize the opportunity and make a go of it." Dave could only hope that he wasn't overplaying his hand and putting Sherry on a plane to Texas. That would be a self-inflicted disaster not worthy of considering.

"Okay, then I'll have my Human Resources team pull together an offer and get it to Mr. Hanson immediately."

"Oh, uh, Joe, it will be best if my name isn't associated with the offer. Edward is a proud man and may not accept my involvement in the spirit I intended."

"No problem. With as much feedback as you gave me in the beginning, I owe you a favor. I'm glad to be able to help out."

"It's greatly appreciated. I'll get Edward's contact information to you later this morning." Dave was pretty certain Sherry had listed Edward as an emergency contact on her application. His information might be outdated, but between Dave and Joe, they'd be able to get the updated telephone number and address without Sherry's knowledge.

Chapter 40

Dave had his legs crossed on top of the long conference table. A night had passed since his family left and the loneliness was strangling. Madeline was so angry at him that she'd packed the kids up and left when they'd gotten out of school yesterday. Although he didn't see them much at home, he spent every night in the same house with his family. Admittedly the rapport wasn't always pleasant, but they were a team. Dave hadn't forgotten them in his heart, and it ached as a result.

He dialed the phone number Madeline had left on the counter. The hotel operator answered and connected him to Madeline's room. It rang and rang until finally the call bounced back to the front desk.

"There is no answer. Would you like to leave a message, sir?"

Dave thought about it, and said, "No message, thank you." He fumbled with the phone receiver for a while before setting it down. He tried concentrating on the business at hand, unsuccessfully. His mind was flooded with years of standing side by side with Madeline in building DMI. She was always at the office with him. Yet, somehow Madeline had managed to keep such close tabs on the kids throughout the day that it felt like he was in tune as well. He never had to feel the emptiness that plagued him today. Madeline had shielded him. Those days of her bridging the gap between work and home were gone. The joy of having long conversations throughout the day and late into the night with her had escaped too.

He'd had enough. Dave had to get out of the office. He got his brother on the phone.

"How about grabbing an early dinner?" he asked Frank.

"Oh, man, you mean I'm going to lose out again? I can't go with you tonight. I have to eat with the wife tonight. She's made plans for us, and you know how that is. I can't dare try to cancel. So, I'm going to put in my time tonight and get a free pass good for another six months. Wish me luck," Frank said, tickled by his own joke.

Dave didn't have it in him to laugh. He'd gladly take a date orchestrated by Madeline.

At least that would imply she was interested in being near him. Frank was more blessed than he realized. Dave said good-bye. Left with no other choices, he went to plan B. He stepped in the hallway and found Sherry at her desk.

"By chance, are you free for dinner? Both my family and my brother have abandoned me." Before she responded, he added, "If you already have plans, I understand."

"I don't. I'm free."

"You sure?"

She nodded in affirmation and he could see her suppressing a grin. "What time were you planning to go?"

Dave peeked at his watch. "I can be ready in fifteen minutes." That would give him a chance to try reaching Madeline once again. His hope of reaching her was low but he'd attempt it anyway.

Fifteen minutes later, Dave and Sherry were walking out of DMI. She was excited and calm at the same time. Sherry was glad to be able to get away from Edward for the evening. If tonight was like last night, he was home looking pitiful.

"Are we going to the café again?"

"If you're interested, I'd prefer to go downtown to one of my favorite restaurants."

"Where?" she asked as they got to the parking lot. If Dave was going, it was bound to be better

than the local diner Edward took her to every
Friday night for dinner.

"The Summit."

"The new restaurant at the top of the skyscraper?"

"That's the one."

Sherry had never been to a five-star restaurant, but had heard plenty about the new place
and the great reviews from food critics. She
hadn't dared to dream about going to such a
place on a weeknight. Who was she kidding? She
and Edward couldn't afford to go any night. The
appetizer probably cost more than she made in
an hour. She was bubbling with excitement, but
didn't want to come across as someone with no
class or exposure to the finer treats of life. She
calmed her reaction, determined to speak with
control.

Dave pointed toward the executive row of
cars, which was at the opening of the garage.
"Why don't we go in my car?" he said.

Thank goodness, she thought. Hers had been
running well since Dave had it repaired at his
shop. She had no complaints, but why take the
risk of pushing the car that she called "Putsy"
fifteen miles each way? Riding with Dave was
definitely the best option. Besides, being in his
company helped her to forget about Edward,

the postponed wedding, and their boatload of problems. Sherry eased into the passenger side of the Cadillac and let her worries stay outside. The next couple of hours were reserved for a good time. She wasn't going to accept anything less.

It was magical, the drive downtown and especially the glass elevator ride up to the seventy-second floor, which showcased the glistening evening lights.

"Mr. Mitchell, I'm glad you'll be dining with us," the host said. Apparently Dave ate at the restaurant often, because they knew him. "Will it just be the two of you?" the host asked, looking past them into the entryway.

"Yes, my wife and children are vacationing at Magic Kingdom in Florida. So, it's just me and Miss Henderson."

"Very well," the host said, grabbing several menus. "Please follow me. I have a splendid table for you."

Dave whispered to her, "You thought the elevator was cool. Wait until you sit down. Every seat has breathtaking views of downtown and Ontario. You'll see."

The candlelight and low tones of people talking set a romantic scene that she'd seen only in movies. Edwards's apartment wasn't as big as the entryway to this restaurant. If she waited for him, many experiences would never happen. Thank goodness for Dave and his taste.

They reached a table along the outer edge of the restaurant. "Madam," the host said, pulling out Sherry's chair. After she and Dave were seated, he handed each a menu. He handed Dave an extra one. "Here's our wine list." He draped cloth napkins across her lap and then Dave's. "Your wine steward will be right over. Enjoy your dinner."

Dave thanked the man and opened his menu.

Sherry was bursting inside. She was too excited to eat. "You were right, the view is incredible." As the restaurant slowly turned, she took in every ounce of ambiance.

"Miss Sherry Henderson, tell me something I don't know about you."

She should have been nervous and there was some of that, but mostly Sherry was free. For the first night in her life, she was enjoying the finer perks without having to worry about what bill would be sacrificed next week to cover the splurge. "Thank you for inviting me to dinner. You have no idea how special this is for me."

"I should be thanking you. Eating alone isn't fun. I'm glad you're here," he said, lightly brushing the backside of her hand.

"I am too."

Chapter 41

The next morning, Sherry felt like a princess, living out a dream. A year ago, she didn't dare waste brain cells fantasizing about sitting in the Summit. Her path had taken a huge turn for the better, and she was pleased.

"What did you think about the restaurant?" Dave asked, headed to his office.

Her words were tripping over one another as she sputtered a response. "It was wonderful. I never knew Detroit and Windsor were so beautiful."

"Funny, when you see just about any city from the top of a skyscraper, it's incredible. That's why I love the place," he said and eased away.

Sherry was making it her new favorite restaurant too; although, she might not ever be able to eat there again if she waited for Edward. The reality of their finances tried to swoop in and erase her memory of an enjoyable evening. Sherry started typing, intending to push away the brewing unpleasantness. At about eleven o'clock, she looked up to see Edward walking toward her desk. She froze. He hustled briskly to her desk. She scanned the area to see who might be watching.

"Edward, what are you doing here?" she said, standing and whispering while rapidly scanning the area again.

"I have great news," he said, extremely happy.

She wasn't happy having him pop up at her place of employment. He was jeopardizing her job and that wasn't acceptable. She had to let him know. "Edward, you can't just show up here. I'm working here, don't you understand that? We can't afford for me to lose the one job we have between us," she spoke harshly. She didn't mean to hurt his feelings, but he had to know.

"That's why I'm here. I got a job," he said so loudly that Dave opened his door.

Sherry wanted to die from the embarrassment. She prayed Dave wouldn't fire her.

"Is everything okay?" Dave said, coming toward her and Edward.

Sherry's pulse raced to the point of throbbing. She was totally unnerved. "We're fine, Mr. Mitchell. I mean, Dave." She was so confused that there was no telling what words were going to come out of her mouth. "Edward was telling me some news."

"Oh, so this is Edward," Dave said, extending his hand.

The men shook hands as Sherry watched. The awkwardness didn't vanish, actually it intensified. She wanted to hide, but there wasn't an obvious spot. "I'm Dave Mitchell."

"He's my boss," she stammered.

Edward said hello, and thanked Dave for giving Sherry the job. "Nice meeting you, Mr. Mitchell, and I also want to thank you for helping my fiancée when her car broke down last week."

"It was my pleasure, and please call me Dave." Edward gave a single nod to Dave as they shook hands.

"Edward, I have to get back to work. I'll see you later," Sherry said.

"This can't wait, we need to talk. Can you go to lunch with me?"

Sherry typically went to the cafeteria between eleven-thirty and twelve. It was almost that time. She didn't need Dave's permission, but for some reason, having him standing there seemed as if she did. *What a mess,* she thought. Sherry didn't really want to go to lunch with Edward, but she didn't want him to get upset, either.

"Is there anything you need me to do before lunch?" she asked Dave, hoping he could rescue her with a simple yes.

"Excuse me, Dave, this is important. Please let her off so she can come to lunch with me."

"Not a problem. I don't need anything before lunch from you, not at all. Go, have a good lunch."

"Thanks," she said, mustering up a fake smile.

Dave extended courtesies, said good-bye, shook Edward's hand again, and left the area.

Sherry couldn't decide if she wanted to be mad or join Edward in his excitement. She'd wait to see what was so important that they had to talk right now.

As soon as Dave was gone, Edward's energy soared again. He twirled her in the air.

"Put me down. I'm at work for goodness' sake." Forget about being happy. Unknowingly he was rapidly shoving her toward getting mad. Edward took her hand and tugged slightly, indicating he was ready to go. "Wait a second, let me grab my purse." She got it and held her tongue until they were in the lobby, safely removed from her boss's presence. "Where are we going?"

"Somewhere nice."

"Really." She stopped and stared at him. "With what?" The thick air rushed against her face as they exited the building.

He scooped her up again. She didn't bother resisting. There was no point.

"That's what I've been trying to tell you. I got a job today, a good job."

"With another temp agency?" She couldn't believe Edward had taken two or three buses to her building, blowing money he didn't have and trying to impress her with lunch at a local dive. Her decision was made. He had officially made her mad. "And you couldn't wait for me to get off work and tell me? What's the big deal, Edward?"

"This couldn't wait. This is a real job. A company in Texas has offered to put me in their supervisor's training program, starting at thirty-two thousand a year, car allowance, full benefits, and an annual cost of living bonus."

Sherry was shocked. "I didn't realize you'd applied for jobs out of state."

"I didn't, but apparently they must have gotten my information from one of the applications filled out at the unemployment office. I guess they send your information everywhere. Look, I don't care how they found me. The bottom line is that they did. This is our ticket out, Sherry. Our luck is finally changing. Now, I can take care of you like I'm supposed to. Can you believe this? I can't." Edward was so hyped that he kept talking, not allowing Sherry to get many words in. That was fine with her. She was speechless anyway. "We can get back on track. We can use the bonus for our wedding. After we get settled in an apartment for a while, we can buy a little house, maybe have a few babies," he said, taunting her as they walked.

She pretended to be happy but the news was overwhelming. She'd grown accustomed to him being depressed and struggling. She didn't recognize the man standing next to her. He was filled with too much bliss. "Sounds like a great opportunity, Edward. Are you taking it?"

"Are you kidding me? Of course I am. As a matter of fact, I already told them yes."

"Without talking to me first?"

"I know, but, Sherry, I had to take this job. We need this. You've been carrying our load for almost a year. It's time for you to get back in school and let me handle the finances. The only hesitation I had was the move to Texas, but I figure it will be a brand new start for us, a clean slate. What do you think?"

Sherry was still pretty quiet, trying to process how quickly her world was changing. One fact was certain. She had no desire to move to Texas. She had established her life in Detroit and was developing a career at DMI. She couldn't leave, not now, not when Dave needed her most.

Chapter 42

Dave had checked Sherry's desk several times. She hadn't returned from lunch by the time he'd left for a one o'clock meeting with Frank. Normally, she'd be at her desk by twelve-thirty. His gut feeling was that he might have overplayed his plan. He pushed the elevator, pondering, distracted. The primary objective for contacting Joe was to get Edward a job as far away from DMI as possible. Maybe he'd underestimated Sherry's desire to get out of the relationship. He pushed the elevator button again, waiting. But, his sensors kept saying that Sherry no longer wanted to be engaged. He got the impression that she lacked an exit strategy. She had never told him that directly, but it's how he felt. Maybe he hadn't given sufficient consideration to the outside chance that Sherry could leave DMI, resulting in a disaster. He took a sigh and went to the stairwell. When it came to business decisions, he was rarely wrong. He hoped this wasn't one of those rare instances. The loss would be significant, and there was no backup plan.

Frank was in his office when Dave arrived.

"Come on in and have a seat. Let me finish jotting a few notes here," Dave heard, and didn't hear. The debacle with Sherry and Edward consumed him.

"Did you hear me?" Frank said.

Dave was sucked back into the room. "I'm sorry, what did you say?"

"I asked if you want to be involved with that severance case. It's petty and won't take too much effort to squash."

"Can you handle it without me?"

"You know I can. Consider it done." Dave stroked his hand across his forehead, causing Frank to say, "You all right? You seem troubled or something."

"It's nothing, just tired."

"Everything okay at home with Madeline and the kids?"

Dave wasn't in the habit of lying and wasn't going to start now. "Maybe, maybe not, depending on whom you ask."

"I'm asking you."

"We're going through a tough period, Madeline and me. She won't let go of this notion of wanting me home every night before the kids go to bed."

"What, you have troubles in paradise? Say it isn't so, not the anointed Dave Mitchell, the one who God assigns angels to hang out with daily. You're the one who walks into court expecting to win and always does."

"You're laying it on pretty thick, aren't you?"

"Not really. There's no doubt that you're a winner. What you touch turns to gold, always has. Remember when we were kids? You fell out of a three-story tree and didn't have a single broken bone. Mom and Pop checked you over for two solid hours, refusing to believe that you weren't hurt. Do you remember that?" Frank asked. Dave grinned a little. "I fell out of the same tree a month later and broke both legs and my arm." Frank extended his arms and limped around the room like Frankenstein.

"You're crazy," Dave said, letting his disposition lighten.

"I might be, but you're the one looking pitiful. I'm not used to seeing you like this. So, I have to take note when I do." Dave waved him off. "Seriously, you and Madeline have something special. Hang on to her, man."

"I plan to."

"You're not going to do better than her. Don't get me wrong. I love my wife, but she doesn't have the tenacity that Madeline has. If you had to step out of DMI for a minute, I think Madeline could run the company without help from anybody. She's a tough woman. Partners like her don't show up every day. Like I said, you're blessed, or anointed, or awfully darn lucky. I don't know which, but I could use some of what you have."

Normally Dave agreed that peace was abundantly flowing in his life, regardless of what challenges were in progress. The key had consistently been prayer and faith that his Father would work out situations. Oddly, he didn't feel right asking God to remove the stumbling block between Sherry and Edward. Selfishly, he welcomed the divide, hoping it was wide enough to send Edward to Texas and keep Sherry at her desk in DMI. "Don't pay any attention to me. I'm feeling sorry for myself because my family is out of town. I miss them, that's all." That wasn't all, but it was what Frank needed to hear. Sharing more would be dangerous.

"Since you're single tonight, why don't you come home with me for dinner? The wife would be glad to see you. It might take your mind off your problems."

"Thanks but I'm going to pass. I'm not going to be very good company tonight." His mind continued wandering back and forth between the void Sherry would create if she left and what he could do to keep her. Seeking God's wisdom never crossed his mind. His spirit didn't dare. When he was in the will of God, peace and that unexplainable sense of confidence saturated him to the point where he literally felt invincible. Dave didn't have that feeling as he reflected on sending Sherry's fiancé to Texas and trying to keep her on board at DMI.

"You look like a little lost puppy dog with your family gone. You might as well come to dinner. What else are you going to do but keep looking pitiful or somehow manage to get yourself in trouble?"

"There's no concern there. If all else fails, my relationship with God is solid and my spirit is strong."

"So you say, but what I know is that no matter how religious you are, you're still a man living on earth. As they say, the spirit might be strong, but the flesh is weak." Dave discounted Frank's appeal. "Be careful, that's all I'm saying. Madeline and the kids will be home soon, and you'll iron out your differences," Frank said, patting Dave on the back.

Perhaps Frank was correct, but Dave couldn't think that far ahead. He had to deal with a more immediate issue and left his brother's office anxiously.

Chapter 43

Dave didn't wait for the elevator. He hustled up two flights of stairs, stopping to gain composure before stepping into the open area. He hadn't lost his awareness of being CEO. Exhibiting leadership and strength weren't going to be compromised, even in his mild state of confusion about what was going to happen with his secretary. He intentionally slowed his pace approaching his office. Once he saw Sherry at her desk, it was easier to take controlled steps. His anxiety withered.

"How was your lunch?" he asked.

"It was okay," she responded, lacking enthusiasm. For a woman who'd just received great news about the betterment of her fiancé, Sherry didn't appear thrilled. Dave didn't want to presumptuously read any more into her reaction than was there. He'd have to wait and see.

The afternoon passed as Dave feverishly fine-tuned the presentation for Tri-State and

a proposal for the Mid-Atlantic Federation
of Churches, an account Madeline had begun
courting before stepping down. Dave set the pen
down and let the moment bring satisfaction. The
vision God had given him was coming to fruition
as he sat in his seat. Spreading wisdom across
the land was happening in the Midwest, South,
on the East Coast, and soon the West Coast.
There was no stopping the move of God. He
lifted the pen and began writing again, although
frequent glances in the direction of his door created a distraction not easily suppressed. Around
four o'clock, Dave couldn't take the suspense
anymore. He went to Sherry's desk, grabbing a
couple of folders en route.

"Sherry, do you have a minute?"

She lifted her gaze slowly and said, "Yes, of
course."

"Are you okay?" he asked.

"I am," she said, offering no more.

Dave was fully aware of the reason for her
somberness. She couldn't ever know he had a
role in getting Edward the job. He set the folder
in the center of her desk. "Can you copy this for
me today?"

Her eyelids widened. "Sure, the documents on
top?"

"The entire folder, everything in both?" The
stack was guaranteed to take at least two hours.

That was the best time to talk, when most of the staff was gone. The phone would stop ringing, and interruptions were few. He'd wait for the right moment to find out what was going on with Sherry. He had to know.

Her eyelids widened again as she thumbed through the top folder. "But I've copied most of this one in the past for legal."

"A backup won't hurt, but if you're too busy," he said, reaching for the folders, "don't worry about it. I'll have you do it tomorrow."

She reached for the folders, grazing his hand. Both she and Dave pulled away instantly and said no more. Her phone rang. "Excuse me, Dave, let me get the phone."

"Sure," he said and went to his office. On the way, he heard Sherry's muffled voice and knew it was Edward. Dave took tiny steps, acting as if he wasn't listening.

"I'm happy for you, honestly I am, but I'm not going to jeopardize my job. I told you that already." She rattled off a series of no, no, no, and then said, "Fine, I'll get off as soon as I can." She said good-bye and gently set the phone on its base.

Dave turned toward Sherry's desk, pretending to have forgotten to tell her something. "Sherry, one more request, can you make two copies

of both the Eastern Lutheran Group and the
Georgia Evangelical contracts. You might as
well throw in the COGIC too." It was one of
their thickest files in the office. "I'll give Frank
an extra copy of each for his records. With the
multitude of lawsuits that we've handled, an
extra copy comes in handy." Those contracts
had settled months ago. Dave knew they didn't
need the bogus copies, but he had to get Sherry
to stick around long enough to get a gauge on
her commitment to staying. Dave had dug a hole
for Edward without realizing he too would be
wading through the aftermath. Sherry appeared
puzzled. Dave read her unrest and didn't feel
right letting her stew in awkwardness. "If you
can't stay late, I understand. We can do this
tomorrow."

"Thank you, Dave. I really appreciate you
letting me off. I just made plans with Edward
and wouldn't feel right cancelling on him. He's
very pleased with his new job and wants us to
celebrate. This is a big day for him."

From Dave's perspective, Sherry didn't exude
a celebratory mood. Edward's glee didn't automatically equate to a moment of joy for her, as
Dave had hoped.

Chapter 44

Sherry didn't want to go to Edward's. There was no choice. She knocked on the door and braced for his reaction, not sure what to expect or what she wanted to happen. Sometimes she'd have to wait for him to open the door. Not tonight. He flung it open and beckoned for her to enter. Her gaze honed in on the suitcase sitting on his sofa bed. "You're packing already?"

"That's why I had to see you tonight. The company is flying me out early tomorrow morning to get my employment paperwork done so that I can start my orientation on Monday." He folded a shirt and placed it in the neatly packed suitcase.

"You're taking the job without us discussing it?"

"What's there to discuss? I've been out of work for almost a year. I finally have a good job that can take care of us both and you want to talk about what?" He went to his dresser and pulled out a wad of socks.

"It looks like you're taking all your clothes."

"Every piece that I can carry."

Sherry was overwhelmed. Edward was moving too fast. She had to sit. "How can you leave without having a plan for us?" Sherry was confused and didn't know exactly what she wanted from the relationship any longer. Edward owed her the chance to express her feelings, and she wasn't going to let him walk out before being heard.

"I plan to stay at the hotel in Texas this weekend. That will give me a couple of days to get a little familiar with the area ahead of time, so that I won't have to find my way on Monday. Maybe I can even look around for a place."

"Sounds like you have this all figured out, but what about me? What about us?" she said, too confused and angry to shed a tear.

"Don't worry," he said, coming close to her. "By the time your two-week notice is up, I will be settled into my orientation program. I'll know the area better and we can find an apartment together, if I haven't already found one by then."

He hadn't taken her feelings into consideration. Edward was all about what he wanted. "That's not going to work for me."

"I'm sorry, I didn't mean you'd have to wait two weeks for us to be together. I can take my security deposit from this room and buy a ticket for you to come down next weekend," he said, wrapping his arms over her shoulders. "Sound like a plan?" Happiness oozed out of his pores, and she wiggled from his grip, not wanting to get any of it on her. "I can't believe how fast our situation has turned for the good. On Monday I was unemployed and wondering where my next dollar was coming from. Wednesday, out of the blue, I get a call for a dream job. How crazy is that," he said, giving her a peck on the cheek and returning to his packing.

There wasn't any nice way to say what had to be said. She wanted to say it and get the matter behind her. "I'm not coming with you," she blurted out.

"Not this weekend, I know. I'm sorry I don't have the money to take you with me, but you can best believe that I'll have you a ticket in the mail by Tuesday."

"Edward," she said, going to him. "I'm not moving to Texas, not this week or ever. I'm not leaving Detroit. I'm not leaving DMI. I'm just not leaving. I'm sorry, but this move is for you. It's not for me."

His anguish hurt her. The love and relationship they'd shared for three years had somehow vanished without their knowledge. She'd love

and care about Edward forever, but that yearn-
ing to be together as husband and wife didn't
exist for her. She had to let him go and let him
pursue a more meaningful future without her
tagging along and being miserable. He deserved
better than she could give him.

"You can't be serious. This is our breakthrough,
our ticket to success. We can live comfortably
now. And as far as the wedding goes, we can
use my bonus to have the biggest or smallest
wedding that you want. It's your choice. Shoot,
we can get married next weekend if you want.
Instead of you flying to Texas, I can fly home
Friday night. We can get married Saturday, and
then go to Texas together, as husband and wife."
Before she could answer he continued talking.
"That will only give you a one-week notice, but
who cares. You won't need that job again. Don't
worry about it. I'm certainly not."

Maybe not, but he should be worried, she
thought. Maybe he should have read the signs
along the way, the ones highlighting her discon-
tent, the ones where she was begging for more.
Neither had taken care of the relationship and
there they sat, divorced before they got married.
Her heart sank, but she refused to let a tear
drop. She couldn't let him feel any worse than he
already did or was going to.

"The answer is no, I'm not going, and that's final." She slid the engagement ring off her finger and gently placed it in his palm, closing his fingers around the ring, and peering into his eyes one last time. "I'm truly sorry," she said and ran out, this time letting the tears have their way.

Chapter 45

Sherry stared at the illuminated numbers on her alarm clock. Two-fifteen in the morning. She rolled over and closed her eyelids tightly, hoping to drift off to sleep and leave her worries behind.

A noise startled her. She immediately glanced at the clock: three forty-five. She flung the bed-spread back and sat on the side of the bed. Why did the night have to torturously drag on for hours? Finally, she'd had enough. She eased into her slippers and went for a glass of milk.

In the short distance from her bed to the refrigerator, Dave and Edward had bantered back and forth in her mind. She wrestled with her old feelings for Edward Hanson and new ones for Dave Mitchell. There was no indication that Edward wanted to end the courtship and none that Dave wanted to start one. He was married. She wasn't going to spend her night on adulterous fantasies. It would be ridiculous. Dave was married to a woman he loved very

much. Sherry reflected on his special gift to
Madeline. Men didn't go to so much trouble
unless they were truly in love. Admittedly, she
desired to have such a caring husband, but not
one who was already married. She'd wait for her
own.

Sherry finished the milk and eventually went
to bed, falling asleep just before daylight. When
her alarm clock rang at six-thirty, she immediately hit the snooze, expecting to hit it several
more times before thinking about getting out
of bed. She was exhausted. Her eyelids felt too
heavy to lift. A low-grade headache seemed to
be percolating, too. She wanted to bury her head
and grieving heart deep under the sheets and
stay there until the pain was gone.

After a few nods in and out of sleep, the light
of day finally arrived. Sherry felt lousy and
considered taking the day off. She looked at
the clock once more and jumped from the bed.
After reflecting on the roller coaster of emotions
she'd experienced over the past couple of days,
Sherry preferred going into the office to keep her
mind occupied. If she stayed at home, Edward's
absence would be too much to bear.

She was rushed getting dressed and driving
in, but Sherry scooted into her desk chair barely
five minutes after nine. Hopefully Dave hadn't

noticed. She'd get to work quickly so that, if he did come near her desk, her tardiness wouldn't be obvious. A few hours passed and she was in second gear, equivalent to getting by, but not sailing along like usual. She'd tried reaching Edward with no answer. She'd keep trying, although it was pretty evident that he wasn't in his rented room. By now he would have answered the phone. She refused to dwell on him being gone. She couldn't accept the death of their relationship, not the way they ended. When she gave him the ring back last night, her decision made sense, or Sherry thought so. Feeling the emptiness of him being gone didn't feel right. She had to find him and figure out another way. She snatched her purse from the lower desk drawer as Dave surfaced.

"I have to take a long lunch today. I have a serious personal emergency to handle."

"Is there anything I can help you with?" he asked, appearing genuinely concerned.

She didn't dare explain her situation to him. Edward would be embarrassed and so would she. "No, I'll be fine; thanks."

She bolted out of DMI and went straight to Edward's rooming house, knocking repeatedly on his door until her hand hurt. Someone must have called the maintenance man, because he showed up, asking her to keep the noise down.

"Excuse me, but it's an emergency. I have to get in there to see if my fiancé is hurt." Sherry prayed he hadn't done something stupid to himself after she broke off the engagement. She felt sick.

"He cleared out early this morning."

"He's gone," she said as if it was a total surprise. Actually it was. She didn't expect him to walk away so easily without attempting to see her or to reclaim their love. Reality tackled her in the hallway, causing Sherry to fall against the wall. "Are you sure Edward left?" she asked, clinging to denial as her crutch.

"He's definitely gone," the man assured her as he dangled a ring of keys. "He took his bags and handed me the key."

Edward was gone. It was the only fact allowed in her head. Everything else was shoved to the recesses of her mind. She wasn't ready to hear that he was actually gone. She thanked the maintenance man and exited quietly, feeling her way down the corridor and staircase among a flurry of warm tears. Somehow Sherry managed to make it outside to her car. She was ripped in half. She didn't want to go to Texas but, deep down, Sherry didn't want Edward to go without her. They had a bond, no matter how fragile. Last night her choice didn't seem as dire. Standing in the trenches of the day after, she realized he meant more to her than she'd remembered.

Sherry sat in her car as the sun peaked in the noonday and headed toward the western sky. She was oblivious to her surroundings. She couldn't give an answer as to why she was sitting there for several hours. Maybe it was wishful thinking that Edward would change his mind and return. Maybe it was simply a foolish fantasy. She didn't care. Either way he hadn't returned by two o'clock. Sherry drove to the nearest pay phone and called into the office. The receptionist was covering Sherry's calls and answered the phone.

"Can you tell Mr. Mitchell that I won't be back today?"

"Are you sick?" the receptionist asked. In a way she was, sick about how her engagement ended. "Oh, Sherry, I almost forgot. Mr. Mitchell has been trying to reach you. Let me forward you directly to his office."

Sherry wanted to end the call and retreat to her apartment, close the curtains, and bury her head in a pillow. She had no choice but to wait until Dave was on the phone.

Before she got a chance to ask for the rest of the day off, he said, "Sherry, thanks for checking in. I need your help big time this afternoon. How soon can you get back to the office? I have an urgent series of meetings that need to be scheduled and a couple of packets that have to make the four-thirty courier service pickup."

Sherry was dejected. She didn't want to go to DMI. In her condition, there was no way she'd be able to pretend that her world was stable. The despair she felt was bound to spill out over the entire DMI executive floor, seeping right into Dave's office. He had a knack for telling when something was wrong. The stench of her raw wound would give her away. She wasn't going to be able to endure his scrutiny without crumbling. She got in her car and gently tapped the gas pedal. There was no hurry to get anywhere anytime soon. Dave and DMI would have her physical body for the afternoon, but mentally she wasn't showing up.

Chapter 46

Sherry seemed sad after returning from lunch. The day was ending and her disposition hadn't improved much. Dave felt responsible and wasn't willing to let her be miserable without his support. Reluctant at first, he insisted that she let him take her to dinner.

"I don't think so. I wouldn't be very good company tonight."

"Come on; don't let me suffer through another dinner alone. Frank doesn't have time for me. That leaves you. Rescue me from the DMI vending machines." She finally agreed. "You want to go for round two at the Summit? I never get tired of the place."

"I can't go there," she said, shaking her head. "Can we stick to a smaller restaurant, maybe not as formal?"

"Sure, I have the perfect spot."

Dave took her to a quaint Italian restaurant in Southfield.

The trip was much more sullen than their last dinner together. She picked over her salad until the waiter took it away and stirred the minestrone soup without taking a sip. "Do you want to talk about it?" Dave asked.

She told him that Edward had left without giving her a chance to sort out her feelings. Sherry burst into an emotional state Dave wasn't expecting. "I'm sorry," she said, taking the napkin from her lap and dabbing the rims of her eyelids. "I can't stay for dinner. Can we go?" she said, sounding choked up.

"Of course we can," he said, standing and pulling out her chair. She bolted to the door. It took him several minutes to get the waiter's attention and the check. He felt compelled to see about her. After all, his meddling was at the core of Edward's abrupt departure. If Dave hadn't gotten the job for him, Edward would still be in town. Sherry could never know that Dave had orchestrated the pain in her heart. Using the credit card would take too long. He pulled a money clip from his front pocket and peeled off a hundred dollar bill. *That should generously cover the bill,* he thought, since they were leaving before the main course was served. He placed the cash in the center of the table and hustled outside. Sherry was standing off to the side. He could tell she'd been weeping. "Let me get you home."

"My car's at the office. You can take me there. I can get home on my own."

"I can't let you drive home in the condition you're in. Don't worry about it. I'll drop you off at home."

"What about my car?"

"Your car will be safe in the lot. I'll have a driver pick you up in the morning."

"I don't want to be a bother. Take me to the nearest bus stop."

Sherry continued resisting but Dave was able to convince her that his suggestion was best. She directed him off the Lodge Expressway to the Davidson. Twenty minutes later he was parked in front of her building, in what appeared to a better-to-visit-in-the-daytime neighborhood.

"At the risk of sounding preachy, you know tomorrow's going to look much differently. You never know, Edward's decision to leave might be the single best gift he could give you. It was pretty brave of him to walk away and not force you to choose his path."

Apparently Sherry didn't agree, because she began wailing uncontrollably. "I was silly to let him go without me. I was so stupid," she said, struggling to get her words out. He plucked a handkerchief from the pocket of his blazer and handed it to her. "Look at me, sitting in my boss's car, weeping like a baby because my fiancé and I broke up. I'm so embarrassed," she said, choking out the words and wiping her eyes. "I'm going inside. I'll see you in the morning."

Dave felt guilty. Even if Sherry wasn't aware of the role Dave played in her despair, he was. He felt awful seeing her so distraught. Not now, but later, she'd be glad the day's events played out the way they had. In the interim, he had to do more than give her a ride home. "Wait, let me get the door for you," he said, jumping out and running around to the passenger's side.

Sherry got out of the car and went practically limp in his arms. "Edward is gone. I'm alone," she cried out. She leaned on him, sobbing with each step.

"What unit?"

"Number two," she said, pointing down the hallway.

"Do you have the key to your apartment?" he asked. She fished inside her purse and handed him a ring with three keys. The two car keys were obvious, indicating the last one was for her apartment. He jiggled the key in the lock while balancing Sherry with the other arm.

She was so despondent that he basically had to lay her limp body on the couch and place a pillow under her head. He sat on the edge of the couch, attempting to console her. One emotion led to another and in the blink of an eye, Sherry was pulling Dave close and they kissed. One kiss led to another. Over an hour later, Dave was tucking in his shirt. Sherry was clutching his arm and asking him to stay longer.

"I can't," he said and left.

Chapter 47

Street lights, traffic signs, and passing cars were a blur. Jumbled images pounded Dave as he entered the house. His mind was bouncing between Florida and shame. He wasn't quite certain how long the ride had been to get home. He was bent on blocking out his transgression, but the act of infidelity was a heavy boulder sitting in front of him. He couldn't take a step without tripping over the bitter taste of dishonesty. God had always been his source of direction. Tonight his willful disobedience had been his guide. Lives were involved. He could say that the decision to be with Sherry just happened, but it wouldn't be true. He allowed his flesh to pin down his spirit, the one he'd spent a lifetime knitting to the ways of the Lord. But, he wasn't going to dwell in darkness. The deed was done. Dave fell to his knees, going to the only place he knew for forgiveness and strength: to his Almighty Father.

"Father, I have sinned and fallen short of your glory," he wailed on the steps as if his heart were literally being ripped from his chest. The agonizing sound of a wounded animal before death couldn't have been more piercing. Dave had betrayed Madeline. Worse, he'd betrayed God, his first love. "I am not worthy of your calling, Father. I am a poor, wretched sinner. My weak flesh isn't able to overcome temptations. My naked shame is exposed before you, Lord. Yet I come to you, Father, because I have nowhere else to go." He prayed earnestly. "You are the only one who can cover my nakedness." He schlepped up the stairs, very slowly, plopping down near the top. "Father, I repent and ask for your forgiveness," he cried out. Dave sat quiet for a while. The weight of his recklessness began lightening with each breath that he took.

A gush of zest filled his loins and Dave scrambled to stand, barely able to keep up with his feet. He ran to the nightstand and found a piece of paper containing the phone number for the hotel in Orlando. He dialed rapidly. When the hotel operator answered he immediately ended the call, realizing it was ten minutes before midnight. The children were most likely asleep. He'd hold off until morning, but they were getting a call after daybreak.

Dave planned to shower, pack a bag, and get a few hours of sleep. He prayed Madeline had changed her mind and was willing to let him come to Florida and be with the family for the weekend. He'd go into DMI around five to make arrangements for the day. It should have been dicey with the Tri-State meeting looming, but weakness had clarified his priorities. He could be with his family in less than twenty-four hours. Even if Madeline didn't agree, he had to get out of Detroit and erase the gap between him and her this weekend, no later. Otherwise the divide might grow bigger than he could repair.

Chapter 48

Daylight broke and it was the day after. Dave was keeping to his plan of getting to Florida. Calling and calling Madeline's hotel room was a bust. Letting her know he was showing up was preferred but not required. He was going regardless. After several more attempts, she answered.

"Madeline, where have you been?" he asked anxiously, relieved. "I've been calling and calling. What's going on with you and the kids?"

"What does it matter to you? Dave, I have four children desperate to get to the pool. Can't we talk later?" she said, extending no grace. Dave was in for a tough appeal, but he had no choice. Madeline had to take him in.

"Come on, Madeline, can't you give me a break? I admit it. I didn't work hard enough to get my schedule cleared for you. I'm sorry."

"It wasn't for me. I'm grown. I can handle disappointment. This was for my children."

"Don't you mean our children?"

"I didn't stutter," she said. Dave didn't see the thick blanket of separation thinning. Madeline was madder than he was prepared for her to be after four days. It was going to take some doing to get her to loosen up.

Dave heard a knock on his office door and ignored it. "Okay, I give up, you win. I accept my lashing from you and the kids. Give me a chance to make it right. Let me join you and the kids for the weekend. We can make it into a surprise for them."

"Why would we do that? I told you from the beginning that we can't constantly be at the bottom of your priority list. These children deserve a father every day, not just when it's convenient for you." He agreed but opted not to interrupt. At least Madeline was speaking in full sentences instead of a few words here and there. He'd take it as a positive sign. He heard the knock again, louder, and continued ignoring it. "I'm sorry, Dave, no way. The children will be disrupted if you show up for two days and then leave. I'm not going to let you jerk them around."

"Come on, Madeline, work with me. I'm really trying to make this right."

"You don't seem to get it. I was very serious about all or nothing. You're gone all the time, why bother jumping in for a coffee break? If you can't stay for the whole week, just don't bother coming down here. The children are used to you being gone, me too. So, stay gone." Dave was dejected but not beaten. "I have to go. I'll talk to you later," she said, saying good-bye.

"Wait, I can come for the week," he said out of sheer desperation, a position totally foreign to him.

"How can you free up a week on a whim? What's wrong with you?"

"Getting to Florida is that important to me. I need to be with my family more than you know. I miss you, and I can't wait to see you." He didn't have a clue as to how the presentation was going to be handled next week. At a point of compromise, he was going to lose on one side or the other. Sherry had him compromised while Madeline forced his hand. He felt an undeniable pulling between the two women. One kept him hostage on the phone and the other kept him held up in the office.

"I have to go Dave," Madeline said apparently unwilling to haggle. Dave finished the call knowing what had to be done.

Sherry called into his office through the intercom. He couldn't avoid her forever. Besides, he was running a business and she was his secretary. They were going to have to talk, eventually. *Might as well be now.*

"Yes, Sherry, can I help you?" he asked after pressing the talk button.

"You're supposed to have a phone call with Mr. Stenton this afternoon about expanding his contract. He wants to get the rest of his staff trained."

"From the Lutheran Group?" They had been a tough sale in the beginning, wanting deep discounts. Dave knew that once they began interacting with DMI, the remaining sales would be effortless—it worked every time.

"Right, he wanted to move your meeting back an hour this afternoon. After I couldn't reach you, I told him we'd have to reschedule. You're free Monday at three or anytime Tuesday afternoon. Which one is going to be better?"

"Sherry, can you come into my office, please? Thank you." She stepped right in and began closing the door. "Oh, you can leave the door open," he practically yelled out before gaining composure. He was still CEO and had to appear in control even when he wasn't. "I'm going to be out of town over the next week." Sherry shifted her weight from one leg to the other and squinted. He avoided eye contact, hoping not to discuss what happened last night. "I'll have to get you to clear my schedule, move everything around."

"But what about Tri-State? That's been the primary focus here for months. You're going to cancel the meeting?"

"Yes," he said. "See what you can do to get it moved to another day. You were right in moving the Lutheran Group, too. I'm not available at all today or next week."

"This is so sudden. What can I tell people?"

"That I have a personal family emergency," which was true.

"Is there a problem with your family?" she said, coming toward him.

Dave jumped from his seat and moved away, toward the window. He was on edge every minute Sherry spent in his office, refusing to succumb to the awkwardness.

"I miss my family and they miss me. My judgment has been off ever since they left. I'm not balanced, and I have to fix that. So, do the best you can with the changes. If someone can't change, cancel them indefinitely." He turned to her and with absolute control said, "I am going to Florida to be with my family, and nothing, I do mean nothing, will stop me today. It's where I belong and it's where I should have been last night."

"I see," she said, standing in the middle of the floor with her mouth slightly open. She ran from the office and he let her go. His decision was firm but it didn't stop him from feeling awful about hurting Sherry. She was twenty years his junior, a nice girl. But to reach out to her at such a vulnerable moment was bound to lead down a path he had no intention of travelling again. He'd repented, his mind was free, and temptation had been buried.

Dave scrolled through the Rolodex, stopping at a travel agency business card. He quickly called to book a flight and car service for the evening. There were better options leaving tomorrow morning but that would mean spending an unprotected Friday night in Detroit, one he couldn't afford. He didn't have time to worry about what-ifs. He had to burn his energy on scrambling together a makeshift plan that the staff could use in his absence. He took the shortcut, and called Frank. He was CFO and was equipped to handle the fallout of Dave's abrupt departure.

Chapter 49

Dave had everyone in high gear as they prepared for him to be out of the office. Sherry had been there nearly a year and he'd never taken off more than a few hours. He was always there, a certainty she'd come to rely on. It was weird to explain, but he was her closest friend really. Yes, he was her boss too, and that was for sure, but they were more. She had to believe they were much more. Dave had walked by her desk countless trips in the past two hours with nothing more spoken than two or three project requests. He was coming her way again. She acted busy.

"Sherry, I almost forgot, here's another list of meetings that you'll have to reschedule. Thanks," he said and went into his office, closing the door on her breaking heart. He hadn't looked at her directly. She normally felt comfortable around Dave but today was different. He was completely focused on preparing for his impromptu week out of town and being with his family. Sherry

didn't know if she should knock on the door
and have a quick chat with him or to continue
pretending that nothing was wrong. She wanted
to crawl under the desk and become invisible.
Despair was determined to be her best friend,
sticking close, allowing her minimal breathing
room. Sherry didn't know how to shake it other
than having Dave affirm her presence. She
wanted, needed, him to acknowledge their time
together last night. She needed him to validate
her feelings but he hadn't. Sherry cringed in
shame meshed with regret. Edward had cast her
aside and now Dave too. She wanted to burst
into a sea of tears but was able to hold on.

Throughout the afternoon, her strength
waned. She went back and forth about whether
to ask Dave a question, anything, something to
hear his voice and have him confirm that she
mattered. The hours had passed and his door
remained mostly closed. Nothing came. On top
of the depression she was battling from Edward's
departure, the coldness coming from Dave was
more crushing. Her tears swelled but nothing
materialized. It would wait until she got to the
ladies' room.

Chapter 50

Dave was on the run. He'd landed in Florida an hour ago and was becoming anxious. The hardest task lay before him, and that was getting Madeline to soften. He wasn't exactly sure what to expect during his stay. He'd soon find out as the limousine barreled down the interstate lined with signs for Disney World—Magic Kingdom. A fairy tale ending was precisely the outcome he desired.

He was hopeful but realistic. At best, a grand reunion with his wife and children wasn't going to erase the stench of last night.

Dave toughened up, reflecting on what he believed. He'd sinned. There was no question there, but he'd also repented. By faith, he knew in the depths of his spirit that God had forgiven him. If the Word of God was true, and he believed wholeheartedly that it was, then he was completely forgiven. No matter how terrible his infraction, it was hindsight and he had to walk accordingly, not allowing it to hold him hostage. Dave shook off the lingering unrest and sat back in his seat, more relaxed than he'd been since rising from Sherry's bed last night. Harmony was flooding in, convinced that yesterday was gone and today was anew.

Unfortunately, his act of betrayal did have other lingering implications that he couldn't faith away or discount. The enormous question before him was whether he should tell Madeline now, later, or never. The answer wasn't automatic. He pondered for a bit and came to a decision. Right or wrong, he'd spend the week enjoying his family and put the fractured pieces of the puzzle together afterward. Dave lay back and let images of Mickey and Minnie Mouse sweep in, as the dirty crevices of his mind were instantly brushed away, thank God.

Madeline had heard every word Dave had said a few hours ago. Sure, he was coming to Florida. That much she'd give her husband. He did what he said he was going to do. That wasn't the source of their problem. She needed him to do more of what benefited the family and not only the fulfillment of his self-absorbed calling. She'd heard that sermon enough times to choke on the

Bible, God, and his freaking calling. If he was so bent on purpose, Dave should have understood the significance of being a hands-on father. Yes, he'd get to Florida, but would he be willing to sacrifice an entire week away from DMI for his family? That was the million-dollar question Madeline wanted to see answered.

"Mommy, can we get a snack?" Tamara asked.

Madeline snapped out of her daydreaming and got back to reality. Burning brain cells on Dave and what he was going to do was ridiculous. She didn't have time for such nonsense.

"It's almost ten o'clock. I think it's too late, young lady."

"Please, I'm really hungry," she said, rubbing her chest.

Madeline was sure it was a scheme. She didn't have the heart to tell Tamara that hunger pains resided in her stomach and not her chest. The insight wasn't worth putting a damper on her daughter's zeal. "I guess you can have a snack. Get the boys and we'll walk up to the snack shop. Put your shoes on quickly. I think they close at ten."

Her daughter went ripping out the room, yelling out the names of Sam, Andre, and Don. Madeline got up to get her shoes when the doorbell rang. With a three-bedroom suite, the bell

had come in handy. She slipped on her sandals
and went to the door, wondering what guest
services wanted this late at night. Whatever it
was, they'd better be quick because she had four
anxious children thirty seconds from plowing
through the front door. "Who is it?' she asked.

"Me, Dave."

Dave, she thought and let her body fall
against the door. She'd forgotten that fast that
he was coming. Honestly, she wasn't prepared.
Madeline drew in an extra-long breath and
gripped the door handle, opening very slowly.
Once the door was open, there he stood, in the
flesh, the man she'd spent her entire adult years
loving, and the past couple of months despising.
What was she going to do with him?

"I see you made it," she said, lacking passion. They knew one another well, rendering no
reason to pretend. Their relationship was built
on honesty. It was the one bond they'd shared
throughout the entire marriage and had become
their glue. She wasn't going to cheapen it by
pretending to be thrilled with his arrival. She
owed him more than empty words and fakeness.

"I told you I was coming tonight. What, you
didn't believe me?" he asked, dropping the bag
inside the unit and opening his arms.

"Humph," was the best she could offer. She didn't fall into his embrace. It wasn't a happily ever after ending. They were living the trauma of a strained marriage and she couldn't muster the ability to accept his reconciliatory gesture. Constantly coming in second and third in his life didn't generate gushing feelings of love for her any longer. She was hurt; simple as that, and it was going to take patience on his end to restore their relationship.

Dave must have gotten the message. He dropped his arms and gave her a peck on the cheek as he entered the suite.

Andre and Sam came barreling into the living room with their little brother keeping up. Tamara strolled in too, which was no great surprise. Wherever Don was, she was bound to be nearby.

"Dad, you're here," Don and Tamara cried out, running to Dave, practically tackling him with affection. The older boys said hello and asked if they were still going for snacks, showing no significant interest in seeing their father. Madeline told them to wait a minute. She didn't think Dave deserved the celebration, but she was beaming inside for her younger children. If they were happy, she was happy, which was precisely why she didn't want Dave there. A week wasn't long enough for him to get to know the children intimately. It was just long enough to lure them into a false sense of time and attention, only to have it snatched away next week. She couldn't subject her children to the emotional roller coaster.

"Let's go, let's go," Tamara echoed, grabbing her Dad's hand. "We have to get to the snack shop before they close. "Let's hurry."

Madeline felt a bit guilty having given Dave the ultimatum. Watching Dave walk out the door with Tamara holding one hand and Don holding the other. Madeline was reminded of how much they loved him, unconditionally. Whereas she wanted loaves of his love, they seemed content with mere grains, far less than they were entitled to have. Now she had to deal with the penalty of forcing Dave to stay for an entire week or possibly longer. *Ugh,* she thought, and closed the door to her casket of despair.

Chapter 51

It was Monday, and Sherry was a mess. She didn't want to be in the office since Dave wasn't there. The awkwardness she'd felt on Friday was crippling and confusing. Thursday, she and Dave were perfectly fine. In an instant, their relationship had changed from boss and employee to something else. She wasn't sure what they'd changed to. Sherry contemplated calling Dave and pretending it was for DMI business. At least she would hear his voice. With further consideration, she decided not to call.

Sherry busied herself, determined to stay calm, yet the constant barrage of negativity kept coming. She hadn't given any consideration to the possible fallout of her actions. Dave might tell Madeline, and then Sherry was out of a job for sure. She'd never worked with Madeline directly in the office. When Sherry first started, Madeline came in once in a while. Sherry had always taken notice of how firm Madeline was.

She wasn't shy and didn't hold back. The few times she'd seen Madeline in action, she was on the phone talking tough to the clients who had been demanding deep discounts. Madeline and Dave had different styles but they were both very good at their jobs, an observation that made Sherry feel worse. She was certainly out of a job. The more she dwelled on her situation the more evident the outcome became.

Oddly, there was going to be a heavy price paid for unleashing her heart and allowing love to roam freely. Sherry negotiated a reasonable explanation that she could live with. When she thought about it, Dave was the one who'd come on to her. He was the one who'd initiated their intimacy. She wasn't completely to blame. He had his part, although that wasn't going to matter to Madeline. It had to be easier casting aside a secretary than the husband she'd been married to for years. Plus they shared a company and four children.

Sherry had saved some money for the wedding. Maybe that could hold her until the placement office could find another job. Even after putting the pieces together and rationalizing what was going to come next, she didn't regret the connection with Dave. Truthfully she felt the opposite, acknowledging a deep sense of longing that wasn't going to be satisfied with her in Detroit and Dave in Florida. Sherry slumped, depressed.

The phone rang. Sherry rushed to get the phone, desperately hoping it was Dave. Her greeting soared with excitement then began floating to the ground.

"Edward, it's you," she said, actually glad to hear from him. He wasn't Dave but that wasn't a truth he could change. So she didn't blame him. "I have been worried sick about you," she whispered into her phone, scanning the area to see who might be close enough to hear. The coast was clear but she'd be watchful. "You left without saying good-bye. How could you be so cruel, Edward? I've been an absolute wreck since you left."

"I know, and I'm sorry, Sherry. It's just that you hurt me badly when you gave my ring back. I admit it. I was so angry that I wanted to get away as fast as I could. I took the airline ticket and got out of town. The way I left wasn't right. I know it, and I'm sorry. But at the time, it was all I could do from going berserk." Sherry was really glad to be talking with him. She'd missed him and was relishing in the love he was pouring out over the line. "As mad as I was at you, I realized that nothing has changed for me," he told her.

"What do you mean?"

"Miss Sherry Henderson, I love you as much today as I did last week, last month, and last year. You are the woman for me. I love you like I've never loved anybody."

The longer he spoke, the worse she felt. Edward was a good man, and he deserved better. Instinct said to apologize and work out a reconciliation. "After I didn't hear from you for days, I figured you didn't want to have anything to do with me."

"Oh no, I still want you to move to Texas with me. We can have a great life together here. I'm finally where I need to be with a good job under my belt. I can take care of you properly and treat you like the queen you are."

She gobbled up each kind word, using it to bury Dave's rejection. As the darkness in her day showed signs of brightening, she pondered. Perhaps she could move to Texas, get married, settle down, and start a family. She wanted to speak out and say yes about moving to Texas, but Dave kept muscling his way into her emotions, snatching her from Edward's sincere embrace. She couldn't resist Dave, his commanding presence, his intelligence, and the way he made her feel valued and important.

Sherry was confused, being jerked back and forth between Dave and Edward. She didn't know what to do. For now, she'd keep Edward on the phone as long as possible. He was a soothing ointment on her singed soul.

Chapter 52

The weekend had crawled along. Monday, Tuesday, and Wednesday had passed, putting Thursday front and center. Dave was stretched out on the couch. His neck was a little stiff, having slept in an awkward position. He'd been too tired and discouraged to let out the sleeper. After the fifth night of distance from Madeline, his picture was clear. Dave lay pondering their situation. He should get up and go home but his determination wasn't allowing him to give in. He was in Florida for one reason: to be with his family. It wasn't going to be easy mending fences but that's what he had to do.

He finally planted his feet on the floor, rubbed his head, and stood for a stretch, rolling his shoulders, buying time before confronting the storm in his life. Dave meandered down the hallway toward Madeline's bedroom. He stopped at the doorway, bracing but still determined. It was nearly nine o'clock and no one was stirring.

A minute elapsed before Dave knocked on her door. It was already cracked open. He walked in slowly and saw Tamara and Don sleeping in what should have been his spot on the bed.

"Madeline, are you asleep?" he said, going to the bedside of his kids and squeezing in. She rustled around without responding. He didn't call her again, concerned that she might get irritated. Their rapport was that tenuous. Dave rested his head against the headboard, letting one foot remain on the floor. The kids were sprawled out, leaving only a small amount of space for him. He fit in where he could.

"What do you want, Dave?" Madeline said in a muffled voice, flinging the sheet over the kids and intentionally excluding him. Not a cover of the sheet touched him.

"What do you and the kids plan to do today?"

She sat up but kept her back to him. "We're going to spend the day at Tomorrowland. Sam and Andre are bent on setting a record on Space Mountain. So, that's where we're going."

"What's Space Mountain?"

"Oh, it's a roller coaster ride of some sort that scares them to death."

"Wow, that sounds intense," Dave said, amused.

"Well, that's where they want to go."

Don and Tamara stayed asleep with little to no movement. "Can the little ones go on a ride like that?"

"No, Dave," Madeline snapped at him. "Duh, come on."

He didn't react. Dave was going to keep feeding Madeline chunks of calm despite what she hurled at him. "If you'd like, maybe I could take the boys for you and you could take Don and Tamara on rides they like."

Madeline whipped around and shot a look at Dave that screamed. Then she said, "You think I can't handle four children? By now you ought to know better."

"I'm just trying to help out while I'm here."

She rose up from the bed, sitting straight up. "Don't you get it? I don't need your help. I've gotten used to not getting it. You spend your time living and breathing DMI, and then you think you're going to hop a plane, come down here, and take over." Her voice was getting loud, causing the kids to fidget, but they didn't wake up yet. "Do you understand that's not going to happen? Not today, not tomorrow, not ever." Her gaze pierced his soul. She was really mad, not just upset, but bitterly angry. Dave wanted to cast a rod of unity, but Madeline wasn't taking the bait.

"What can I do, Madeline? Tell me and I'll do it."

"N-o-t-h-i-n-g."

Dave sat for a while and then got up. Before walking out he said, "Obviously you don't want me here." Madeline gritted her teeth and rolled her eyes. She'd spoken; additional words would be redundant. He walked out accepting where she was. He'd give up on trying to appease her and shift his focus to spending the remaining time with his kids. Unfortunately the number of days was completely in Madeline's control. She'd decide when he had to go. Dave didn't hang his head. Instead, he went to the kitchen, willing to prepare breakfast for anyone interested in sharing a meal with him. He was pretty sure Don and Tamara would. The rest of the family was a monumental question mark, one he hoped to convert to a comma, representing a continuation of their bond.

Chapter 53

Dave limped into the living area, wounded but not defeated. He'd set his family woes aside to tackle battles where his strength never wavered, at DMI. Thinking of the office, Sherry did trot across his thoughts. There was no way around her. If he was going to get updates while out of town, they'd have to talk. He would be okay with continuing their boss-and-employee relationship while blotting out their brief indiscretion. Last Thursday night was in the past for him, completely buried. He wasn't sure if she felt the same way. He claimed a quiet spot at the kitchen table, next to the wall phone. Dialing DMI, soon he'd find out.

"Sherry, it's Dave. Thought I'd check in before the day gets too hectic for you there."

"Hi, Dave," she said, without him detecting any awkwardness. There was bound to be some but nothing yet.

"So, what's going on in the office? Any major news?"

"Only the Tri-State expansion meeting. I have tried and tried to get a new date set but no confirmation so far."

"Well, keep trying." Andre walked into the kitchen and went to the refrigerator without saying a word. Dave felt invisible. He figured it was because he was on the phone. Maybe his imagination was in overdrive, but for several days he'd sensed that Andre was avoiding him. Dave covered the mouthpiece on the phone and said, "Good morning, son." Andre returned a weak wave. "Sherry, hold on please." He directed his conversation to Andre. "Come on, surely you can do much better than that, young man."

"Hi," he said, agitated.

Dave didn't get mad. He was sad seeing the sting of Madeline's anger transferring to the kids. He was helpless. Here he was a man brokering million-dollar deals with a long line of top executives, movers, and shakers. Yet, he couldn't manage the lackluster response of a ten-year-old.

"Dave, are you there?" he faintly heard coming from the phone.

Sherry. He'd forgotten she was on the line. "I'm here," he said, fumbling to get the phone up to his ear. "Now, what were you saying about Tri-State?"

"We still have to get the meeting rescheduled."

"Shoot for next week."

"That's been the problem. They're bent on coming in this week. They wanted me to check with you and see if there was any way you could come in this week. They offered to pay for the plane ride."

Dave laughed out loud for the first time in days. It felt good.

Out of nowhere, Madeline entered the kitchen while he was laughing.

The call was innocent, but it didn't feel that way. He knew why. The grand plan had been to come to Florida, find the right private moment with Madeline, and tell her the truth about what happened with Sherry. He hadn't found either the courage, the time, or both. Every day that his secret remained buried, the roots were spreading. He realized that unless he unearthed the issue, it would eventually grow too big to conceal and manifest at the most inopportune time. He couldn't let that happen. He'd tell her, soon.

"Who are you talking with this early?" Madeline asked, opening the cabinet.

Dave hesitated and then said, "Sherry."

"It figures," she snapped at him. "You can't leave DMI for a few days without checking in." Dave adjusted the phone to reduce the chance of Sherry overhearing. Madeline bent down and whispered into his ear. "Who are you fooling? This isn't where your heart is. Do us all a favor, *go home,*" she drilled into his ear.

"Sherry, tell the Tri-State clients thanks for the offer, but I have a family commitment the entire week," he said to Sherry, intending for Madeline to hear him too. "I'm here until further notice."

Madeline slammed the cabinet drawer shut.

"Humph," she muttered, storming out.

"I'll let them know what you've said," Sherry told him. Dave was ready to end the call when she said, "Dave, can we talk when you get home?"

"About what?" he asked, sitting up in the chair and scanning the room. A family member might enter at any time. His conversation had to be clean.

"Kind of personal."

"Sure, why don't you get a meeting on my calendar," he said a bit louder. "We can discuss the details then," he said, intentionally vague. He had to protect home. Sherry would have to understand.

Chapter 54

Don and Dave tumbled around on the floor playing silly games. Tamara sat close by waiting her turn, jumping in every now and then. Madeline watched off to the side. She was enraged, to the point where her head was hurting. She massaged her temples gently with no results, forcing her to apply more pressure. She'd go and lie down, hoping to get relief. Madeline stumbled to the bedroom, not quite sure what to do. She'd spent most of the first week with the children, alone. They'd established a routine and it worked for her. Dave popped up on short notice and was trying to dominate time with the children. She had to lie down, relax, and let the anger dissipate. Besides, the only person in pain was her. Dave and the two younger children were getting along nicely.

Rest didn't come easily. Perhaps a cup of tea would help. She wandered into the kitchen to find Dave on the phone again.

"I haven't seen a fax machine here, but I'll check and let you know," Dave said to whoever he was talking to. If Madeline had to guess it was DMI.

"Don, Tamara, go get your things packed," she told them.

"Why, we don't leave until tomorrow?" Miss Tamara said. Madeline wasn't in the mood to negotiate her request, not today.

"Go do what I said, young lady."

"Okay," the little girl said, stomping each step. Tamara stopped and displayed a look of discovery, like she'd found out a big secret. "What about Andre and Sam? Don't they have to pack too? Can I go get them?"

"Yes and no."

"What?" Tamara asked, looking lost.

"Yes, they have to pack and, no, you can't go find them. I'll get them."

Dave got off the phone.

"Daddy, are you coming to pack with us?"

"What's this business about packing?" he asked Tamara, picking her up to shoulder level and twirling her in the air.

"Mommy said we have to pack."

"Why are they packing so early? I was planning to spend the day with the kids."

"We're going home today," she barked at him without making eye contact.

"Today, why? I thought we were leaving tomorrow."

"We're leaving today. Now go and get packed," she yelled at the children and then eased up, because it made her headache hurt worse.

"That's not fair," Tamara said, crying and clinging to Dave.

"Life isn't fair, young lady, now go," Madeline said, pointing in the direction of the bedrooms.

When Don and Tamara were gone, Dave asked, "Is this about me? Are you so mad that you're going to rob the kids of their last day here? This isn't like you, Madeline. What's going on?"

She didn't have enough energy, interest, or pain relief to adequately address his question. Plus it would be redundant. He already knew why she was upset. Dropping in wasn't acceptable. She'd told him from the beginning what was best for the children. Selfishly he disregarded her request and showed up for a mini visit. Her children needed a full-time father, not one who squeezed them into his schedule like a client meeting. They deserved more and she would make sure they got it.

"If you can tear yourself away from the phone for ten minutes, I'd like to make a call to the travel agency."

"You're really going to do this to the children?"

Madeline shot a stare at him that pierced deep inside. "Don't you even think about going there."

"You know how much the change is going to cost you in airfare? Why spend the money when we can wait one more day and fly out together tomorrow?"

"I am not concerned about a few dollars when it comes to my peace of mind. Staying in this hotel one more night with you is going to drive me insane. At least Mayweather Lane is my turf, and I'm not so bothered with you being around."

"Okay, Madeline, if you want to end the vacation on a sour note, be my guest." Dave handed her the phone with nothing left to say. She took it and made the call.

"I'd like to change my reservations for tomorrow and get a flight to Detroit this afternoon." She gave the agent her confirmation number and waited. "They're full-fare tickets. So I should be able to make changes with no problem, correct?"

The agent agreed. Madeline waited and waited until finally the agent returned and gave an update.

"Mrs. Mitchell, there's a flight at three o'clock, but it doesn't have five seats left in first class. There's only one."

"Are you sure?'

"Positive, I called the airline to confirm."

Madeline was dejected. "I really needed to get home today. It's an emergency," she said, which had enough truth to justify the comment. If she didn't get away from Dave immediately, words might be spoken that couldn't easily be erased. Better for her to go home and let Dave have the suite and the entire state of Florida if he chose. "What other options do I have?"

"First class is basically full, but there are five seats available in coach."

"Ugh," Madeline responded. Her headache was heating up, which was why she said, "I'll have to take those unless there's another flight later today or tonight."

"Psst," was the sound Dave made attempting to get her attention.

"There's a flight at two-thirty with two seats. There's also one at six and another at eight-fifteen, but both are also fully booked. As a matter of fact, the three o'clock flight with the five seats is your best bet."

Madeline contemplated briefly and then said, "I'll take it."

"Psst," Dave continued.

"What?" she asked him.

"Change mine too, please."

"Humph," she said, shaking her head for no. "You have to take care of your ticket after I finish," she said, holding the phone away from her mouth with an outstretched arm.

"Please hold on while I make the changes," the agent told her.

"Sure, thanks," Madeline said. While on hold she turned to Dave and said, "This flight is full except for one seat in first class." Before he remotely considered taking the seat, she added, "And I don't expect you to be in first class when the five of us will be in coach."

Madeline concluded the transaction to her satisfaction. She'd be on Mayweather Lane sleeping in her bed tonight. Her headache was already easing. She handed Dave the phone. He'd have to find another flight home, because the one his family was on had no room for him.

Chapter 55

By five o'clock Madeline was sailing through the Detroit Metropolitan Airport, rejuvenated. This was her dominion, and she stepped with the confidence that said so.

"Mom, can I get a drink from the store?" Sam asked.

"Sure, everybody can get something from the store," she said amid a wave of screaming approvals. The children floated around the store picking up a few things. She was drawn to a stack of magazines on the counter with Dave's picture. Then she recalled him mentioning an article being done on him a few weeks ago. She bought a copy and tucked it away for the limousine ride home.

Secure in the car and on their way, Madeline plucked the magazine from her bag. Her heart began warming, melting the chunks of ice she'd let form toward Dave over the past week. She stared at the handsome photo blanketing the cover. Dave infuriated her at times, lately it was most of the time, but the truth of the matter was she adored him. They'd pieced a life together, and after calmly reflecting, she wasn't willing to throw her hard-earned work in the trash. The more she thought about it, Dave was worth a second chance. She'd talk when he got home and figure out how to move forward, to restore the best of what they had. She was willing. Hopefully he would be too. Her headache subsided.

Feeling good about her decision, Madeline flipped to Dave's article. The children were preoccupied with their treasures from the gift shop. She used the semi-silence to read.

The headline read: LOCAL MILLIONAIRE HAS THE MIDAS TOUCH. A few minutes into the article, Madeline slapped the magazine down on her lap, steaming.

"Are you okay, Mom?" Andre asked.

"Yes," she said, lying. She wasn't going to alarm the children. They wouldn't understand anyway. She'd save her dissatisfaction for Dave and him alone. *How dare he* was what kept roaming through her head, meshed with lines from the article. *Much of Dave Mitchell's recent success can be attributed to the support of his right-hand man, or more appropriately labeled, his personal assistant, Sherry Henderson.*

Going on and on about Sherry was bad enough, but adding a photo of her and Dave standing in his office was ridiculous. Madeline's headache was flaring up again. He was quoted as calling Sherry "invaluable." A four-page article and not a single mention of Dave's wife—not a word. She slammed the magazine down again, this time shoving it into her bag.

"Mommy, can we stop for ice cream?"

"Uhn hmm," she said without offering her full attention. They could have asked for just about anything and gotten a yes. Her mind wasn't in the car. Madeline's outrage was manageable, so long as Dave reprimanded the magazine's editor for the mistake. They'd also demand that the magazine reprint another four-page spread, highlighting Dave and his wife as they should have done in the first place. She'd settle for not a word less.

Chapter 56

The limousine pulled into the circular drive-way. Madeline hadn't allowed the ride to water down her temperament. She was as hot pulling up to the front door as she'd been reading the magazine. It would get straightened out. She'd table the issue until the children were settled inside. Since Dave was taking a different flight, she hoped he was already home. She preferred not to serve her resentment cold.

"We're home," she said, attempting to sound engaged and upbeat with the children as they collected their suitcases from the front walkway. The driver left. "Aren't you glad to be home?"

"No" was tossed at her from each child in harmony. No one responded positively about being back.

"Andre and I were planning to go on Big Thunder Mountain and ride Space Mountain two more times. We were going for a record, but you made us leave early."

"Yeah, for no reason," Miss Tamara said.

Madeline was trying to be cheerful for them but she wasn't interested in petty debates. She couldn't spare the nerves. Hers was needed for a much larger battle. She opened the door and saw Dave's suitcase at the foot of the staircase. She exhaled, feeling good that he was already home. She didn't have to wait long for their talk, which was perfect. She wanted to convey her sentiments while the disdain was fresh.

Andre and Sam dropped their suitcases and backpacks by the door and tore in the direction of the kitchen.

"Oh no, come and get these bags. Take them upstairs." Whining followed, which she ignored. "Let's go, you too, Don and Tamara."

"But we can't carry our suitcases. They're too heavy," Tamara whined.

"Yeah, it's too heavy," Don mimicked.

"I'll get it," Sam said.

"Good, Andre, you take Don's. Tamara and Don, both of you can at least carry your backpacks, right?"

"Yes, I can, Mommy," Don said, taking his steps slowly as he balanced the load on his back.

Madeline rushed the brood up the stairs and got them squared away in their rooms. Next stop was Dave's office. He was probably in there on the phone with Sherry. Actually, she was surprised he hadn't gone straight to the office.

She made a pit stop in her bedroom to drop off her bag and then hit the battlefield. She opened the door and found Dave sprawled across the bed. Before organizing her thoughts, Madeline lashed out, slamming the door behind her. "When were you going to tell me about Sherry?" she said, admittedly angrier than the article warranted. She'd psychoanalyze later.

Dave sat up on the bed and let his head hang down. He clasped his hands together and said, "Madeline, I'm sorry."

"You're sorry. Is that all you can say?"

He kept looking at the floor. "What else is there to say? I made a mistake that I regret."

"You better believe you made a mistake," She wailed.

He looked up and continued. "But I can promise you that it only happened once. Last Thursday was the only time, and I would take it back in a second if I could."

Madeline felt a rush of uneasiness. Her deposition shifted from anger to confusion. Dave couldn't possibly be talking about what it sounded like, no way. "Exactly what did you do with Sherry?" She had to be absolutely certain.

Dave sighed. He must have assumed she knew what he was talking about and began rattling off details. "If you need to hear it, I'm willing to say the words; whatever it takes for us to work this out. The only explanation I can offer is that I was weak. My lust got the best of me and it happened. I could say that it didn't mean anything, but that would be cruel. What I can say is that it wasn't worth risking my marriage and family," he said, fixating his gaze on hers.

After Dave delivered the crippling revelation, a stunned Madeline managed to extract the magazine sticking out of the side of her bag. She hurled it at Dave. "I was talking about the article." Her control was short-lived once the revelation took root. Dave had actually cheated on her? She stared at him, unable to move an inch.

"I know you want to say something. Go ahead, I deserve it. I can take it," he said.

She didn't know what to say. The words and images were rushing forward, scrambling to get out first. They were too jumbled to make sense. A jilted feeling dominated, knocking the other emotions aside. The amount of support and sacrifice that she'd given to Dave and to the establishment of DMI was pressing forward too. "Dave, how could you be so reckless? You not only put our marriage at risk, you've jeopardized the company's reputation. All because you didn't control your hormones. What were you thinking?"

"I wasn't. I messed up, and I'm sorry. I've repented and asked God to forgive me too. Now I'm asking you to forgive me."

"I can't think about forgiveness. I'm still in shock that you were so weak. Where was your God when you took your behind somewhere with Sherry and did your business? Huh, tell me, where was your God?" Her words were getting organized and taking center stage.

"Madeline, you know God wasn't with me in my sinful act. It was my choice and I accept full responsibility."

She went to the bed, on the opposite side of Dave, and sat down. "You of all people have supposedly committed your life to helping churches and ministers get their acts together, so they can represent the Lord with integrity," she said, making quotation marks in the air with both index and middle fingers. "Well, where's your integrity, Mr. Dave Mitchell, the mighty man of God?"

"I'm not perfect, that's for sure. I sinned. I repented. God has forgiven me, and I have to move on. I can't reclaim the past, and I won't spend time trying."

"How can you be so sure God has forgiven you? Because I haven't."

"I'm a hundred percent sure God has forgiven me, because that's one of his promises. By faith I believe it, no matter how big or little my sin is."

"Don't talk about faith with me, Dave Mitchell. I believed you'd be faithful in our marriage, but that was obviously wrong." Madeline wanted to lunge at him, rip the hurt resting on her soul, and stuff it down his throat, but she didn't. Her body was too limp to make any moves, but her tongue was strong. It would have to continue fighting for her. "How can you throw our marriage away for a roll in the hay with a woman almost twenty years younger than you are? What can she do for you? Oops, excuse me. That's a silly question. We both know that answer." Dave was silent as her tirade extended. The mixture of disbelief, anger, and confusion kept her fueled. "This is too much to handle. I need you to leave."

"Madeline, we're talking. I'm willing to listen to you without defending myself. I owe you that and more."

"What you owed me was faithfulness. Apparently that was too much for you. So, I need you to get out. Go."

"Where?"

"I don't know," she yelled. "You didn't ask for my advice about how to pursue Sherry. You don't need my advice now. Figure it out so long as it's outside of this house. Go," she yelled again. "Get out."

That forced him off the bed and out of the bedroom. Madeline wanted him out until she could make sense of their jumbled situation. Hopefully he wouldn't be gone long.

Chapter 57

Dave had tried reasoning with Madeline unsuccessfully. It was barely after five o'clock; so he opted to drive into the office. He could camp out there for several hours until Madeline gave him the okay to come home. He went into the building expecting Sherry and the rest of his staff to be gone. Riding in the elevator, his mind rested on Madeline. He acknowledged her pain and was sensitive to it, but he wasn't going to dwell on guilt. It bared no fruit.

The elevator door opened and there was Sherry carrying a stack of papers. "Oh, you're here," he said, caught off guard.

"I might as well stay late since there's no reason to go home early. Edward is gone and you were too," she said. "I don't have anyone to go home to."

Maybe her being there was a blessing. They had to talk. "Can you please come into my office?" She set the papers down and followed him into the office. Dave started to close the door but decided not to. "Have a seat," he said, pointing to a chair at the table. He intentionally sat on the other side, several chairs away. Distance was necessary.

"I didn't expect you in the office until Monday," she said.

"We decided to come home early." He wasn't interested in small talk. The critical issue had to be addressed directly. "Madeline knows what happened."

Sherry gasped. "Oh no, how did she find out?" She appeared terrified.

"I told her," he said. The revelation hadn't been intentional, definitely not in the way it transpired. That wasn't Sherry's business and he didn't tell her.

"I'm so sorry. How did she react?"

Dave smirked. "Not well, as you can imagine." He leaned his elbows onto the table. "Sherry, I have to apologize to you and ask for your forgiveness too."

"No, you don't owe me an apology. I knew what I was doing. And, Dave, I have to tell you, I don't regret the time I spent with you."

"It was a mistake and can't happen ever again."

Sherry maintained her disturbed demeanor. "I guess this means you're going to fire me?"

Letting her go hadn't entered his mind. She needed the job before. After her fiancé relocated, he figured she needed the job even more. He didn't feel right firing her because of his mistake. He was the boss, the older one out of the pair. He should have known better. Dave's compassion kicked in. He wouldn't have Sherry double penalized. They'd have to work out how to function together in close proximity, but he was willing, even if it meant moving her to another department. "You can keep your job here as long as we both set aside the past and move forward appropriately. Is that something you can do?" he asked.

"Yes," she whispered.

Sherry wasn't convincing but he'd accept her response for now. Each day would determine how much further they'd be able to go.

Chapter 58

A month passed and the bitter sting of his adultery hadn't lessened. Madeline hadn't allowed it. He'd let her have the space required to heal as long as she understood that Dave wasn't giving up on reconciliation. He straightened the sheets on the queen-sized bed in the smallest of the two guest rooms. The solitude would normally be refreshing, but his equated to isolation. "Father, let your will be done. I am born of flesh and my strength comes from you. Let my decisions today be pleasing before you, God. Let me walk in your ways," he prayed. "Let your will be done in my marriage." Dave sat alone in the room, soaking in the quiet.

He heard a noise at the door and looked up to see Madeline standing there. "Are you busy?"

"No," he said, leaping to his feet. He couldn't remember the last time she woke up this early in the morning.

"Can I come in?" she stammered.

"Absolutely," he said, maneuvering toward the doorway. In September they'd celebrate thirteen years of marriage, but in that moment they were like teenagers on a first date. Their awkwardness lingered and he didn't mind. Having her talk to him after a month of virtual silence was not only an answer to his prayer, it was encouraging.

"Can we talk?"

"Yes," he said, patting a spot on the bed for her to sit. He bounced around to the other side, automatically assuming she didn't want him too close. He'd gladly accommodate. Keeping the dialogue flowing was his goal.

"I'm not going to beat around the bush. You screwed up, that's the bottom line."

"You're right," he said.

"But I've invested too much into this marriage, into the company, and into you to let a teenybopper sneak in and steal our way of life. I'm not letting that happen. You're my husband, and if little Miss Sherry Henderson thinks she's moving in, she's got another think coming."

"You don't have to be concerned about Sherry. I spoke with her right after you found out and made it clear that our one-time mistake wasn't happening again. She was in total agreement. I'm not sure if this matters to you, but Sherry feels awful about what happened too."

"Uhn hmm, right," Madeline said. Dave might have been smart in business, but he wasn't immune to flattery. Sherry had the power to bat her eyelids, and open the gate wide for her lying tongue to flow. Madeline had seen her kind and was on alert, especially since her husband wasn't. She decided that his so-called anointing only applied to business. No worries, she'd make up the difference. "If we're going to work this out, I have a few requests that are non-negotiable."

"And what would those be?"

"You've used your one and only chance to be forgiven for infidelity. This can't happen again," Madeline said firmly, harshly, to be certain he understood that she was serious.

"It won't."

"I mean it, not ever again."

"Done," he said. "What else?"

"The second requirement is that you have to fire Sherry. She has to get out of DMI. I don't ever want to see her again." Madeline wanted the freedom of stopping by DMI any day, and she didn't want the wayward woman making her visit unpleasant. No question, Sherry had to go.

Dave shut his eyelids and let his head drop. "Do we have to fire her? What happened wasn't her fault. I take full responsibility."

"She's a grown woman. You didn't force yourself on her, did you?"

"Absolutely not," he rose to say. "You shouldn't have to ask me that question. You know me."

"Thought I did, but you've proven me wrong." Madeline felt tinges of anger slowly percolating and chose to ignore them. She wanted to stay in a positive place with Dave. Her anger had spoken loudly by keeping silent for a month, but her love for him was real. She let her heart do the talking for a change.

"If Sherry has to be fired, then it's done."

Madeline could tell Dave wasn't convinced that Sherry had to go, but he'd better not say it, otherwise the harmony floating between them would evaporate instantly. Sherry wasn't getting the slightest consideration. As far as Madeline was concerned, when Miss Henderson chose to lie down with the head of the company, she should have been prepared to get up looking for a new job. There was zero compassion being spent on her.

Dave continued. "I want you to be okay with this going forward. Like I said before, I'll do what needs to be done to make this right between us. You're my wife and I love you."

There was a long pause in the room. Madeline hadn't expected Dave to agree to her demand so quickly. She was prepared to fight and none came, causing her to be unsure. Should she celebrate or remain cautious? She simply didn't know. Dave broke the silence. "Before Sherry and I caused a stir in our marriage, we had problems. You know it and I know it." Madeline fidgeted. "If we truly want to fix what's broken in our relationship, let's go the full distance. We can get counseling, go away together, I'm open to suggestions."

Madeline spoke without fully processing what Dave was saying. She only heard the part that said their marriage was already in trouble, making it easy pickings for a floozy like Sherry. "Our marriage is like any other long-term marriage. We have our ups and downs but don't think for a minute that our problems gave you a license to cheat."

"That's not what I said."

"That's what it sounds like to me." She was annoyed at the accusation and her tone reflected the agitation.

"I'm only saying that we have other areas to improve in our marriage. That's all I'm saying."

"Tell you what," she said, standing. "Let's handle one problem at a time since, according to you, we have so many. Sherry is the number one priority. Fire her behind and then we can talk about the number two priority. That works for me," she said, crossing her arms and letting the words marinate with Dave.

Chapter 59

Dave was putting home at the front of his decisions. Negotiations were finalized with Madeline, and he drove into the office prepared to close the deal with Sherry. He prayed. "Lord, even in my calamity, you are the God of peace. Even when I fail you, God, you lift me up, dust off my transgressions, and renew my faith in you. Where I am weak, thou art strong and I rest in you."

Since the conversation with Madeline had taken awhile, it was already well after eight o'clock. Dave was pleased finding Sherry sitting at her desk. She'd been out sick for several days.

"Good morning, Dave," she greeted him in what appeared to be an upbeat tone. "I know your calendar is full today, but when you get a minute, can we talk?"

"Definitely, as a matter of fact, this is a great time." Best to get the unpleasant matter behind them, give her a powerful recommendation, and let Sherry get on with her life. This was best for her in the long run. Might not feel so good at the moment, but the day would come when she'd have no regrets about leaving DMI.

Sherry followed Dave into the office as he closed the door behind them. She took her usual seat at his table.

"Thank you for meeting with me."

Dave sat down. "It's not a problem, and I needed to talk with you anyway." Dave could have prolonged the inevitable but didn't. "Madeline and I have talked and come to an agreement about how to restore our marriage. The only way I see this working is to let you go." It wasn't in his heart to be so harsh. But Madeline's position in his heart was much greater. She had the outright edge. Sherry was quiet. "I hope you understand. It's just that my family is very important to me, and I have to protect my marriage and my children." Sherry was still quiet. "I will make sure you get a generous severance package and a glowing letter of recommendation. If you need help finding another job, just let me know. I'll do the very best I can to help you get relocated." To Dave's surprise, the discussion was going smoother than expected. Sherry wasn't yelling or crying. He felt pretty good. "And, Sherry," he said, wanting to touch her hand and offer comfort, but decided it wasn't a wise move. "I'm very sorry about how this has turned out. I pray that you've forgiven me, and I wish you the best in your future." Bringing the meeting to a close he said, "Is there anything you'd like to say?"

"I'm pregnant."

"Excuse me?" he said, pulling up to the table.

"I'm pregnant."

Dazed, he went for the only relief available, hoping it was true. "Is it Edward's?"

"No, it's yours," she said very calmly.

"How can you be so sure?"

"Because I haven't been intimate with Edward for months, long before he left for Texas. And we've only spoken a few times since he moved. That relationship is over. There is no one else but you."

Now, Dave was the one sitting quiet. He really was speechless. Many thoughts swirled, none positive. Going home to tell Madeline was at the top of his list, and it wasn't a task he wanted to undertake. She was going to be a handful.

Besides facing his soon-to-be irate wife, he reflected on his faith. The obvious question would be where was God? How could God let this happen if He'd truly forgiven him? But Dave didn't need to ask any of those questions. He rested on his reality and allowed wisdom to think for him.

Had he been obedient to God's commandments, he wouldn't be dealing with the aftermath, but the deed was done. Repenting had cleansed his soul, but there were circumstances that netted unchangeable consequences. Sherry's pregnancy was one. A moment of weakness was planting seeds for a lifetime of discord.

"Are you sure?"

"I'm positive. It's yours."

He drew in the longest sigh of his life. "Then we'll have to figure out what comes next."

"I can't lose my job. I'll have no insurance or income."

The legal implications bombarded him along with the other factors to consider. They could be significant, but paled in comparison to the backlash coming from Madeline. He honestly didn't know what to do.

He didn't have to wait long. There was a knock with the door opening simultaneously. "Madeline, what are you doing here?"

"I came to make sure that this little tramp gets fired today," she said, approaching the table as each word was enunciated.

"I am not a tramp," Sherry fired back, which seemed to fuel Madeline.

"As far as I'm concerned, you are. I took your behind off the street and gave you a job when you were practically homeless, and this is the thanks I get. You sleep with my husband. You knew he was a married man which makes you a tramp."

Dave hustled to the door and closed it. By that time, Sherry and Madeline were standing toe-to-toe. He rushed over to get in the middle. "Ladies, let's all take a breath and calm down. We need to discuss this like adults."

"Discuss what? We're already discussed what's going to happen. She needs to pack her stuff and get the heck out of here, end of discussion," Madeline said, spewing disgust in Sherry's face. "We don't ever want to see you again."

Sherry took a step back and rubbed her belly. "Dave is always going to be a part of our lives."

"What are you talking about?"

"Ask Dave."

Dave cut in, terrified that Madeline was going to find out in the wrong way. He had to get them separated and attempt to regain a semblance of control. "Sherry, please don't do this. Can you step outside and let me talk to Madeline, alone?"

"That's right, step out of this office, out of this building, and out of our lives. Bye," Madeline said, giving a wave to Sherry as she left the office. Dave closed the door.

Madeline sat down, appearing to cool down. "Good, finally, she's gone."

Dave wished there was a way to avoid what had to come next. He contemplated, considered his options, and thought some more. There was no other way out. He had to tell her. "Madeline, Sherry's pregnant."

"Great, she and her fiancé can go away and raise their offspring somewhere. They won't ever have to look back at us," Madeline said glibly.

Dave wished he could drop the conversation there. He trudged on. "She says the baby is mine."

Madeline swung around in her seat and belted out, "Pleasssse, that's the oldest trick in the book. I have to give it to her, though. She's good, real good, but Sherry didn't count on having to deal with me. We've handled so many ridiculous lawsuits in the past. She will just be one more pathetic money grubber looking for a payday. I'll have an attorney take care of it. You won't have to be bothered. I'll handle this with pleasure."

"She might be telling the truth."

"She better not be," Madeline barked.

Dave had to be honest. Denials and lies weren't going to erase the truth. "I have a strong feeling that it's true," he said, drawing close to Madeline. "But this doesn't change what we talked about this morning. If this turns out to be true, we'll do right by the baby, but that's where the relationship with Sherry ends."

"Have you lost your mind? You're struggling with taking care of four legitimate children. One more isn't remotely an option. More importantly, when I told you I never wanted to see Sherry again, I meant it. I can't imagine having to deal with her and a baby. It would be a constant reminder of your betrayal. I couldn't handle it, Dave, no way," she said, breaking down in tears.

"We'll figure this out."

"Don't come home until you do."

"I know you're upset, rightfully so, but let's not make any hasty decisions until we get home and talk this through, calmly."

"The decision was made on our wedding day, when you agreed to love and honor me. That includes honoring our bedroom, which you haven't done. So, don't talk to me about being hasty, because I don't want to hear it."

"I understand how you feel, but we still need to talk."

"Dave, I mean it, don't come home."

"Where am I going to go?"

"You figure it out. Get a hotel, get lost," she said, turning toward him and sending a piercing gaze. "You can stay anywhere, except Sherry's place. You better not stay there."

Before he could console Madeline, she bolted out. He didn't chase after her. She had to breathe and let the shocking news settle. He'd get a suite at the Westin for a few nights until Madeline changed her mind. Sherry was another story. He didn't quite know what to do with her yet. Wisdom would come hopefully real soon.

Chapter 60

Madeline had to get out of the den of disgust and retreat into her safe haven on Mayweather Lane. It was going to be the one place Sherry's venom couldn't penetrate. Running inside the office was inappropriate, but she hustled as quickly as her high heels permitted.

"Madeline, what are you doing here?" Frank said, catching her coming off the elevator in the lobby. "Please tell me that you're coming back to work. We've missed having you here, especially me."

Madeline sniffled. "Frank, I'm in a hurry." Sherry and Dave had robbed her of the ability to offer common courtesies. Getting out was her single priority.

"You seem upset. Anything wrong?"

"Ask your brother and his trifling secretary." She slowed down but didn't stop. Making small talk was of no interest. She'd barely fought back tears a few minutes ago, and they weren't far from returning. Madeline wasn't going to take a chance on losing composure because she carelessly chewed up time chatting. "I'll talk to you later," she told Frank, escaping through the revolving door.

Frank watched as Madeline left the building, confused about her disposition and comment. Something was definitely wrong, and it bothered him. Madeline wasn't a woman easily shaken. He'd seen her in action. She was tough, especially for a woman. He'd gladly have her on his team anytime. Seeing her unnerved was troubling. He'd go to his brother's office and get some answers.

Frank went upstairs and walked into Dave's office. Sherry was in there crying, with his brother consoling her. "Excuse me," Frank said. "I'll come back."

"No, come on in," Dave said, moving away from Sherry.

"Don't worry about me. I didn't want anything important. I can follow up with you at another time," he said.

"You sure? Because Sherry was just leaving," Dave told him.

"See you later," Frank said and left. He kept walking to the staircase. With each step, Frank hoped that what he'd seen wasn't what it seemed.

If Dave could fall victim to temptation, then there was no hope for him. Frank wished for a miracle. He would have prayed, but didn't really know how. Sure, he could have sputtered off a few sentences, but they probably wouldn't get past the ceiling. It wasn't his strength. He'd solely relied on Dave to handle spiritual matters for him. Without his brother's prayers, he was lost.

Sad or mad; Madeline sat in her Mercedes flipping back and forth between the two, both with equal force. She wiped across her eyelids, certain that her makeup had smeared. She didn't care, figuring her outside might as well be consistent with the ugliness she was harboring on the inside. *What has Dave done* she repeatedly wondered. She shifted the car in reverse and then back into park. She was numb to the core, unable to move. *Do this, do that,* rattled around in her head, with nothing seeming to gel.

Sherry, Sherry, Sherry, also played over and over in her mind. Madeline could push her into the abyss and wipe away the problem. If only she could send Sherry's tacky behind on a ride to the moon. That would be about the amount of distance necessary to feel secure with her around. Since neither of her top choices was feasible, Madeline remained stuck. She attempted to put the car in reverse again, but the rush of chaos overtook her. Madeline eased the gearshift into park. She gripped the leather-padded steering wheel with both hands and let her forehead rest against it.

There was no getting around it. She wanted—no, needed—Dave and his mistress to pay dearly. Conflicted, the next second Madeline remembered what she and Dave had meant to one another for over a decade. She wasn't ready to walk away from her world because of one mistake. Raising four children required her to see the merit in surviving the infidelity. But then, there was the baby, a constant reminder. How could she accept a child born to her husband's mistress? But she couldn't let Miss Nobody crawl in and make a home with her husband. Madeline wanted to scream out, dig deep into the center of her pain, and get some relief. *Get control.* She allowed her emotions to calm the best she could.

A little while passed and Madeline put the car in reverse, this time giving it the gas and making an actual move. She was going backward. But at least from her perspective, she wasn't sitting still and letting misery beat her down. Pride and grace could continue their debate along her thirty-minute ride home. The winner would determine whether she was going to fight or forfeit the marriage. Time would soon tell.

Chapter 61

Frank popped up to Dave's office after six. He had to catch his brother before the day ended. He got to the sixth floor. His brother's door was open and the light was on. Frank bolted into the office without knocking. Dave was sitting at his desk.

"Hey, I see you're still here," Dave said, glancing upward and quickly returning to writing on a notepad.

Frank grabbed a seat and pulled right up to his brother. "What the heck happened today? I caught Madeline running from the building in a tizzy. Then I come upstairs and walk in on you and Sherry hugged up while she's bawling her eyes out. What is going on?" Curiosity had escalated to the point where Frank had to get answers.

Dave looked up, set his pen down, and rested his arms on the table. "I messed up," he said bluntly.

"How?"

Dave's gaze dropped to the floor. He covered his eyes and said, "I slept with Sherry, once." He held his index finger in the air. "And that was enough to create a gigantic nightmare."

"You can't be serious. Come on, Dave," Frank said, not able to process what he'd heard. "It's not possible. You can't be serious."

"I wish I wasn't, but the truth is the truth. Worse yet, she claims to be pregnant."

"Man, you got careless, little brother," Frank said, falling back into his chair. "If they'd told me to list a million men who had or would cheat on their wives, I could have named every man I know, except you. Yours is the only name that wouldn't have been on the list. Even my name would be on the list but not yours." Frank scratched his head. "Anybody else could get away with this, but not you, man. And she's pregnant? I can't understand how you can jeopardize everything you have accomplished." Frank let his head hang down, as the gravity of his brother's carelessness came into vision. "This is unbelievable."

"I told you I messed up."

"How could you fall into one of the oldest traps in the book?"

"What trap would that be?"

"Getting too close to the secretary and eventually committing adultery. That's why I don't have a secretary. I don't plan to get caught."

"It wasn't a trap. She went through a rough patch with her fiancé being out of work for almost a year. I tried to help and instead caused a bigger riff between them."

"So what, you decided to offer a shoulder and one step led to the next."

"Something like that."

"Where's the fiancé now?"

"Gone to Texas. I'm pretty sure they're finished."

"You think?" Frank snickered. "What man wouldn't be once he found out his woman was pregnant by another man?" Frank kept shaking his head. "You shouldn't have taken the man's woman. You said he had been out of work. She was probably the best thing he had going, and you scooped in and took her from the man. That's shameful, and I have to tell you, this doesn't look good. If this gets out, DMI is ruined. Your reputation won't be any better than the slobs we're trying to help improve their images and choices."

"We'll work through this."

"I'm not as confident as you are about cleaning this up and keeping it out of the press. This is going to start a chain reaction impacting most of us. What are we going to do when clients find out and ask questions? So long as you were seen as a godly man, we could hock our religious services. Not now."

"I understand that people may be mad, but the truth is that people, not God, wants me to pay for the same mistake over and over. I know there will be plenty of folks to judge me. I can't stop them. I'm not perfect. But when I fall short, there is someone who can cleanse me and give me a fresh start, even when others don't think I deserve it. That's the role God plays in my life."

"Sounds good, but who's going to buy that crap? Clients expect you to walk the walk even if they aren't."

"I've been humbled. If anything, I will have more compassion for others who have done what I've done."

"Whoopee-do for them, but how's that going to help you?"

"What do you want me to say? I'm not running from my sin. I'm not trying to cover it up or sugar-coat it. I messed up. My actions with Sherry were a stain before God, but redemption has made me whole again, and I refuse to waddle in guilt. It is a heavy weight. I choose to move on and fulfill the purpose in my life."

"Well, good luck with convincing your clients about how stable DMI is with your wife and mistress fighting." Frank laughed. "Your anointing will certainly come in handy right about now."

Chapter 62

Four months concocted more of the same. Dave was a semi-permanent resident at the Westin, costing him a boatload of money. His excuse for extending the stay there was that he didn't have time to find more economical accommodations. Truthfully, he was wishing that Madeline would change her mind and let him come home. Dave was willing to patiently wait as long as it took, but the light of hope was dimming in the marriage. He could hear it in Madeline's voice when they spoke.

Sherry reported to the human resources director on the third floor. Dave thought moving her was the best compromise. He hadn't fired her, because she didn't seem strong enough to handle it. But Sherry couldn't stay near his office if there was any shot at Madeline's heart softening. Out of sight three floors away seemed reasonable to him, especially on mornings like this when his wife was coming into the office. Dave didn't know why she was coming in and braced for the worst, like he had for her past three visits.

"Great, you're here," she said, tossing her autumn jacket onto the back of a chair. "I plan to make this quick," she told him. "I have not changed my mind. I don't want the children at your cramped place. You'll have to keep taking them to the theater, park, or somewhere." His suite wasn't their estate, but he didn't consider 3,000 square feet cramped. He had several bedrooms, three and a half baths, a study, gourmet kitchen, living room, den, family room, and plenty of space for the kids to play, but Dave opted not to correct her. Letting her vent had become the routine. "They're familiar with their home, and I didn't sacrifice my career to stay at home with them just so you could cart them around like little gypsies."

"Okay, then you're saying that you prefer for me to visit the kids at the house?"

"No, I'm not."

"Then what are you saying?" he asked.

"I'm not ready to make any kind of decision. After all, we're talking about the welfare of our children. They come first here."

"I agree, no argument here. As long as I get to see the kids, where we meet is not a problem for me."

"Right now they're confused and hurt. We have to give them a chance to adjust to what's going on."

"But I want to see my kids, Madeline. That's a reasonable request."

"I'm not trying to keep you from your children," she yelled. "But if you think they're going to be around that woman, you got another think coming," she said, locking her hand against her hip.

Frank walked in, closing the door behind him. "Hey, you guys, I can hear you in the hallway. Hello, Madeline." She gave a half-hearted response. "What's going on in here?"

"Ask your brother," Madeline barked.

"I could say this is none of my business, but that's a lie. Look here, both of you are family. You have to pull this nonsense together. You have a team of employees watching every move, and the two of you are in here arguing like high school students. Get a grip, for goodness' sake," he said, leaning on the table.

"We wouldn't have to argue if your brother would do the right thing."

"And what is that?" Frank asked.

"Kicking Sherry's behind out of here. We can't begin to talk about the future or the past until she's out of my company."

"I'm jumping in the middle, and I don't know all the details, but that sounds reasonable to me, Dave. Is there something I'm missing? Because this right here has to stop," Frank said, waving both index fingers at Dave and Madeline.

"Humph," Madeline responded.

"I kept her on board because, legally, you don't want to fire a pregnant woman."

"Why not? And don't get me some lame excuse that you're afraid she'll sue." Madeline clapped her hands together and in a single motion latched them to her hips. "Because I say let her sue. We'll treat her the same way we have the other dogs who are out for our money."

"Do you think she'll go that far?" Frank asked.

"She's never mentioned suing, but why take the chance?" Dave said.

"Why can't you ask her? Obviously you've had pillow talk at least once, maybe more," Madeline said.

Dave sighed.

"Come on, Madeline, this isn't helping us get to a solution. Is it me?" Frank asked drilling his index finger into his chest. "Am I the only one who sees this company going into the dumps because the two of you are constantly fighting?"

"Tell that to him," Madeline said, flicking her hand toward Dave. "He has to get his crap fixed;

otherwise, I'm not listening. You might as well let us fight to the finish."

"I'm not butting out," Frank said, raising his voice to match Madeline's but not pushing too hard. She was mad, and getting loud, but he knew it was from hurt. "I was with the two of you when we cut the red ribbon at DMI. I didn't hesitate to invest every dollar Pops left me to help you get DMI going, and you both know it's the truth. The way I see it, you owe me five minutes to hear what I have to say."

Madeline moaned but didn't refute him.

"You're right, Frank, have your say," Dave said.

"Okay, then here it is. If you let this thing with Sherry end up separating you, then DMI is as good as dead. The reputation of this company is built partially on your image, Dave. The public sees you as a strong, honorable man of integrity."

"Humph," Madeline interjected again, twiddling her fingers.

"Unless you survive this, you'll be just another man out there with flaws too big to be overlooked. You have to hear me. Both of you, please, work this out and let's get back to business. That's it," he said, flailing his hands in the air, "my whole two-minute spiel."

"No offense, Frank. You mean well, but there's only one question I need answered. Dave, are you willing to fire that woman, Sherry Henderson, right now?"

"I'll work it out."

Madeline stepped up to Dave, stood within six inches of him, and said, "Are you going to fire her right now?"

"I will handle it."

Madeline snatched her jacket from the chair. "Well then, Frank, there you go. Your brother can't get any plainer than that. The answer is *no*. He's not going to fire her. So, let me cut this party short. Dave, don't fire her. It's fine, but I want a divorce."

"Madeline, don't do this," Dave pleaded, reaching out to her.

"Ah, sis, come on, Madeline," Frank said.

"Don't bother trying to change my mind. I'm finally seeing you for who you are, Mr. Dave Mitchell. You basically want to have your cake and eat it too—not going to happen. I've put up with you placing God first. I can accept that. I'm no dummy. I can't compete with Him. I even sat quietly and let you put DMI in front of me, but there's no way on earth I'm playing runner-up to another woman."

"Geez, I'll fire her and deal with the ramifications afterward."

"I personally don't care what you do. It's too late, Dave, much too little, way too late," she said, reaching the door. "Once upon a time you were the man, seriously, the one who had it all. Now, you're just plain," Madeline said and left.

Frank stood baffled. Should he go after her or stay and press Dave to fire Sherry? They could give Sherry a hefty severance package to keep her mouth shut. Frank chose to go after his sister-in-law. When he got into the hallway, Sherry and Madeline were both standing near the elevators. He rushed over. "Ladies, we're okay?"

Madeline burst into laughter. "Nothing will ever be okay again, thanks to missy." Frank eased between them. "Don't worry, Frank. I'm not wasting my breath with this woman. She isn't in my league. She is my employee, and I don't fraternize with the help." The elevator door opened. Madeline got on and the door closed.

Sherry looked terrified to Frank. Knowing Madeline as well as he did, she'd better be.

Chapter 63

Dave came into the hallway and saw Sherry. "What are you doing up here?" he asked, realizing Madeline had just left. If she'd seen Sherry there would have been fireworks. He was careful to keep distance between the two women. As much as he regretted firing Sherry, he had no choice. "Can you step into my office please, we have to talk," he told her.

Sherry took a few steps and winced. "Dave, I'm in pain. I think it's the baby," she cried out.

Dave didn't panic. "Do you want to sit down?" he asked, ushering her to a seat nearby.

"Yes," she moaned, doubling over and clutching her side.

Dave reached for her, fearing she was going to fall. "Sherry, here, sit," he said, pulling the chair to her.

"I need to get to the hospital. Can you take me?" she asked.

He didn't hesitate. "Let's go." Dave didn't think about Madeline or Sherry. The baby's health was foremost. The adults could squabble some other time.

Dave rushed her to the nearest emergency room. Sherry was immediately wheeled to an examination room. "Dave, can you come in with me?" She must have interpreted the *no* coming forth and pressed further. "Please, I'm scared and don't want to do this alone," she said, caressing her stomach. He followed the wheelchair. In the room, Dave stood off to the side. He wanted to support the baby without showing false indicators to its mother. A nurse came in to take Sherry's blood pressure and temperature.

The doctor came in, reviewing Sherry's chart. "Mrs. Henderson, I see that you're about twenty-two weeks pregnant," he said, flipping several papers. "And what brings you in today?"

"I'm feeling sharp pains down here," she said, rubbing along the top edge of her skirt.

"Any spotting?"

"No," she said, sounding alarmed.

The doctor jotted notes. "Have you been pregnant before?"

Sherry stared straight at Dave. "No, this is our first baby together."

"I see that your blood pressure is elevated to 150 over 97, much higher than I'd like to see at this stage in your pregnancy. Are you under any stress?"

Dave and Sherry's glances met, both screaming yes. But she answered, "No more than usual." There was an element of honesty in her response, but the full truth was yes. She was at odds with Madeline and from every indication would continue to be for years to come, even after the baby was born. Sherry's stress level at 150 over 97 was only the beginning. She was confident her stress meter would eventually explode, taking her health with it.

"If you can't pinpoint any contributing factors to the elevated blood pressure, then let me order a few tests so we can see what's going on with you," the doctor said, stuffing a pen into the pocket of his white lab coat. "The nurse will be in to draw blood. Think you can give me a urine sample, too?"

"I think so."

"Good." It almost seemed like the doctor was flirting with Sherry. Dave wasn't certain. Oddly he felt jealousy stirring, while at the same time relieved not to be asked any questions. He wanted to be supportive but invisible. The doctor hadn't acknowledged his presence. Apparently receding into the corner and staying in the background was working.

"You want me to step out while they do the tests?" Dave asked.

"Stay, please. I feel so much better with you here." She seemed desperate, causing him to worry. Dave didn't talk to her when they were alone. He was concerned that each glance her way, and the slightest word, would toss a log onto her budding crush. Dave couldn't get caught up again.

The nurse came in to complete the tests. Sherry went to the bathroom for the urine test and was wheeled back in afterward. Dave stayed and waited. Several times, he'd wondered about Madeline. She wasn't his first thought. The baby was, but she was close behind.

When the doctor returned he said, "Well, Mrs. Henderson, I have good news and even better news for you," he said, touching Sherry's hand. "We didn't see any problems from the lab work."

"Ah, that's great," Sherry said, beaming.

"Yes, that's the good news. The even better news is that you'll have a long vacation. I'm recommending that you be put on bed rest for the duration of the pregnancy. I can give you a note for your job or you can discuss this with your own doctor and get a note."

"I'll take your note, and follow up with my doctor, too."

Dave was her boss, and he didn't need the note. He'd see to her having the time off without objection.

"Other than your blood pressure, everything else looks perfect from what I can see. You'll definitely want to follow up with your doctor this week. My suggestion is to stay away from stressful situations. Take care of yourself and that will be the best gift you can give to your baby. Good luck," the doctor told her.

"Mr. Henderson, you'll need to take care of this young lady," the doctor said on the way out. Dave didn't bother acknowledging the mistake with his name, didn't matter.

Dave replayed the doctor's suggestion. As long as Madeline was around, there was no way Sherry could be stress-free. Unexpectedly, Dave felt a connection with the baby more than he'd realized. It was as pure as the one he'd felt for his other kids when they were born. Standing in the corner, Dave vowed that no matter what happened with him, Sherry, and Madeline, he'd always provide for his baby and ensure that the child had the best shot at life. Madeline wasn't going to like his next move, but he'd have to provide for the mother, too. If that meant taking care of Sherry until the baby was born, then so be it.

"Let's go get your things from the apartment," he told her.

"Why, where am I going?"

"You're coming to the Westin with me."

"I am?" she said, wide-eyed and grinning.

"I'll get a suite for you until the baby is born."

"You don't have to do this."

"I know. I want to. You can't be alone. So, I figure if you're going to be on bed rest, I'd prefer for you to be in a place with amenities and services that I can't personally provide. Don't you worry about a thing. I'll handle the details. You concentrate on delivering a healthy, happy baby. Let's go," he said, pushing the wheelchair out of the confines of the room and into the open, visible to everyone.

Chapter 64

Dave was forcing her hand. Madeline was a little surprised that he hadn't taken care of the problem as soon as she made him move out four months ago. It wouldn't have taken her nearly as long. Madeline entered her attorney's office, prepared to wage war. Dave would one day regret not meeting her simple demands, especially after paying with his money and credibility.

"Madeline," her attorney said once the receptionist had escorted her into a conference room. "To what do I owe the pleasure?"

"I'm here to file for divorce," she said, suppressing any visible sign of how she actually felt. This was business and she'd act accordingly.

"I didn't expect you to say divorce."

"Me either, but that's why I'm here."

"I'm sorry to hear it, but I'm willing to help you in whatever way I can."

Madeline set her Chanel purse on the table. "I want my share and then some," she said.

Madeline was determined to leave Dave the least amount of money she could. He could run off with his new family, but they weren't going to live well, not on money that she had helped earn. Let Sherry grovel in the trenches and work her way up like Madeline had. Nobody had given her a million dollars for being young and loose.

"Where do you want to start?" the attorney asked, adjusting the frames of his eyeglasses. "What do you want to walk away with?"

"Majority ownership in DMI, full custody of the children, possession of the estate, and seventy-five percent of our liquid assets and other properties," she said straight out. Madeline wanted Dave where he was in the beginning, before her hard work, loyalty, and sacrifice helped him become a millionaire. She figured he had God and his anointing. She'd settle for the cash.

Chapter 65

Dave laced his shoes. He heard the phone and went to answer, straightening his tie along the way. The size of his suite automatically came with a butler but he'd declined the service. Except for the few times Madeline had let the kids come over, he was there alone and quite capable of taking care of his needs. Often he'd considered moving to a smaller place, but resorted to the notion that Madeline was going to let the kids come over and they'd need the room. He remained positive answering the phone, assuming it to be someone from housekeeping.

"Excuse me, Mr. Mitchell," the caller said.

"There's a gentleman in the lobby to see you."

"Me?" Dave responded.

Other than Frank, no one knew he was there, or so he assumed. "What's his name?"

"He won't say. Would you like for me to ask him to leave?"

"No, that's no problem. I'll be right down."

"Thank you, sir. He'll wait for you at the concierge desk. Please let me know if I can be of further assistance to you."

Dave took the private elevator to the lobby. Speculations jockeyed. *Definitely wasn't Frank. He'd have given his name.* The only other person it could possibly be was Edward. Maybe Sherry told him she was staying at the Westin. Maybe he knew about Dave and the baby. A pack of maybes had his head spinning. If it was Edward, he'd face the fire. Dave saw the man standing at the concierge and approached him.

"I'm Dave Mitchell. Are you looking for me?"

"Yes," the gentleman said, handing Dave a folded pack of papers. "You've been served." The gentleman left.

Dave opened the papers and read. "Petition for Dissolution of Marriage. Madeline Mitchell vs. Dave Mitchell." He stood, paralyzed. He'd prepared for a visit from Edward. He would have accepted that feud over a divorce request. He was crushed taking the elevator upstairs. Besides the sting of divorce, the terms were outrageous. He sat down and contemplated, finally deciding to call Madeline.

When she answered, he hesitated before saying, "Madeline, I got the divorce papers. We have to talk. What if I stop by the house on my way into the office?"

"I don't want you coming here and disrupting the children. They're not doing very well with our separation as it is," she said flat out with no extra discussion. "I'll meet you at the office."

"No good there. I don't want the staff to see any more than they have already," he told her.

"Fine, I'll come to your hotel around nine-thirty, after the boys are off to school."

Chapter 66

Madeline didn't want to go see Dave. He wasn't going to change her mind. She'd grown weary from fighting. She preferred to let the attorneys fight the rest of the way.

It was after nine. Madeline got her coat and gulped a last swallow of coffee. She called Dave to let him know she was running late.

"Good morning, how may I help?" the hotel attendant said.

"Could you please connect me with the suite of Dave Mitchell," she said, balancing the phone between her earlobe and shoulder while stepping into her pumps. Madeline fumbled with the other shoe, waiting for Dave to answer.

"Hello," came across the line.

Madeline froze. "Who is this?"

"Sherry, why who is this?"

"Sherry, what the heck are you doing answering Dave's phone in his hotel room?" She dropped the shoe onto the floor as her hand shook.

"This isn't Dave's room. This is my suite."

"Oh really, and you expect me to believe that? Since when did your DMI check get big enough to cover a suite at the Westin?" Madeline wanted to implode but reined in her total rage. She wasn't going to let Sherry knowingly have the upper hand. "You tell Dave that I'm on my way to the hotel, and I better not see you there."

"Whatever, Madeline," she said and hung up.

It was confirmed. Dave had officially lost his mind. Good for him that Sherry hadn't answered before now, or their children would have never gone to that hotel. Madeline had to cool down or she'd surely blow a fuse. She grabbed her keys and ran to the garage. He hadn't heard the last from her.

She cut the thirty-minute drive to just over twenty. Thank goodness Detroit highways were made to handle seventy-five and eighty mile-an-hour drivers with ease. Slower drivers were in danger with her on the road this morning. She wheeled into the valet and handed over her keys, giving them Dave's name and room number for the charge. Madeline walked hurriedly to the desk.

"I'm here to see Dave Mitchell. He's in the penthouse suite."

"Yes, of course, and you are?"

"Mrs. Dave Mitchell."

"Yes, I see that he has given approval to let you up. Go through the double doors, near the end of the hallway, to the private bank of elevators. There will be a gentleman there to assist you."

Madeline thanked him and got on her way. Upstairs, she rang the bell, ready to have it out with Mr. Dave. He'd embarrassed her for the last time.

"Come in," Dave said, opening the door and taking a step to the side.

Madeline bolted in. "What are you doing, Dave? You're an old man who knows better. Tell me, what are you doing here?"

"Don't you remember? You kicked me out. That's why I'm here."

"Don't get coy with me," she said, flinging her purse onto the living room sofa after entering the open area. "You have the nerve to move Sherry in here with you." Dave pursed his lips. "So, it's true? She's here."

"She's not in my suite, but Sherry is at the hotel."

"When did she start getting paid enough to stay here?" Dave pursed his lips again. "Don't bother answering, I get the picture." Madeline folded her arms. "And when were you planning on telling me? Oh, that's right, silly me. I'm the wife, the last to know."

"It's not what you think. The doctor put her on bed rest for the remaining of the pregnancy. I couldn't leave her in the apartment alone."

"You could have and you should have."

"Regardless of how this happened, I'm responsible for this baby. I have to do the right thing."

"The right thing was keeping your behind at home and out of her bed. The right thing would have been to fire her when I asked you to. The right thing would have been to win me and the children back. So, don't talk about doing the right thing because you have not done right by me."

"I'm sorry you feel this way."

"What did you think? You thought I'd accept you and Sherry living together because her adulterous pregnancy is in trouble? Humph, you have the wrong person if that's what you thought." She grunted again.

"We're not living together, Madeline."

The phone rang.

"Might as well be. You're a few doors or floors apart. Can't get much closer without people talking."

Dave let Madeline finish and then excused himself to get the phone. Madeline heard voices but no one entered the room. She went to the hallway where Dave had gone to get the phone and overheard him talking.

"Don't worry. You're not in this alone. I'm here. Don't stress yourself or the baby. I'm calling the ambulance and then I'll come right down."

Madeline stepped away so Dave didn't know she'd heard. When he returned, she acted unaware, although her soul was bleeding. Hearing him comfort Sherry was a knife slicing at her core, but pride held her together in his presence.

"I'm sorry, but we have to talk later. I can meet wherever you want, but I have an emergency," he said, walking fast and talking.

She could have delayed him, asked questions, or made him confirm what she already knew. She chose not to do anything. Her pain was too deep to mask, seeing Dave show devotion to another woman and their child.

"Madeline," Dave stopped and said, "I'm sorry."

After he left, she stood in the hallway, alone and empty. She lingered in the suite long after Dave was gone, reflecting. She was sorry too, sensing in her spirit that the chapter on their marriage had closed at the precise moment when Dave turned the handle and walked into his life with Sherry and their baby. Her heart and soul wept in unison over the loss.

Chapter 67

Dave trailed the ambulance in his car, arriving fifteen minutes after Sherry had gotten to the hospital. He rushed to the emergency room admission desk. "I'm looking for Sherry Henderson."

The nurse checked the monitor. "Are you a family member?"

"Yes, I guess I am," he said, convincing enough for the nurse to direct him to exam room number four. He thanked her and hurried to find the room down the hall. "Sherry," he called out, entering the room and seeing her lying on a gurney. She had a series of cables linked to her and several monitors. Her moans carried into the hallway.

"Dave, it hurts so badly," she said, extremely emotional. She reached for him as he entered. He didn't want to get in a compromising situation again, but the main purpose for being in the hospital was to provide the support she wanted.

He came close to rub her forehead. His touch seemed to quiet her.

The doctor entered but his body language didn't sit well with Dave.

"Miss Henderson, are you still in pain?"

"Yes," she said, trying to talk while crying.

"I'm going to take a look," the doctor said, grabbing a pair of gloves.

"I'll leave," Dave told Sherry.

"Don't go," she told him as the doctor asked Sherry to place her legs in the stirrups. Dave stayed, careful not to get in the way. Silently he prayed to God that the baby and Sherry would be healthy and well.

A nurse entered and closed the door behind her. Dave didn't watch the actual exam, but he couldn't elude Sherry's moaning.

Dave didn't need a medical degree to read the look of concern on the doctor's face as he completed the exam.

"Can you get the neonatal unit down here?"

"What's going on?" Sherry cried out.

"Your cervix is dilating."

"But it's too soon," she said frantically.

"I'll attempt to slow the contractions down, but my concern is that the baby appears to be in distress."

"Is my baby going to be all right?" she pleaded.

"We'll do everything we can."

"Oh," she wailed, pressing into her belly.

Several other medical people squeezed into the room. Dave was buried in the back. They talked among themselves, pressing buttons, reading charts, and talking with Sherry.

"Sherry, we don't have a choice. You're going to have to deliver the baby today," the doctor told her.

"I can't. It's way too soon. My baby won't survive if it's born this early. I can't do it."

"You have no choice. The baby's heart rate is dropping and has to be delivered now."

A nurse popped her head in and said, "We're going into operating room nine. They're prepping for the cesarean." A flurry of movement kicked off. They wheeled Sherry out of the room in a swoop.

Dave twirled his wedding ring without noticing. The nurse saw him and said, "Mr. Henderson, there's a waiting area on the second floor near the operating rooms. You can wait there. The doctor will come out and give you an update on her condition as soon as he can. Why don't you go on up," she said, winding the cord attached to the fetal monitor. "You'll be more comfortable up there."

Maybe, but he knew of a place where he was guaranteed to find comfort. "Where's the chapel?" The nurse told him, and Dave ran to the Lord. It was the only help he knew that could move mountains and calm the troubled heart of a baby. There was no machine, surgery, or physician on earth more equipped to perform a miracle than His God. Dave called out to his Father, believing for more than he deserved.

Dave entered the chapel, approached the makeshift altar, and fell to his knees. "Father, it's me, your sinful son, the one who has failed you time and time again. The one who is not worthy to call you Father, but by your grace I call you Daddy. I call you the great I am. I call you the King of Kings and the Lord of Lords. I call you Jehovah Rapha, my baby's healer. I ask for your mighty touch on the tiny body of my newborn child. Let the baby live so that it can grow up knowing you as his Savior and giving glory to your name. I ask for your mercy, Lord. Let my child live," Dave pleaded, burying his face into his hands and howling. He lay stretched out on the floor, not caring if anyone came into the room and found him wailing at the altar. He had nowhere else to go but to God. "Father, let your will be done." After a short while, Dave rose to his feet, relieved. It was finished for him. He made his appeal going as far as he could. The next move was on God.

He returned to the waiting room renewed. The doctor must have been searching for him, because he came over immediately. "Mr. Henderson."

"It's actually Mitchell, Dave Mitchell," he interjected, no longer bound by speculations.

"I'm so sorry. Mr. Mitchell, Sherry delivered the baby. It was a boy, but we couldn't save him. He was stillborn."

Dave digested the unsettling news. "Okay, thanks," he replied, completely composed.

"She's been calling for you. If you'd like to see her, go to the end of the hallway, make a left, and ask someone at the nurse's station to direct you to her recovery room. She will be moved to a room upstairs shortly."

Dave extended his hand. "Thank you, Doctor, for what you did. It's appreciated."

"Well, sir, under the circumstances, I wish there was more that I could have done. Unfortunately this was out of our control."

But it wasn't out of God's, Dave affirmed. He found his way to the nurse's station. Before getting there, he leaned against the wall and wept openly. He dried his eyes and reclaimed composure. God had spoken. Those were the only tears he'd shed.

He went to Sherry. She wasn't as composed. Devastated, she rambled on, calming minimally when he entered her room.

"I lost our baby, Dave," she said hysterically. "I lost our baby."

They tried calming her unsuccessfully. She held tight to her grief. The medical team decided to sedate her, giving Sherry a chance to rest and regain her strength.

She dozed off to sleep, and Dave went to a pay phone in the lobby. He called Frank.

"I'm at the hospital with Sherry."

"Is she having the baby?"

"Actually, she already had it, and the baby died."

"Oh, man, I'm sorry. I don't know what to say." He paused. "Is there anything I can do?"

"If you could please sit in on a meeting for me this afternoon, it would free me up to stay here the rest of the afternoon with Sherry. She's not doing well."

"I can only imagine."

"Let me run. Sherry might wake up and I don't want her to feel alone."

"Hey, Dave, I hate to say this, but losing the baby might be a blessing in disguise."

"How?"

"At least this way you and Madeline won't have Sherry's baby standing between you. If you want your marriage, this might be the break you need."

Dave didn't respond. He didn't see the death of his son as a blessing or a punishment. It was God's will and no further explanation was required.

Chapter 68

Madeline had slowly made her way home, oblivious to the surroundings. In the house, she meandered aimlessly, without motivation.

Tamara was getting ready for school. "Mommy, what am I going to wear?" she asked, finding Madeline in the master bedroom.

"Darling, you can wear whatever you want today."

"But I can't choose. I need your help."

Madeline couldn't help Tamara, because she couldn't help herself. "Please, Tamara," she said, about to yell at her daughter but caught it in time to pipe down her tone. She told her to ask Ms. Jenkins for help.

"Okay," the little girl said, stomping from the room. Madeline let her go, unable to comfort her. She stretched out across the bed, pulling the pillow over her head in hopes that sleep would whisk in and rescue her.

"Mom, Mom," she heard, awakening to see Sam standing near the bed.

She jumped up. "What's wrong? What are you doing home so early from school? Did something happen to you?" she asked hastily, grabbing his arms and checking him over.

"Mom, it's after four o'clock. We've been home over an hour. I've already done my math and vocabulary and most of my science, but I need help with the last two questions," he said calmly.

Madeline searched frantically for a clock to confirm the time. She couldn't have slept the afternoon away. Locating the clock on her nightstand, it said she definitely had. Sam continued talking but she didn't hear anymore.

Dinner, homework, and the typical chaos came and went, too, with Madeline remaining out of sorts well into the evening. "It's time to get ready for bed," she told her children.

"Not for us, it's only eight o'clock, and we get to stay up until nine," Sam reminded her.

"Tonight everybody is going to bed at eight." The faster they got to bed, the sooner she could get back to sleep. It was the only place she seemed to steal away from Dave and the divorce. She hurried the children along, despite protest from the older boys. "Let's go," she said, tucking each child into his or her bed and kissing them good night.

Finally, they were down and she'd be next. She stood outside Sam and Andre's room, realizing the nights when their father would poke his head in to see them were no more. Her heart shattered.

She humbly returned to her bed, with images of Dave and Sherry bombarding her. She couldn't hide. There was nowhere to run from the surreal pain of Sherry's pregnancy and Dave's concern for his other family. Her marriage was over. Madeline tried shoving the pain away, but it wasn't budging. She began sobbing uncontrollably, drawing her knees into the fetal position.

Tears kept gushing. In the midst of her cry, it sounded like a thud came from outside the door, causing her to sit up. She quietly waited to see if the noise repeated. It didn't but she went to the door anyway, after being overcome with curiosity.

Don was sitting by her door, clutching his blanket and bawling.

She instinctively set aside her needs and comforted her son. "What's wrong, Don?" she asked, falling to the floor and drawing him close, letting his head rest against her chest.

"I had a bad dream, Mommy."

"Oh, I'm sorry. Why didn't you come in?" He seemed afraid. "Don, Mommy is here now. You're safe," she said, hugging him tighter.

He seemed to relax. "I wanted to come in your room, but I heard you crying, Mommy, and it made me sad," he said, ready to cry again.

She lightly pressed her hand against his head, keeping him close until his fear was gone. She waited patiently until he seemed ready to go back to his room. She tucked him in once more. This time he was asleep before she reached the threshold. Madeline went to her room. She was more cautious this time, closing the door behind her. Madeline turned up the TV volume in her room so she could cry without disturbing or frightening the children. She had to suffer. It was inevitable, but she'd see to it that her children didn't.

Chapter 69

Sherry's eyelids slowly opened. For a few seconds she felt anxious and unable to figure out where she was. Desperately searching the room for any sign of familiarity, she caught a glimpse of Dave slumped over in a corner chair. She breathed easier and called out to him as the hospital room came into focus. He must not have heard her. "Dave," she softly called again.

"Yes, what," he said, startled from his sleep.

"What time is it?" she asked.

Dave tried reading the face of his watch but it appeared difficult for him. It was somewhat dark in the room. So she reached for the light button and winced in pain. Not as much pain as she'd expressed at the hotel, but discomfort for sure.

Dave jumped up. "Hold on, let me get that for you." He came around to the side of the bed closest to her and reached for the controller tucked next to her leg. He found the light button and turned it on. Glaring at his watch he told her, "It's ten-fifteen."

She was surprised. The day had gone. "When did I fall asleep?"

"Right after the surgery."

As soon as he said "surgery," a tsunami of emotions and aches gushed in, overtaking her. Events of the day were fuzzy, as if it had been a dream. The only fact she could recall was having a baby. "I know it's late, but I want to see my baby." Dave gently laid the controller next to her leg. He stared at her without speaking, displaying a funny expression. He was taking too long for her. Sherry wanted her baby. "Dave," she said more forcefully, "I'd like to see my baby. Can you get the nurse for me please?"

"Sherry, the boy died."

"What, no, I want my baby," she said, becoming agitated and confused. "Get the nurse," she said, fumbling with the buttons on her remote, pushing practically every one, determined to get help. She must have hit the right one because a nurse entered the room.

"Can I help you?"

"Yes, I want to see my baby," she shouted.

Dave cut in and told the nurse, "She's very upset. Is it possible to get something to help her relax?"

The nurse peered at Sherry's chart and responded, "I'll check with her doctor. Shouldn't be a problem though."

Sherry wailed, unable to control herself. She wanted to die too if her baby was dead. Dave attempted to calm her down but nothing worked. "It was a boy?" She asked through her moans.

"Yes," he said reluctantly.

"Our son is dead," she screamed. "Why aren't you upset, Dave? You're the father. Don't you care about our son?"

"I do, but he's gone. No amount of anger or caring is going to bring him back."

"I don't know how you can talk so nonchalantly about him."

He stepped away from the bed. "I prayed and prayed for the baby to live. Once I realized the baby had died, I accepted the fact that God had spoken. His will was done. I could question why, but what good would it do?"

"At least I would feel like the baby mattered to you," she said, unsuccessfully reaching for a tissue.

Dave hurried over to get it for her. "I'm not going to dwell on the past. It's out of our control. I prefer looking to the future, where I can make a difference." He handed her a tissue. "I suggest you do the same."

Sherry wasn't as willing to accept their baby's fate and definitely wasn't as satisfied with God's decision as Dave was. "I can't forget about my baby as easily as you've been able to do. I need time to accept the loss of my first child."

"I understand. Don't worry about anything. I'll make arrangements with the funeral home."

Arrangements hadn't dawned on her until he said it. The revelation spurred Sherry to ache both emotionally and physically. She didn't want any part of a funeral. Yet, Sherry couldn't bear to miss the only opportunity she'd ever get to care for her child's needs.

"I want to take care of the arrangements for our baby. Please, don't do anything until I'm out of the hospital," she pleaded, wiping her eyes and nose.

He acknowledged her request, offering a slight sense of relief as she laid her head on the pillow and closed her eyes to rest. If she never woke up again, that would be perfect.

Chapter 70

Chill was in the air. Summer had passed and autumn was on the way out as Christmas approached. Madeline reflected on how much her life had changed. One short year ago felt more like a lifetime. She vividly recalled making the tough decision of choosing Dave, DMI, or the children, with room for only two. Back then, she chose Dave and the children without hesitation, believing that her only challenge was figuring out how to be superwoman without becoming overwhelmed.

Madeline strolled down the long hallway, peering at one family photo after the next. She stopped at the most recent addition: the one with Dave, her, and the three children taken before Andre arrived. She stood staring and reminiscing. Her pride soared staring at the faces of Don smiling, Tamara beaming, and Sam being a little man. Sadness touched her lightly. They weren't the family in the photo anymore.

Her world had changed to an unrecognizable state. She brushed her hand along the rim of the picture frame, similar to the way a person patted a casket just before walking away from a gravesite.

She moved into the foyer. Her mind was set. Confusion had waged a solid war, tossing her back and forth, in and out of marriage for months. Madeline had worn down just about the time when her decision was becoming evident. She was no longer conflicted about the divorce, having spent many days and nights pondering and sobbing. Sherry and Dave had driven her to the brink of insanity. It would have been simple to blame the divorce dissolution on the baby. She didn't, realizing that Sherry's baby hadn't been the sole factor preventing her from reconciling with Dave. If it was, they'd have gotten back together after the baby died last month. They hadn't and she was experiencing a fair amount of peace being away from Dave and the fallout.

Thinking about the decision now, she would have never guessed that DMI and the children would be her life, void of Dave.

She had to move forward expeditiously with the divorce and get on about the business of living. She'd wait and call Dave in the morning to tell him about her decision.

Chapter 71

Dave eagerly agreed to meet Madeline when she'd called earlier. She'd opted to meet at DMI, mid-afternoon, and he was most accommodating. He'd checked the clock several times between one and two o'clock, expecting to see Madeline coming through the doorway. He began to doubt that she was coming. Just as he was about to give up hope on her, she rapped on the door. It was already open. He leapt to his feet and beckoned for her to come in. She did.

"I was beginning to think you'd changed your mind," he said. "Can I get you anything?" Dave asked, partially sitting on a corner of his desk.

"No, nothing, thanks. I couldn't help but notice that you have a new secretary out front. What happened to Sherry? Did you finally fire her?"

He hesitated, not wanting to derail their positive interaction. He carefully chose his words. "No, I didn't."

"Then where is she? Because I know you know."

"Before she had the baby . . ." he said, stumbling a little over his words. "She was moved to human resources quite awhile ago." Dave could see a slight change in Madeline's disposition, precisely what he didn't want to happen. They were at least talking and that was more than he'd realized in weeks.

"I better cut this visit short, because honestly, I don't want to run into her today. I'm feeling too good for drama."

"You don't have to worry about her interrupting." Madeline looked perplexed and he wanted to ease her concern. Whatever he could do to keep her in his office and talking, he would do. "She's in a short-term care facility."

"For what?" Madeline asked. He couldn't discern if she was asking out of a modest level of concern or pure curiosity. Either way, he was going to tell her.

"After the baby died, she had a psychological break."

"You mean she's in a psychiatric facility?" Dave nodded in affirmation. "Hmm, that's too bad." Dave was touched getting a glimpse of the old Madeline, the loving and caring woman he'd chosen to spend his life with. "As a mother, I feel for her. As a wife, all I can say is that she made her bed and now she's lying in it." Dave kept quiet. "Her fiancé is probably just as hurt as I was about the baby."

"I don't know. She hasn't mentioned him to me, not that there would be any reason to. I'm not involved in their relationship."

"You don't mean that, do you?" Madeline asked.

"Yes, I do. My only involvement with Sherry is covering her expenses until she's recovered and stable."

"You're obviously spending time with her, too."

"I visit her if that's what you mean. I figure it's the least I can do since I did contribute to her situation. I'm not making excuses, but she comes from a very small family and is practically alone. My visits seem to be helping. So, I go."

Madeline waved off the comment. "Whatever. I didn't come here to talk about Miss Sherry Henderson. I came here to talk about us."

Dave's hope sparked. He took random glances at her, remembering what an attractive woman she was. Especially today, the suit fit her body like a glove and her hair was curled, hanging down onto her shoulders. She was quite pleasing in his eyes. "I don't know if this is the right time or place, but I want you to know that I miss you. I would love for us to give the marriage another shot. What do you think?" he asked.

Madeline sat on one of the chairs closest to his desk. "Dave, I miss you too." The words were a treat for him coming from her. He was hopeful. "But too much has happened. We can't turn back the hands of time. Mistakes have been made, hearts broken, and this is where we are, but I'm not mad right now. I'm just ready to move on," she said, pausing, and then going on to say, "without you."

"That's not what I was hoping to hear from you." He truly believed they needed more time to let the troubles dissipate before taking such a monumental step toward severing the marriage. That's what he believed but certainly wasn't going to push. "But if there's nothing else I can say or do—"

"There isn't," she said, interrupting and grinning. "Let it go, I have."

Maybe she is right, Dave pondered. "Then I will make the settlement as painless as possible for you." Dave placed both feet on the floor as he leaned against the desk's edge. "I'll let you have whatever you want; but Madeline, you know I can't give you DMI." Without his family, the company was all he had left. Managing DMI was his calling, and he'd continue leading the charge through the many battles left to fight. "But I've been meaning to create a board of directors since we've grown to a significant size. How about a seat on the DMI board?"

"Sounds interesting," she said, appearing intrigued, and then she took on a serious tone. "And I want my job back."

"Done, it's yours," he said.

"Yeah, right, for how long? Until a new Mrs. Mitchell wants you to kick me out?" she said, smirking.

"Won't ever happen."

"Which part, your getting remarried or me getting kicked out?"

Dave didn't dare answer her no-win question. Instead, he did what his heart said. "I will put it in writing. You will have an executive-level role here as long as you want."

She was instantly chipper, a sight that pleased him. "Really, you mean I don't have to fight you on it?"

"Not at all, you helped build this company. It's partially yours anyway. The least I can do is to make your permanent involvement official. You can be here until death do you part. Neither I nor anyone after me can make you leave. God has a plan for DMI, and you're a part of it."

"I'm not trying to be funny or insulting, but with the way your life is playing out, are you still convinced about God's so-called anointed plan? It doesn't seem to working too well for you."

He scratched his chin and said, "It's the only fact that I am certain about. As unfair or crazy as this may sound to you, God's plan didn't change because I made a mistake. He knew before I was born what I'd be doing, what I'd do well, and where I'd fall short." Madeline didn't seem interested but he continued anyway. "He'd already factored in my sinful, weak nature."

"Well, then you have to explain to me why the anointed plan for you has caused so much hurt for everyone else?"

Dave didn't return the answer he could have given, convinced nothing would pacify her thirst for restoration and healing. Telling her that it was him, and not the Lord's plan that failed her, wasn't going to alleviate the anguish. Instead he said, "Madeline, I apologize again for hurting you and betraying your trust. We've had many great years together. I don't know what the future holds, but I can honestly say these have been the best years of my life." He took several steps toward her with his arms extended.

At first Madeline didn't move. Then she took several steps toward him too and leaned into his embrace, with no other words spoken between them. Dave felt her heart beating in rhythm with his. He only had admiration for Madeline and harbored no sorrow about loving and partnering with her for so many years. He held her tighter, as tightly as she'd let him. Minutes seemed like hours. He accepted that it would be the last time he'd be able to hold her as his wife.

Their moment of togetherness evaporated, and Madeline was leaving.

"Can you close the door behind you?" he asked her.

"Sure," she said on her way out of the office.

Madeline left Dave with his memories. He went to the windows and peered into the majestic sky. DMI's reputation was going to pay as a result, but those consequences weren't his primary concern as he stood there. Failing as a husband and father was where he felt the grief. His hands covered his face as he wept over the loss. "My God, deliver me. Let my life be pleasing before you," he said, continuing to stare into the heavens, the source from where his peace and restoration would have to come without Madeline by his side.

Reading Guide Questions

Makes You Go Hmmm!

Now that you have read *Anointed,* consider the following discussion questions.

1. Who's your favorite character and why?
2. Dave was very clear about his calling and never wavered about what took precedence in his life. Given that he loved Madeline, was marrying her the right decision?
3. Should Madeline have left DMI to become a stay-at-home mom? How did the change affect the bond with Dave?
4. Looking back at the relationship between Dave and Madeline, there were signs of problems brewing. In your opinion, what was the primary reason for the breakup between Dave and Madeline: infidelity, unwillingness to forgive, or was it the distance they'd both allowed to creep into the marriage?

5. Is Sherry a calculating "home wrecker" as Madeline sees her or is she a victim of circumstances and vulnerability?

6. How can Dave be a solid man of God and sin so easily? Does his mistake dilute his relationship with God?

7. Can a couple survive adultery? If not, why? If yes, how?

8. Did Madeline make the right decision in kicking Dave out and filing for divorce? What would have been the benefits or sacrifices associated with staying in the marriage?

9. Do you think it's a smart idea for Madeline to go back to DMI with Sherry there?

10. Frank adored his little brother and saw him as a godly man with the "golden Midas touch." He was very disappointed in Dave's fall from grace and began losing faith in the future. What's the danger in placing your hope and faith in a person as opposed to God?

11. We watched Sherry and Edward grow apart. Can the couple rekindle what they had?

12. How did you feel about the efforts Edward made in paying Sherry's bills—should or shouldn't have?

13. The Mitchell family drama is loosely based on King David, a mighty Biblical warrior who had God's favor and a distinctive purpose, but was also plagued with personal problems, family failures, and sinful choices. Because of his willingness to repent and to forgive, he was deemed a righteous man, able to forget the pain, anguish, and bitterness associated with mistakes of the past. Why is forgiveness so important to both the offender and the offended?

14. Forgiveness isn't easy but can be liberating, healthy, and powerful. Is it difficult to embrace a joyous future while holding on to wounds of the past? Is there anyone you need to forgive in order to embrace your future?

15. If *Anointed* was a movie and you were the casting director, who would play the role of Dave, Madeline, Sherry, and Frank?

Author's Note

Dear Readers:

Thank you for reading *Anointed*. I hope you found the story entertaining. Look for **Betrayed**, the next book in the Mitchell family drama series, followed by *Chosen, Destined,* and *Broken*.

I look forward to you joining my mailing list, dropping me a note, or posting a message on my web site. You can also friend me on Facebook at Patricia Haley-Glass or *like* my Author Patricia Haley fan page.

As always, thank you for the support. Keep reading, and be blessed.

www.patriciahaley.com
phg@patriciahaley.com

UC HIS GLORY BOOK CLUB!

www.uchisglorybookclub.net

UC His Glory Book Club is the spirit-inspired brainchild of Joylynn Jossel, Author and Acquisitions Editor of Urban Christian, and Kendra Norman-Bellamy, Author for Urban Christian. This is an online book club that hosts authors of Urban Christian. We welcome as members all men and women who have a passion for reading Christian-based fiction.

UC His Glory Book Club pledges our commitment to provide support, positive feedback, encouragement, and a forum whereby members can openly discuss and review the literary works of Urban Christian authors.

There is no membership fee associated with UC His Glory Book Club; however, we do ask that you support the authors through purchasing, encouraging, providing book reviews, and of course, your prayers. We also ask that you respect our beliefs and follow the guidelines of the book club. We hope to receive your valuable input, opinions, and reviews that build up, rather than tear down our authors.

What We Believe:

—We believe that Jesus is the Christ, Son of the Living God.

—We believe the Bible is the true, living Word of God.

—We believe all Urban Christian authors should use their God-given writing abilities to honor God and share the message of the written word God has given to each of them uniquely.

—We believe in supporting Urban Christian authors in their literary endeavors by reading, purchasing and sharing their titles with our online community.

—We believe that in everything we do in our literary arena should be done in a manner that will lead to God being glorified and honored.

—We look forward to the online fellowship with you.

Please visit us often at:

www.uchisglorybookclub.net.

Many Blessing to You!

Shelia E. Lipsey,

President, UC His Glory Book Club

ORDER FORM
URBAN BOOKS, LLC
97 N18th Street
Wyandanch, NY 11798

Name (please print):_____

Address:_____

City/State:_____

Zip:_____

QTY	TITLES	PRICE

Shipping and handling: add $3.50 for 1st book, then $1.75 for each additional book.
Please send a check payable to:
Urban Books, LLC
Please allow 4-6 weeks for delivery.

ORDER FORM
URBAN BOOKS, LLC
97 N18th Street
Wyandanch, NY 11798

Name (please print):_____

Address:_____

City/State:_____

Zip:_____

QTY	TITLES	PRICE
	3:57 A.M Timing Is Everything	$14.95
	A Man's Worth	$14.95
	A Woman's Worth	$14.95
	Abundant Rain	$14.95
	After The Feeling	$14.95
	Amaryllis	$14.95
	An Inconvenient Friend	$14.95

Shipping and handling: add $3.50 for 1st book, then $1.75 for each additional book.

Please send a check payable to:

Urban Books, LLC

Please allow 4-6 weeks for delivery

ORDER FORM
URBAN BOOKS, LLC
97 N18th Street
Wyandanch, NY 11798

Name (please print):_____

Address:_____

City/State:_____

Zip:_____

QTY	TITLES	PRICE
	Battle of Jericho	$14.95
	Be Careful What You Pray For	$14.95
	Beautiful Ugly	$14.95
	Been There Prayed That:	$14.95
	Before Redemption	$14.95
	By the Grace of God	$14.95

Shipping and handling: add $3.50 for 1st book, then $1.75 for each additional book.
Please send a check payable to:
Urban Books, LLC
Please allow 4-6 weeks for delivery

ORDER FORM
URBAN BOOKS, LLC
97 N18th Street
Wyandanch, NY 11798

Name (please print):_____

Address:_____

City/State:_____

Zip:_____

QTY	TITLES	PRICE
	Confessions Of A Preacher's Wife	$14.95
	Dance Into Destiny	$14.95
	Deliver Me From My Enemies	$14.95
	Desperate Decisions	$14.95
	Divorcing the Devil	$14.95

Shipping and handling: add $3.50 for 1st book, then $1.75 for each additional book.

Please send a check payable to:

Urban Books, LLC

Please allow 4-6 weeks for delivery

ORDER FORM
URBAN BOOKS, LLC
97 N18th Street
Wyandanch, NY 11798

Name (please print):_____

Address:_____

City/State:_____

Zip:_____

QTY	TITLES	PRICE
	Faith	$14.95
	First Comes Love	$14.95
	Flaws and All	$14.95
	Forgiven	$14.95
	Former Rain	$14.95
	Forsaken	$14.95
	From Sinner To Saint	$14.95

Shipping and handling: add $3.50 for 1st book, then $1.75 for each additional book.

Please send a check payable to:

Urban Books, LLC

Please allow 4-6 weeks for delivery

ORDER FORM
URBAN BOOKS, LLC
97 N18th Street
Wyandanch, NY 11798

Name (please print):_____

Address:_____

City/State:_____

Zip:_____

QTY	TITLES	PRICE
	From The Extreme	14.95
	God Is In Love With You	14.95
	God Speaks To Me	14.95
	Grace And Mercy	14.95
	Guilty Of Love	14.95
	Happily Ever Now	14.95
	Heaven Bound	14.95

Shipping and handling: add $3.50 for 1st book, then $1.75 for each additional book.
Please send a check payable to:
Urban Books, LLC
Please allow 4-6 weeks for delivery